UNDYING DESIRE

A Novel of the Enclave

JESSICA LEE

Entangled Publishing, LLC
2614 South Timberline Road
Suite 109
Fort Collins, CO 80525
Visit our website at www.entangledpublishing.com.

Edited by Erin Molta
Cover design by Kim Killion

Manufactured in the United States of America

First Edition April 2014

To Mr. Lee: none of this would be possible without you. You amaze me, and I'm the luckiest woman in the world. Love you. Always.

Chapter One

There are times in life when saving something or somebody you care about requires taking the risk that you'll lose it all and have nothing in the end.

Guerin's friendship with Kenric St. James, master of the Enclave, was a prime example of the possible nasty consequence. But it was a chance he had to take to keep his leader and best friend from once again getting screwed by his sire, Marguerite.

Even after her death.

Like a foreboding message, Guerin's last conversation with Arran, the only Enclave warrior who knew the real reason he'd left, rolled to the forefront of his mind.

"So what will you do when you cross the pond and find Eve isn't what Marguerite claimed she'd be, her vengeful, spiteful mother's daughter? Will you wrap her up like a present and bring her back to her father? Kenric will never forgive us for keeping Eve's existence a secret from him."

It had been a valid question, but it was a decision he didn't believe he'd truly need to make.

"She's Marguerite's spawn. How can the female be anything but evil?"

"Yet," Arran responded, *"if Marguerite was telling the truth, she only possesses half of Marguerite's genes. There's a part of her that's Kenric as well."*

"Kenric never had a chance to be a part of her life, to impart any kind of moral compass for the female to follow." Guerin had glanced over his shoulder and dread had settled like an anchor around his neck. *"I wish like hell this wasn't my journey to take. But what kind of friend would I be if I didn't do this for him? No man should ever be asked to kill his own child."*

The bell tower chimed once, then twice, announcing the late hour to the empty, wet streets of Nuremberg, Germany. Guerin swiped the rain from his face and off the shadow of a beard that had grown during his ten-hour trek across the Atlantic. He picked up his speed as he made his way through the aged passageway, his boots splashing through the puddles littering the street. The weatherworn buildings attested to decades spent enduring the unyielding elements. Guerin understood all too well the harsh effects of existing for too many years.

The edifices were old—but he was older.

Guerin inhaled a lungful of the icy breeze, attempting to shrug off the heavy blanket of isolation that was trying to suffocate him. It had been more than a century since he and Kenric had teamed up and formed the Enclave. At first, it had been only him and his best friend defending the humans on the coast of South Carolina. Through the years, Kenric had recruited a select few males who'd demonstrated a strong desire to keep their darker side in check and protect others from those of their kind who couldn't resist the urge to kill while feeding.

The Enclave had grown to five male warriors until earlier that year, when they'd lost Logan during the rescue of Arran's mate and her sister. And then there was Markus. Physically, the bastard was back inside the Enclave's walls, but the vampire's head was so screwed up from Marguerite's manipulations that Guerin doubted Kenric would ever be able to reach him.

With the high level of risk associated with his mission, crossing the Atlantic onto a master's territory without notice and hunting down a vampire on foreign soil—a vampire none of them knew anything about—Guerin really should have his team at his back. Or his head examined. But this was something that had to be handled alone. There was no other way.

Slowing his pace, Guerin sampled the air once more. His informant was already here. He'd sensed the other's presence a moment ago when he'd turned into the corridor. The vibrations and scent given off by another vampire were hard to miss, if they wanted to be found, that is.

"Guerino Lombardi?" A sultry female voice drifted from the shadows.

"Depends on who's asking." Guerin halted and fisted his hand around the hilt of his dagger. The steady pelt of the rain on the cobblestones drummed in his ears as a figure emerged from the darkness.

Long waves of cinnamon-brown hair draped the shoulders of a woman who appeared to be about a head shorter than his six-foot-two frame. A dark-crimson cape enveloped her, brushing her ankles and shielding her from the cold night of the early Bavarian winter. She reached up and pulled its hood over her head as she glided forward and slowed to a stop before him. Her eyelids shuttered, and her lips parted on a deep inhale. A sensual display, and one he was sure was for his benefit.

"Mmm…" She opened her eyes, and a flash of red circled her pupils. "My, you are an old one," she said in a thick accent that hinted of a Russian heritage. The tips of her fangs glinted from beneath her upper lip. "I am Ana."

Arousal and blatant lust rolled off the female like a tsunami wave and slammed into Guerin's senses. He bit back a groan. One not formed from mutual desire, but of distaste.

"If you're Ana, then yes, I'm Guerino. The one sent by Markus to locate Eve for his Mistress," he said, omitting one small detail—Markus's Mistress, Marguerite, was dead. She also didn't need to know that Markus was in a silver-plated cage, wasting away like a fucking ice cream cone under a midday summer sun. Not that the Enclave's master wasn't trying to save him. Shit. For the past month, Kenric had attempted to feed him every other day, but for some reason, Markus had developed a damn martyr complex. Guerin swiped a hand through his hair, pushing back the rain-slicked layers dripping onto his face. *Damn.* He hated how cold the rain was in Europe. "Do you have the information?"

"Ah, yes…Marguerite." Ana lifted one brow and painted a smile on her red lips. "And how is dear Marguerite? It's been too long since last we…played."

"She's eager to find her daughter. Marguerite lost contact with Eve after leaving the country, and you're the only other person who knew of her existence. She's counting on your cooperation."

Ana *tsk*ed. "So impatient for one as old as you." She closed the distance between them, reached up, and trailed her fingertips in a slow exploration down his chest. "You and I could have fun getting to know each other." Her hand dipped below his belt. Guerin hissed, seized her wrist, and jerked her hard against him. The breath whooshed from her lungs in a cloud of vapor.

"You want to get to know me?" Guerin growled, dropped her wrist, and gripped Ana's chin. "Lesson number one: I don't fuck vampires."

"Fine." Ana pulled free of his hold and stepped back. "We don't fuck."

Guerin took a deep breath. *Shit. Get a grip.* He needed her. She was his only lead to finding Eve.

"Sorry," Guerin said through clenched teeth. "Nothing personal."

Ana huffed. "You're lucky I'm loyal to Marguerite, or I'd tell you to go screw yourself."

"Like I said. Nothing personal, Ana." Guerin shrugged. "Just a preference." He stepped closer. "Now, do you know where Eve is?"

"I do." She smiled. Ana brushed past him with a come-hither rock of her hips, then circled him like a cat parading its kill before its master.

Yes. Finally a lead. The blood surged in Guerin's veins, but he forced back the adrenaline rush. He didn't need Ana suspicious over his reaction.

"So where is Eve Devonshire, Ana?" It was all he could do not to grab her and demand an answer. He had to find her. Kenric, his best friend—his only family for the past century—didn't deserve to live through another one of Marguerite's choreographed nightmares. For a moment, his mind flashed back more than a hundred years ago to the night he and Kenric had met.

Guerin had only been in the low country of South Carolina for about six months when one evening, he stumbled upon a lone human going up against several crazed DEADs on the docks. Five against one. Those kinds of odds weren't much to his liking—then and now. So Guerin had decided to crash the party and help the poor male.

For the first few minutes, everything had been going fine. In fact, he'd been kicking some ass and rather enjoying himself, until one of them pulled a knife and sank the blade into his flank. That's when a stranger, with powers unlike any he'd witnessed in years, appeared out of nowhere. A wicked windstorm kicked up that knocked him back into a pillar and temporarily clouded his vision. Guerin had realized immediately that he was in the presence of a master vampire. Gurgling cries sliced through the air, and as quickly as it had all begun, the storm ended. The strong winds ceased, leaving only the sounds of the harbor surrounding them.

The powerful new vampire stood up from where he'd been checking the victim for signs of life, but the human's wounds had been too great. As he turned and approached, the male's dark coat billowed around his ankles in the sea's slight breeze, and hair the color of a raven brushed the sides of his face. He closed in on Guerin and stopped, his pale blue eyes meeting Guerin's. Energy, a strength only another creature of the night could detect, radiated off the male in palpable waves. Whoever he was, Guerin had known that the male was someone he didn't want as his enemy. What the master did next, though, had caught him by surprise. As if they'd just met at a social event and not after having battled several DEADs, the master vampire stuck out his palm in a gentleman's offering. "The name's Kenric St. James, and who might you be?"

Ana pressed her shoulder into his, jarring Guerin back into the present, and came around his left side, stopping in front of him. Her bloodred cape swayed around her ankles. Hundreds of raindrops beaded on her shoulders like diamond dust in the moonlight, giving her an almost angelic appearance. A deceptive illusion he knew the lethal beauty used to her advantage. "Actually… She was here—last I saw her. Just outside of Nuremberg."

"Where exactly?" Guerin couldn't believe his luck.

"Der Roses Dorn."

"The Rose's Thorn? What is that? Some sort of club?"

"Yes," Ana replied. "One that caters to those with a taste for the more…exotic in sexual pleasures. It's the last place I saw her." She turned to move away. Guerin reached out and gripped her forearm. Ana whirled. "What else do you want?" Her gaze flicked up to his. "I've given you what you came for. Now you can inform Marguerite that she owes *me* one." Ana tugged at his hold on her wrist and dismissed him with a turn of her head.

"Not so fast." Ana was loyal to Marguerite, but it didn't mean she wouldn't be compelled to run her mouth about this little rendezvous, especially if she walked away with nothing to show for her cooperation. When she'd come on to him earlier, he had shut her down colder than a bare ass in Siberia. He could kill her and make for damn sure no one learned of his arrival in Germany. But one woman to assassinate was enough. Guerin took a deep breath. Ana had come through for him.

"What?" The heated glare Ana tossed his way declared she still wasn't too happy with his earlier rejection. "You don't want to fuck me, but you do want to stand here in the cold and freeze your balls off. *Pfft*." She gave a slight jerk of her chin. "Americans."

Guerin seized Ana's other arm, and faster than she could utter another complaint, he shoved her under the cover of the building's overhang.

"What are you doing?" she cried out as he took her farther beneath the shadows of the building's roof.

"If you stop complaining, you might find out."

He wedged Ana against the solid steel door that the shadows and the narrow covered passage hid from anyone passing by the mouth of the alley. Guerin braced one hand beside her head and leaned in. Her ragged breaths gave evidence to how much he'd rattled her. *Good.* Knowing he'd unnerved the vampiress was a bit of a rush.

"I said I wouldn't fuck you," Guerin began. "But I do have something I'm sure you'll enjoy just as much." He lifted his free arm and brought his wrist to his lips. Ana's eyes widened and fire swirled in her pupils as he curled his upper lip back and exposed his fangs. Without hesitation, he sank them into his flesh, opening his vein. Warm, thick liquid coated his tongue. Guerin pulled his wrist from his mouth and held it up to Ana in offering.

Her upper lip curled back on a hiss, and she struck. Without mercy, Ana latched onto his open vein, drawing the essence from his body with hard pulls that nearly buckled his knees.

He groaned.

It'd been years since Guerin had fed another, and it was a trip down memory lane he'd rather not travel. With damn good reason. Those memories were an ugly road full of pain, betrayal, and foolishness on his part. His stomach roiled with Ana's repeated sips and licks at his vein. She rocked into him, pressing her hips into his, and a vibrating mewl emanated from the back of her throat.

This bad idea needed to die a quick death. Now.

Guerin reached out with his mind and slipped easily into the distracted vampiress's head. The quickest and most *humane* way to get a vampire female off your vein: take her down the shortest path to fulfillment. A journey she would no doubt appreciate to help satiate the growing arousal from her meal.

A mind fuck.

He stroked the bundle of neurons near her brain stem, signaling the pleasure center of Ana's mind. She shuddered against him, gasped, and sent a rush of cool air skating across his wrist.

"Oh God, yes…" She moaned and pulled away, bumping her rear into the door. "I thought you didn't fuck vampires?"

Guerin brought his wrist to his mouth and sealed the wound. He watched as Ana's eyelids lowered and her head fell back. "I don't."

"What? But…" As if she were in the throes of a wet dream, Ana lifted her hands and slowly unzipped her cape. The crimson cloth fell open; she reached in and cupped both breasts with her palms.

"You were so very helpful, Ana," he rasped. "Allow me to give you what *you* want."

Her fingers tightened, sinking into her ripe flesh, squeezing her breasts as though she could milk the pleasure straight from her pores. "Oh, God…more!"

Ana's heart pounded like a bass drum inside his head, and the scent of her arousal flooded the space between him. But unlike with human women, the pheromones she released did nothing for his libido.

With a mental tug on her pleasure cortex, he gave her more. Guerin increased the pressure, massaging her neurons into a pulsing fury of sensation. Ana's hips bucked as if he'd thrust deep inside her core. She cried out and dropped a hand, reaching for the apex of her need.

"That's it, Ana," he whispered inside her head. *"Let go."*

Guerin followed the path of her hand with his gaze as she pulled up her dress and exposed her black lace panties and garters to the night. He had to admit, she was lovely. But she was a vampire, and no amount of satin and lace could cover up that bitter fact.

She trailed her fingers over the lace covering her sex, clamped her palm over her mons, and ground the heel of her hand over the hidden bundle of nerves. Her breath hitched, and her back arched. Ana's mouth fell open on a silent cry. Guerin held on to Ana's mind, increasing the pleasure until her every muscle contracted, buckling her legs. He snaked an arm around her waist, taking the weight of her body, and she slumped forward onto Guerin's chest. Warm, rapid pants of air heated his neck.

"No fair, vampire," she mumbled lazily at his throat before lifting her head. "You play dirty. I didn't get to finish my meal." She licked the residual traces of his blood from her lips.

"Maybe…but you did enjoy your reward."

"True." Ana gave him a hint of a satisfied smile. She pushed away, tugged her dress down, and zipped her cape. "Pity you're so opposed to making the experience a reality."

Guerin flipped the collar up on his coat. "Not really." He turned and made his way out onto the cobblestone.

"Bastard," Ana shouted behind him.

In every sense of the word, *yes*, he was. And if Eve proved to be anything like her mother, she was about to meet the biggest bastard of her life.

Chapter Two

The vodka slid down Eve's throat on a fiery trail and erupted inside her chest like a volcano. *Yes.* This was exactly what she needed to burn off the chill that had infiltrated her bones tonight.

"Mistress Fallon." Eve lifted her gaze from her shot glass to the full-figured blonde who neared her table. She could almost hear her shift manager squeak as she approached wrapped in a black latex bodysuit. The outfit squeezed her ample breasts like pressure-filled balloons.

"*Ja*, Ingrid."

"A man is at the bar asking to speak with the owner," she said, her German accent turning her "thes" into "zees."

Eve scanned the area in front of the massive brass-and-wood bar. "Which man?"

Ingrid pushed a lock of platinum-blond hair behind her ear and nodded in the direction of the tall man leaning against the far end. "That one," she said. "Black leather coat and shoulder-length dark hair." His back was to Eve, preventing a glimpse of his face. "I haven't seen him here before, Mistress. But I would be happy to take care of our visitor any way you'd like." A knowing grin spread across her lips.

If the male was one of Seth's spies, turning him away would only ignite more suspicion. Besides, Eve knew how to handle nosy scouts.

"No." Eve poured herself another shot. "Send him over." She tossed another dose of heat to the back of her throat. It was a shame the bitter liquid never made her drunk. To experience one night of bliss-filled oblivion and have all her problems disappear would be nice. But no matter how much of the stuff she filled her gut with, it only provided a little warmth. That, too, was a rare find outside the bottle.

Eve ran her fingers through the long tresses of her red wig as the stranger rounded the bar and headed in her direction. The male strode toward her to the beat of Rihanna's "S&M," slicing through the crowd of dancers as though *he* owned the place. His body language screamed alpha male. A female didn't have to be a two-hundred-year-old vampire to recognize a male who took what he wanted and made sure the woman enjoyed every minute of the taking.

Her nipples hardened into sensitive peaks. They brushed the lace of her bra with each breath, sending electric pulses straight to her sex. Eve crossed her legs, and her grip tightened on the empty shot glass.

The mere sight of a handsome man should *not* have her squirming in her thong. But males who looked like him didn't stroll through her club every night, and her bed had been empty for much too long. Unfortunately, finding a lover—one she could trust when her eyes were closed—was a difficult task. And the anonymous sexual games played at the Rose's Thorn had long since lost their appeal.

On a deep breath, she reached inside her mind and repressed the part of her DNA courtesy of her mother. He wasn't close enough yet to detect if she was a vampire or not. But he was a stranger, asking for her, and Eve couldn't afford to be careless and wave her hybrid ancestry around like a red flag. Except for her mother, whom she hadn't heard from in far too long, she was alone in the world. So her best defense was offense. No one could hurt her if they couldn't find or detect her. And with her secret heritage suppressed, any vampire within sniffing distance would register a human.

He came to a stop at her booth, his long black leather coat brushing against the dark jeans at his calves. The metal buckles on the sides of his boots glinted in the halogen spotlights that circled the perimeter of the club's ceiling.

Eve slowly lifted her gaze. The layers of leather, denim, and cotton did little to hide the strength of the man beneath.

"Like what you see?"

The deep rumble of the question jerked Eve's attention from her perusal. She glanced up and into a lopsided smile. The man's dark complexion hinted at a Mediterranean descent, and wavy, dark-chocolate hair curled along the sides of his face. Long sooty eyelashes framed eyes the color of rich molasses—eyes that held a depth of wisdom well beyond the thirty-something years his appearance led one to believe.

Mysterious and provocative.

A lethal combination.

Not for him, but for the many women she was sure he

lured into his bed with those looks.

She cocked a brow in his direction. "As a matter of fact—I do." Eve tilted her head and tossed him a smile. Over the past two centuries, she'd been accused of a lot of things, but coy wasn't one of them. She despised that particular quality.

If you liked something—wanted it—be woman enough to admit it.

"That's nice to hear. Then perhaps this could be the path to a beautiful friendship." He reached out, took her hand, and lifted it to his mouth, yet stopped as the warmth of his breath heated her skin. His gaze moved from their fingers and connected once more with hers. "And I do mean beautiful," he uttered, before lowering his head and brushing a kiss over the surface of her knuckles. Her breath hitched at the contact, and Eve captured her lower lip between her teeth.

Damn. He was good.

She could easily imagine him scratching her itch in every conceivable way or position.

Eve tugged her hand from his grasp and went for her bottle of Stoli, doing her best to squelch the tremble rolling from her stomach to her fingers. *Shit.* He was already starting to piss her off. No one got under her skin, especially a man. And the fact that this one had from the moment he'd walked across the room was unsettling her.

"So how can I help you, Herr…?" She poured another shot and returned the bottle to the table.

"Lombardi. Guerino Lombardi."

"Herr Lombardi." Eve gave a slight nod and brought the glass to her lips for a sip. The lingering spicy scent of man and sandalwood drifted off her fingertips. Eve inhaled deeply—and froze.

Son of a bitch.

How in the hell had she missed the unmistakable pheromone?

He was a creature of the night. She knew he was too good to be for real. Eve was slipping. She should have picked up on the scent of her own kind—or half her kind— the moment he'd stopped at her table. But she'd been too enamored by the whole alpha male aura and good looks. A mistake that could have had deadly consequences.

Oh, she had plans for this rogue.

"So what brings you to my table?" Eve downed another sip of vodka, then licked the remaining traces of alcohol from her lower lip. She didn't have to look to know he watched her every move. She could feel it.

"I'm looking for a woman."

Curiosity killed the cat. But just wait and see, Guerino Lombardi, what happens to overly inquisitive vampires.

Eve glanced up. "And you need *my* help? Strange," she said. "I would have taken you for a man who didn't need the help of others in that matter."

"Smart and beautiful. I appreciate those traits in a woman." He smiled and placed his hand on the back of the seat opposite her side of the table. "May I sit?"

She nodded.

He slid onto the cushion, and the confined space of their two-seater booth showcased his large build. *Yum.* Such a damn shame he had to be one of Seth's scouts.

"You think I can help you find this woman, Herr Lombardi?"

"Please, call me Guerin," he said, and propped an arm along the length of the backrest.

"Guerin?" Eve quirked a brow in his direction. "Hmmm... Friends already, are we? My, you do work fast."

He released a short but deep chuckle. "A less formal approach is a much nicer way to communicate. Don't you agree, Mistress Fallon?"

"Yes...it can be." She smiled. "On occasion." Eve moved forward, resting both arms on the table and lacing her fingers. "So tell me, Guerin, who is this woman you're looking for?"

"Eve Devonshire." Guerin dropped his arm and placed his forearms on the table. "Can you tell me where to find her?"

"Eve Devonshire..." She shook her head. "I don't believe I've ever heard the name." Eve held his gaze. She knew from years of practice that hers remained unreadable. After spending more years than she cared to remember on her own and in hiding from those who wanted her either dead or only alive long enough to take her apart piece by piece, she'd learned how to mask her expressions and her emotions. "Can you describe her?" She shrugged. "Perhaps I've seen a woman who might match the description."

"No. Unfortunately, I can't."

"You're searching for a woman, but you have no idea what she looks like." Eve eased back, placing some distance between them. "Sounds like you are searching through quite the haystack for that proverbial needle."

"True." Guerin stroked the dark shadow of a beard at his chin. He studied her, his dark eyes drinking her in, sliding over her skin like warm melted chocolate, making her feel just as decadent. "But for some reason, Fallon, I get the feeling you might be the one person who could narrow the search."

"Do you, now?" Eve lifted her brows. "Then I suggest you see someone about those…'feelings,' because they're leading you astray."

"Well, damn." Guerin slowly shook his head. "Guess a man's instincts can't be right all the time." He rose from the table with a nod. "It's been a pleasure." A smile tugged at his lips as he turned and moved toward the bar.

Eve's gut twisted. Would it never end? She scanned the club for Ingrid and found her a few tables over with one of the regulars. As if sensing she was needed, Ingrid's gaze drifted in Eve's direction. With a lift of her chin, Eve called Ingrid to her table. Eve grabbed the bag sitting beside her on the bench. She reached inside and pulled out a notepad and pen. Quickly, she jotted down a message—one that was short and to the point.

"Ja, Mistress," Ingrid said as she neared Eve's side.

"Remember our visitor who wanted to speak with me a moment ago?" Eve checked to the side of Ingrid, making sure she wasn't being watched by the man—vampire—of whom she spoke. She spotted him tossing back a shot at the bar, his attention tuned to the crowd and not in their direction.

"Ja. How could I forget?"

Eve ripped the note from her pad and folded it in half before handing it to her manager. Ingrid clasped the slip of paper between her fingers and glanced back at Eve with an inquisitive look.

"In a few minutes, I want you to give this to tonight's bartender and ask him to place it in the hands of our handsome guest. "Do not"—Eve gripped Ingrid's hand—"I repeat, do not say it's from me. If asked, tell the bartender to say that perhaps the gentleman has a secret admirer."

Ingrid nodded and tucked the paper inside one of her long bloodred gloves. "Right away, Mistress." She turned on her heel and weaved through the crowd.

Eve poured another round for herself, and without hesitation, tipped it to her lips. The slow burn rolled over her tongue and down her throat. If only the fire could incinerate the empty feeling inside. Or at least numb her mind, so she didn't have to endure the ugliness that was about to be her life once more. There were times she hated her other side. But if she wanted to stay alive…unleashing that beast was an unavoidable evil.

• • •

She was good.

Very good.

But Guerin had been playing the game a hell of a lot longer, and he knew when someone was trying to shovel a lie his way. The moment he'd mentioned the name Eve to Mistress Fallon, tension had swelled so thick and sour he could've tasted it in the air. Her heart rate and respiration never changed, though. Highly unusual for a human who was lying. He couldn't shake the feeling that something didn't seem right. She knew more than she was willing to share.

Guerin turned his beer up for another swig as the bartender stepped up to the counter. He leaned in, the halogen beams bouncing off the silver loops piercing his nipples. Without a word, he pushed a folded slip of paper his way.

"What's this?" Guerin held it up between his fingers.

"Secret admirer," the other man replied, his words thick with a heavy German accent. "Maybe, ja?"

"Right…" Guerin unfolded the note and gazed down at the lines of red ink.

If you want to know about Eve…
Meet me in five minutes.
Behind the club. Alone.

Adrenaline slammed into his system, kicking his heart rate into a pounding percussion in his head. Guerin shoved the slip of paper in his coat pocket and cranked his head around in Mistress Fallon's direction. She appeared engrossed in a stack of work an employee must have placed in front of her.

Had she sent him the note?

He fisted his beer, then tossed back another swallow. Guerin pulled out his cell, checked the time, and section by section, continued his survey of the crowd around him. Most of the club's patrons were focused on the various activities available in one of Nuremberg's hidden fetish nightspots. The others, a couple of women and a few men who'd met his gaze, looked more interested in coaxing him to play than divulging information. He shoved his cell back inside his coat's interior pocket.

The sound of leather cracking across flesh split the air of the club and sent a chill down Guerin's spine. A loud moan followed, and Guerin jerked his head toward the pleasure/pain-filled utterance. His gaze landed on a St. Andrew's cross that stood spotlighted in the back corner of the club. Shackled to each upper limb of the device hung a blindfolded, shirtless man with his back to the crowd. His thin pale arms, wet with sweat, glistened in the harsh light. A crowd formed a semicircle around the display, fixated — mesmerized — by the petite bare-chested brunette and her submissive.

Before Guerin realized he'd even moved, he found himself working his way to the front of the group of voyeurs.

Crack.

The whip sang out before its Mistress hit her mark with expert precision across her sub's right shoulder blade. The man writhed and groaned as another red welt blazoned to life across his back, followed by a trickle of blood from the thin slice in his flesh.

Arousal rolled off the humans in waves, mixing with the sensual and haunting melody emitting from the sound system like a hypnotic spell. His cock swelled to life. At that moment, a songstress crooned something about the devil making us sin. *Shit.* If Satan were the only thing he had to worry about, Guerin's existence would be much less complicated.

But there were darker creatures of the night that didn't exist merely in the fiery pits of hell. They walked the streets and were capable of getting inside your head, creating a craving within your soul that even a century-long abstinence could never cure.

Crack.

The single tail uncurled through the air once more and struck its target. The sub shuddered, threw his head back, and released a loud groan. Guerin's pulse roared in his ears. His breathing was reduced to pants, and his fingers curled at his sides into tight fists. *Christ.* He had to get the hell out of here.

Swinging around, he barreled through the crowd,

heading straight for the club's main entrance. Beads of per-spiration formed on his brow, and he swiped them away with a muttered curse. How many decades had to go by before he could let go of his past? Before the sights and sounds of what he'd just witnessed didn't crawl under his skin and press every one of his *fuck-me* buttons.

Focus.

He had to stay on track. Remember why the hell he was there in the first place. Guerin jammed his palm against the club's front door lever and stepped into the cold night.

Five minutes, the note had said. He reached inside his coat, pulled out his phone, and glanced at the display. Right on time: 1:15 a.m. The cell vibrated in his palm, signaling an incoming call. The screen lit with a single name: Arran. Guerin shook his head. *Dammit.* He didn't have time to deal with the warrior right now. Guerin slid his index across the lower half of the screen, answering the call.

"What?" he barked into the cell.

"What do you mean, what?" Arran growled. "You were supposed to report two hours ago."

"Well, excuse the fuck out of me, Daddy." Guerin spat the words out through clenched teeth. "I've been a little busy." He sucked in a calming deep breath. He knew Arran was in an ugly situation as well, keeping their secret from Kenric. Not an easy task. Silence lingered between them for a few tense moments, each man reining in the need to lash out. Guerin was about ready to chew out an "I'm sorry" when the sound of a prolonged exhale reached through the phone, and Arran broke the ice.

"Where are you?"

"A club called the Rose's Thorn on the outskirts of

Nuremberg. The female Markus arranged for me to meet said this was the last place she'd seen Eve." Guerin shoved his hand in his pocket, going for the crumpled note inside. "At least the asshole has been good for something besides a fucking knife in our back."

"Solid lead, then?"

"Maybe…" He tightened his grip on the thin slip of paper. "When I know more, you'll be the first."

"Guerin, how long—"

"I can't do this right now." He was already late. "I gotta go." Guerin tapped end call, not bothering to wait for a reply. There wasn't time for an explanation. He dropped the cell back inside his pocket and flipped the collar up around his neck, eliminating some of the cold bite of air against his exposed flesh. If all went well in the next few minutes, he'd have something to call home about.

Rolling his shoulders, Guerin attempted to loosen the knot of muscles between them and headed toward the rear of the club. His boots thumped against the damp concrete, but there was no reason to mask his presence. This particular informant had sought *him* out, knowing Guerin wouldn't pass up the opportunity.

The question was: if this meeting wasn't with Mistress Fallon, how the hell did he or she know he'd come looking for Eve?

No one in Germany was aware of his exact reason for being in the country except for…Ana. His mind raced back to the cinnamon-haired vampire from the previous night. But if it was Ana, why the game? The female could have told him all she'd known twenty-four hours ago.

Except for the low-level thump of the bass vibrating off

the club's walls, the rear lot appeared quiet. A lone black Mercedes sedan sat backed into the only available parking slot, its bumper sitting inches from the rear of the building. A run-down two-story dwelling filled the other side of the lot. The bottom floor seemed deserted. The few small windows facing the club from the second level were dressed with curtains and blinds, though no light shone from the inside.

Guerin reached beneath his coat and slid the dagger free from between the waistband of his jeans and lower back. He palmed the hilt of the blade, enjoying the warm, smooth feel of the metal against his skin. He stepped into the spill of white light illuminating the rear half of the Rose's Thorn's back lot—and stopped. The fine hairs at his nape lifted, sending a tingle down the center of his back. He straightened his spine, and his fingers tightened around his weapon. But his boots remained firmly planted. Guerin pulled in a lungful of air through his nostrils.

Human.

Interesting.

"I'm here," Guerin announced. "So the next move's yours." He rotated on his heels, and froze.

Definitely not Ana.

The woman standing in front of him stole his ability to breathe.

Beautiful. The word formed on his lips, but no sound emerged. Long waves of midnight hair spilled over her shoulders and framed a delicate heart-shaped face. A face that caused his fingers to itch with a desire to caress. She tilted her head slightly, and full red lips lifted at the corners into a semblance of a smile. Except he couldn't help but notice it failed to reach her eyes. His gaze locked with irises the color of pale-blue tropical waters. *So familiar.* Guerin's pulse quickened. *Son of a bitch.*

Eve!

"Looking for me?" Two pearl-white fangs dropped from beneath her upper lip.

Guerin tensed, surged forward, and slammed into a wall of pain. A roar tore from his throat. His head was going to explode. He stumbled back, dropping the dagger from his hand. Lights swirled around him in a blur of dizzying color. *Shit.* Guerin grabbed his head and blinked rapidly, trying to bring the night back into focus.

What the hell was she doing to him?

His knees buckled. Down. *Fuck.* He was going down... The lights flickered.

Then faded to black.

Chapter Three

A groan vibrated at the back of Guerin's throat. His shoulders throbbed and his wrists burned. Damn, his head felt as if it had been used in somebody's perverse version of kickball. He would have laughed at the mental image if his brain didn't hurt so fucking bad. Guerin dragged his eyelids open, and intense white light stabbed into his retinas. He jerked, slamming his lids shut. *Shit.*

"Excellent," a female voice stated from behind him. "You're finally awake."

Keeping his eyes closed, Guerin tilted his head in her direction. "I haven't had my coffee yet," he said, his words hoarse, coming out of his parched throat. "So watch out. I might bite."

Guerin shifted the millimeter his restraints allowed and hissed. Manacles laced with silver seared the flesh surrounding his wrists and ankles.

He parted his eyelids once more and surveyed his

situation.

Though from the all-too-familiar stance, Guerin didn't need his sight to know the deal. He'd been cuffed to a St. Andrew's cross, both arms raised and spread wide. His parted legs formed a perfect upside-down vee, and were secured to the lower half of the contraption. Except instead of facing his kidnapper, his cheek and chest were pressed into the wood of the cross, gifting his captor a full view of his naked back. Cool air caressed his skin, and he realized his briefs were the only item left covering his ass.

"Enjoy your moment of humor, vampire." His captor's hand snagged the hair at his nape, wrenching his head back. The tug at his roots sent a sharp twinge down his spine. The combination of the cross and the pain brought his cock roaring to life. *Fuck.* This was definitely not the time. "For it will most certainly be short-lived if you don't tell me who sent you looking for Eve."

With her body next to his, the warm scent of vanilla spiked with cinnamon tantalized his senses. *Mistress Fallon?* The same fragrance had invaded his nostrils and teased his dick when he'd spoken with her at the Rose's Thorn. Not a big surprise, considering she'd been the one to set him up, and he'd walked right into her trap.

The next obvious questions: where the hell was Eve, and how the fuck was he going to get his ass off this cross?

"Why don't you go first?" Guerin yanked his head out of her hold and tried to snag a glance of his kidnapper over his shoulder. But the moment he caught a glimpse of long dark hair, she stepped out of sight. *Dark hair?* Fallon had been a redhead. Could it be...?

"Eve," he continued. "I know it was you who hit me with

some kind of pulse last night. So I take it you and Mistress Fallon are one and the same?"

The crack of leather echoed through the room a split second before the silver-studded tendrils of a flogger seared his back. Guerin hissed. Silver was the only explanation for the level of pain exploding across his shoulder blades. The residual burn radiated through his flesh as if a dozen cigar-smoking bastards had used him for an ashtray.

"I believe you've somehow gotten the wrong impression that this is a two-way question-and-answer session." Another *snap* filled the air. Guerin sucked in a harsh breath, and his cock throbbed, straining against the material covering his pelvis, waiting for the next blow. But this time, only the lingering sizzle of the first strike licked at his nerve endings. "The only words I want exiting your mouth are the name and location of who you're working for."

"Or what?" Guerin growled.

Snap!

Another searing strike of the flogger landed across his back, followed by a lungful of sweet vanilla and cinnamon. Pain arced through his nerve endings, drawing his balls tight and boiling the cum inside. Guerin's fangs burst from his gums, stabbing into his lower lip, and flooding his mouth with the metallic taste of his own blood. *Son of a bitch.*

His body was out of control, responding as if he'd never walked away from this. From the pain. Like an alcoholic who'd swallowed his first taste of liquor after years of sobriety, the need was back and raging in the forefront of his mind. Wanting nothing more than to beg her to strike him one more time—hell, a hundred more times.

Christ. He'd vowed never to allow himself to succumb

to his darker desires. Especially with a female vampire. Not after Daniela. His sire and former Mistress had wielded his passion for pain and his submissive nature, when it came to sex, as a cruel weapon. She'd used and manipulated him until there was nothing left but mangled pieces of his heart—his trust—on the dungeon floor. He'd been nothing but a toy.

His submission a joke.

"Or pain will be the only thing you know until the moment you do. It's not as if I don't already know the answer. But I want to confirm my suspicions before I—"

"Kill me?" He swung his head around, searching for another glimpse of his captor. "Then you should be prepared for murder," Guerin spit. "Because I will never submit and give you what you want to hear."

"Oh really?" A blur of color danced before his eyes, and then she was there, in his face. Layers of sinfully dark hair fell over her shoulders and soft curls teased her cheeks. Eve's vivid blue gaze snagged and held his. She leaned in. Close enough that the urge to reach out with his tongue and taste the luscious curves of her lips was nearly irresistible. "Is that a challenge, vampire? You don't believe I can bring the walls down inside your mind?"

Guerin pulled in a deep, stabilizing breath through his nostrils. The scent of her arousal barreled into his brain, knocking out what little defenses he had left. In its wake, white-hot lust surged through his veins. *Oh, shit!* Guerin curled his fingers, digging his nails into his palms.

"Call it what you want, Eve," he growled, surprised at his ability to form a coherent sentence. "But know this before you continue with your little plan: pain will never break me." Guerin narrowed his gaze on her and licked the last drop of blood from the corner of his mouth.

One perfectly arched brow lifted, and she stepped back. "Now how could I resist a dare like that?" Eve stroked the tassels of the deep purple flogger in her hand—and disappeared.

Less than a heartbeat later, the leather tendrils sprawled across his back, punching the air from his lungs.

Over and over Eve worked the silver into his flesh. How long it went on, Guerin had no damn clue. He'd lost all sense of time. The smell of smoldering flesh and blood and the heady scent of arousal filled the air. His and hers. Guerin rolled his head over his shoulders. *Yes!* His brain—his cock—sipped on the endorphins racing into his bloodstream. He moaned. It was a high like no other.

"Tell me!" Her frustrated demand pierced his eardrums.

"Fuck you," he managed to spout.

Her scream ricocheted off the stone walls right before his wrists and ankles were freed. His knees buckled under his weight, but Guerin rebounded and straightened. She grabbed his arms, spun him, and shoved his spine and the open wounds into the cross's center support post. Guerin's breath hitched. White dots danced in front of his eyes. He blinked, chasing them away, doing his best to focus on the female in front him.

"You bastard," she spat, then reached out and clawed her way down his chest. Guerin's head lolled onto the wood with a groan. Too drained of strength to do anything more, he wrapped his arms around her and hauled her against him. Her lower abdomen slammed against his throbbing erection. *Fuck, yeah.* He rocked into her warmth. Eve hissed. Then she was at his throat, sinking her fangs into his flesh. Hard tremors rippled through her body.

Guerin stiffened, and a roar erupted from his lungs. The climax he'd held at bay burst from his cock. Unable to stop, he pumped his hips against hers. Every brush along his sensitized flesh, every pull at his vein, released another jet of cum from the end of his shaft. God, how long had it been since he'd felt ecstasy on this level?

Never.

Eve pushed free from his throat and arms, eyes glazed. With a thumb and forefinger, she wiped away the smear of blood beneath her lip. Guerin staggered but grasped one arm of the cross to hold himself steady. The lingering effects of his flogging and the most intense orgasm he'd ever experienced wreaked havoc on his ability to stand upright. And judging by Eve's labored breaths, she'd been equally affected.

The hardened tips of her nipples tented the delicate blue silk of her blouse, sending his imagination into overdrive. Were they as dark and rosy as the color of her lips? Would they taste as sweet as she smelled? His mouth watered, and it was all Guerin could do to drag his gaze away. The moment their stares locked, Eve's gaze flicked to his crotch and her nostrils flared.

"Was it good for you too, baby?" He couldn't help the sarcastic tone in his voice that said *I told you so.*

"Asshole," she whispered. Her eyelids drifted closed a second before what felt like the sharp end of a dagger's blade sliced through his skull. He cried out and clutched the sides of his head. *"She is her mother's daughter."* Marguerite's words looped in his brain.

"Eve! Stop...," he groaned. His eyelids sagged, his

ability to hold on to consciousness waning.

Then once more, darkness.

"More," he moaned, his head spinning. "Please… Mistress." He was so close to the precipice.

Daniela smiled, raking her gaze over his naked form while tugging the gloves from her fingertips. "Impressive. Pity I can't honor your request, since I do enjoy hearing you beg. But I want to make sure this continues to work." She fisted the end of his hard length, making sure her nails bit into the hypersensitive tissue.

"Yes!" Guerin's spine arched, rattling the shackles holding him to the cross. The pain should have been enough to buckle any other male, make him beg for mercy. But he wasn't like any other male.

For the last twenty-five years, Daniela had seen to that.

His Mistress knew what she was doing, and the quantity of pure silver embedded inside the cock ring was enough to brand him but not enough to castrate. She enjoyed his dick too much to risk its removal.

"You come, and this will be the last night you spend on my cross for a very long time." Daniela scratched beneath the head of his shaft for emphasis. "Understand, pet?"

Guerin hissed, yanking hard on the reins to his orgasm. "Yes, Mistress." Her threats were never empty, and she knew every one of his buttons. She should, since she'd been the one to unearth them from his psyche. And she played him like a finely tuned instrument. An erotic melody choreographed especially for her pleasure.

Daniela nodded, and with her remaining gloved hand reached over to a nearby table. "I think you'll enjoy these," she crooned. Guerin caught the shimmer of the object *between her fingers right before she clamped it over his erect nipple. The combination of the hard pinch and the sting of silver arrowed straight to his balls, drawing them even more, shoving the ring tighter against his flesh. He bucked against his manacles, squeezing his eyes shut. Less than a breath later, Daniela repeated the process on the other side. The pressure gathering inside his cock was not going to be denied much longer.*

"Mistress…please," he groaned. "Give me release."

"What do I get in return?"

Guerin lifted his eyelids, his gaze finding Daniela's dark eyes, and his heart fisted in his chest. "Anything," he whispered. "You know I love you. I would give you anything—do anything—to make you happy."

A radiant smile bloomed on her face, exposing the tips of her fangs. "I was hoping you'd say that." Daniela spun, her sheer black gown and blond locks fanning out around her like a dark angel. "Bring her in," she called out.

The double doors to their suite opened wide, and two large vampires marched inside, dragging a sobbing girl between them.

"Here," Daniela pointed to the polished wood floor. Her minions dropped the human female, who couldn't be more than eighteen, onto her knees. With her hands bound behind her back, she tossed her matted brown hair out of her eyes and looked up. Eyes glazed with horror met his, and she screamed. Guerin could only imagine what his appearance was doing to her innocent mind: a bloodied nude male chained to a wooden cross.

"Shut her up!" Daniela's vamps launched into action and gagged their prisoner. "Now." She threaded her fingers

through the blond tresses around her face and sauntered in Guerin's direction. "What do you think of her, pet?"

"I think she's frightened as hell," he said, the blood roaring inside his head, jacked up on the scent of her panic and his own adrenaline. "Why not ease her mind instead of stifling her screams?"

Daniela tsked. "What would be the fun in that? I want you to drink in her fear when you kill her."

Guerin's eyelids jerked open. *A dream. Shit.* It had felt so real. As if he'd jumped 250 years back in time. Except it had been his reality, and the dream had actually been a flashback. A wave of nausea sent a rush of bile to the back of his throat. He swallowed hard, scanning his surroundings.

Overhead fluorescent lighting glinted off the thin silver bars of his cell. *What the hell?* How had his ass landed in a cage? He guessed his brain hadn't quite checked back in on the happenings over the last few hours. A disturbance in the air moved over his damp skin and had gooseflesh lifting over his bare chest and limbs. He breathed deep, and the sweet molecules of vanilla mixed with cinnamon sparked Guerin's neurons back to life. The memories of the last few days were unveiled inside his brain like a curtain parting on a stage.

Blood rushed to his groin, and Guerin slammed his eyes shut.

Eve had returned.

Chapter Four

Seth Keller strummed his nails over the thick wooden arm of his favorite chair in front of the fire. They were late. And the crumbling edge where he stood over the chasm called fury grew more fragile with each passing moment.

"Master." The soft voice of his male calyx, or human feeding servant, called from the arched doorway. Seth turned his gaze from the hearth. "They have arrived, sir."

"Direct them below." Seth returned to the flames, mesmerized by the flicker of alternating red, orange, and blue. He'd lived two centuries as a creature of the night, but he'd never grown tired of partaking in a well-stoked fire. The heat and glow reminded him of warm summer days when he used to walk beneath the sun's rays. He sighed, leaned in, and lifted his hand, palm side out, toward the hearth, absorbing its radiance. "Ah, to feel the dawn's light on my skin once more."

He stood, adjusted his black Prada blazer, and shook off

his momentary indulgence in nostalgia. His reflection glared back at him from the large gilded mirror hanging over the mantel. His green eyes shone in the firelight, a stark contrast to his pale complexion and even paler platinum-blond hair. He smoothed the straight, shoulder-length locks behind his ears. It was time to see if the female waiting in his basement knew more than she'd already revealed. If so, evolution was nearly in his grasp, and his fantasy would not be such a frivolous waste of time.

Irate murmurings echoed off the walls and trailed up the narrow flight of stairs that led to Seth's underground chambers. One by one, he sauntered down the steps, allowing the creaking wood to announce his arrival. Conversations dwindled to silence, and all heads turned as he entered the softly lit cavernous space.

"Well now, Ana…" Seth lifted his arms and held them open in greeting. "Thank you for meeting with me tonight."

"Did I have a choice?" Ana lowered the hood of her scarlet velvet cape.

Seth quirked his lips and added a chuckle. "One always has a choice, *liebling*." He ambled over to the large overstuffed chair in front of the three vampires and eased onto the seat. "Albeit, some *options* are more desirable than others." Seth's gaze flickered between his two vampire minions, and he gave a slight nod.

One male seized Ana by the arms.

"What the hell are you doing?" she screeched.

With gloved hands, the other slapped a two-inch-wide silver-plated collar around her throat. Ana wailed and clawed at her neck. Smoke trailed from beneath the metal, and the stench of burning flesh permeated the air. She launched toward the stairs, but the foot-long chain attached to the back of the restraint halted her escape.

Ana staggered, then sank to her knees. "Why are you doing this, Seth?" she cried, her voice hoarse. "I don't understand. What have I done?"

Seth rose, approached her, then reached out and stroked her cheek. "Done? Why nothing, *liebling*." He shook his head. "But that *is* the problem, isn't it." Seth cocked his head, relishing the sheer panic gleaming in Ana's eyes. "Since I suspect you have not shared the very information I've been after for years." He *tsk*ed. "How greedy of you, Ana." Seth dropped his hand and whirled. "I think it's time you were punished until you decide to relinquish what you know."

"What are you talking about?" Ana gasped. "Why would you think I've been holding out on you? I've served you for more than a century—in every way possible."

"That you have." Seth chuckled. "And quite deliciously, I might add." He raked her with his gaze and lowered his voice before continuing. "It is a shame I may have to kill you, *liebling*."

"Seth!"

"Onto the table with her," he commanded. Seth lifted his chin and indicated the wheeled steel slab on the other side of the room, resembling something medical examiners would use for an autopsy. Ana screamed in protest, but his minions did as directed. In seconds, they had her stretched out prone, wrists bound, and a drape of silver mesh placed over her torso.

There would be no way for her to phase now. Not without risking decapitation from the collar and dissection into a million little pieces from the confining cloth.

"Now, Ana," Seth cooed as he neared her trembling body. "Are you ready to start talking about what you know about Eve?"

Ana's gaze darted in his direction. "Eve…? I know nothing about your mystery vamp," she spat, and her lower lip trembled.

"Is that so?" Seth smoothed the fire-kissed brown locks away from her brow. "Then why are your mental walls sealed so damn tight?" He gripped a fistful of hair at the top of her head.

"Because you have me locked down like an animal!" she cried out.

"True…," he began. "But I think it may have something more to do with your attempt to hide the information regarding your meeting with a certain vampire from America called Guerino Lombardi." Ana's body tensed and Seth smiled. *Yes.* Body language was so revealing. Seth patted her head and continued. "You, of all people, should know that no one comes or goes from my territory, *liebling*, without my knowledge. Especially one as old as he. You got sloppy, Ana."

He leaned in, watching as a lone tear rolled down the side of her face. "My informant tells me he was here to see you," Seth whispered. "On behalf of Marguerite Devonshire. Next time, I would suggest not conducting your secret meetings in the open—where anyone could overhear." Seth moved until they were eye to eye. The revelation of his words dug their claws into her psyche. Her pupils swelled, nearly filling the white of her eyes. "Now why would you keep your history with Marguerite from me—unless…" He reached out and seized Ana's face with a punishing grip. "You're hiding Eve's whereabouts for her."

"Please…Seth," Ana begged. "I-I don't know anything."

With a flick of his wrist, he withdrew his hand and whirled around. "Drain her until either she talks or is a lifeless shell. And if the latter, take her head when you're done and get her out of here."

"No!" she cried out. "Seth, please don't do this."

Seth glanced back at her. His minions had gathered around her, and with gloved hands, exposed the vital areas of her body for the exsanguination. Uncovering her lower half, they spread her legs and locked her ankles in place with the attached manacles. The femoral artery would serve them well.

Without hesitation, the vampires tore away the fabric of her dress and lunged. Ana's piercing cry filled the room. Seth's pulse raced at the sights and sounds of the erotic, bloodthirsty frenzy. His cock swelled as fangs burst from his gums. He curled his fingers into a tight fist, claws sinking into his flesh. It was all he could do not to rip the other vamps from her body and feast on her essence himself.

"Seth…wait. I'll tell you what you want to know." Ana's weak telepathic cry drifted into his mind.

"Stop!"

The minions lifted their heads from her open arteries. Crimson fluid dripped from their chins and extended fangs, their eyes black with bloodlust. The vamps trembled with the restraint required not to finish the job and reach their pinnacle in overindulgence. No other high compared with the intensity achieved from draining a human, thus becoming a DEAD, a Death Euphoria Addict. But the volume they would share from Ana—a vampire—would have been enough for a nice head rush.

Seth moved to Ana's side. Her eyes fluttered open. The black had receded, becoming inky pinpoints at the center of now-faded moss-green irises. Seth cupped her chin, thrusting her gaze to meet his. He reached out with his mind and drilled into the recesses of hers. A small gasp followed by a groan escaped her lips under the harsh invasion. Seth could have gone slower, eased into her memories one slight push at a time. But he didn't have the patience to be nice. Too many damn years had passed without a fucking thing to show for it. And all the while, this bitch had had the answers he'd been looking for. To hell with gentle.

Sights, sounds flickered passed his mind's eye in a dizzying array of colors and patterns. Faces, some he recognized, some he'd never seen before, whirled, spinning as if on a carousel inside his head.

Marguerite.

There.

Seth zeroed in on her and opened his mind to all Ana held within her neurons related to the vampiress. The dump of information hit him with full force, swaying him on his feet. He gripped the side of the table for balance as his last meal threatened to crawl its way back up his throat. Seth breathed deeply through his nostrils and slowed the flow of data in his mind. Then suddenly, it was there—the one name he'd been searching for: Eve.

Seth grabbed and pulled on every thread containing her name. A slow grin tugged at the corners of his mouth. *Yes.*

The Rose's Thorn.

Exactly what he had hoped to find.

Straightening, he smoothed the front of his jacket before turning away from the pale figure of the woman lying listless on the metal slab. He stalked toward the stairs. "Finish her, and then get her out of my house."

Chapter Five

Magnificent.

The only word Eve could muster to describe the male lying on the cage floor. She couldn't remember the last time any man had driven her to the point where she'd lost control like the previous night. Nor could she remember the last time she'd experienced an orgasm as intense as the one she'd felt with him. *Damn.* And he hadn't even touched her.

Much less…

Eve chewed her lower lip, suppressing the groan in the back of her throat at the mere thought of having him fill her deep inside. Her gaze strayed from his face, down his bare chest, to the thick bulge at the juncture of his spread thighs. Warmth flooded her core, dampening her panties even more. She leaned in and wrapped her fingers around the silver-laced bars of the small cell. God, how could he still be hard after what they'd shared and the force of the mental blow she'd given him—again?

"Back for round two?"

Guerin's deep voice dived under her skin and lifted every hair on her body. She gasped and jerked away. How did he do that? The effect was unnerving. She was the one in control here—not him. Always. Anything less meant death. She inhaled, settling her heart rate.

"Perhaps...," she said. "I'm surprised you're awake. It's still early in the afternoon," she added in her most nonchalant tone. And she was a master at feigning indifference. Having spent most of her life shifting identities, she'd learned to become whatever person was necessary to stay alive. The fact that she may have cared about anything—or anyone—had never mattered.

"Put the cat down, Eve." Marguerite snatched the *small bundle of dark fur from her arms and tossed it onto the moonlit grass at Eve's feet. "Do* not *get attached to that animal. I don't want to deal with a crying child when you have to leave it behind."* Eve gave her head a slight shake in an effort to erase the unwelcome memory.

Guerin moved into a sitting position. The muscles along his arms and back flexed—rippled—a helpful distraction to keep her tethered to the present. He'd tried to suppress it, but she hadn't missed the slight groan. The combination of a prolonged flogging and the silver cage had to be wreaking havoc on his nervous system.

Why he wouldn't confirm what she already suspected and end this, she'd never understand. Her mother may have enjoyed breaking the humans and males who disobeyed her, but Eve had never taken pleasure in the act. Unless of course, the scene was something on a more personal level, a form of pleasure, not torture. That, she understood and even enjoyed on occasion. But the male before her was unlike any she'd ever seen. He'd taken everything she'd thrown at him. Soaked it up until his lust had become a palpable fog in the air. Her heart raced with the vivid recollection.

He rolled his shoulders. "What can I say? I'm eager to spend another day with you." The smile on his face conflicted with the daggers in his glare. Guerin rubbed his hands over his upper arms, once more drawing her attention to the unusual tattoo on his right pec—an infinity symbol with a dagger piercing its center and dripping with blood. Eve had noticed it when she'd initially placed him on the cross and had wondered about its origin.

"I've never seen a tattoo like that one before." She stepped closer. He stilled, then glanced down at his chest before returning his attention back to her. "What does it mean?"

"Nothing." Guerin shrugged.

Eve met his stare. "I doubt it."

A cocky grin tilted the corner of this mouth. "Then why don't you use some more of your fancy mind mojo, take a look inside my head, and find out for yourself?"

Eve curled her fingers into a tight fist. "You know very well none of this would be necessary if it weren't for the literal force field you've erected inside that skull of yours."

The vampire shot to his feet and launched toward the bars. She almost leaped back, but caught herself when he stopped a breath away from the metal.

"If you can't get what you want, beautiful, then why haven't you killed me?" His gaze narrowed on hers, the dark-amber irises near molten with heat.

Beautiful? The word echoed inside her head, setting off

a tornado of reactions. Physical and emotional. Her breath quickened. Other men had used flattery in the past in an attempt to get what they wanted. But none of it had held the power of Guerin's voice uttering that one simple word.

Jesus…did he actually mean it?

Oh my God. Stop it, Eve.

Why did she even care? He was a spy. Had to be. A mercenary sent by Seth Keller to either capture or kill her. No other explanation made sense as to why Guerin was searching for Eve.

"I don't kill unless I have a very good reason." Eve turned away from the cell. Maybe if she didn't stare at him, she could think with a level head. He did have a point. What the hell was she going to do with him? She couldn't break down the wall in his mind. God knew she'd tried. And obviously pain would not force him to give her answers. Another scene like the previous one they'd shared and she might not be able to resist sampling everything he had to offer. Eve swallowed, trying to regain some moisture in the barren landscape inside her mouth.

"Then maybe you're not so much like your mother, after all."

Eve whipped around, her heart a frozen knot in her chest. "What did you just say?"

"I said, maybe you're not your mother's daughter. Because Marguerite would have already killed me."

Oh, God… He did work for Seth. The hard lump behind her sternum tightened into a painful throb. Rage washed over her in a drenching tidal wave. Eve flung herself toward him and grabbed the bars, rattling the cage.

"You admit it?" she yelled. "You're one of Seth Keller's

spies." *Shit.* Why did being right have to hurt so damn bad?

"That's not what you heard. I'm familiar with the name, though. It pays to know whose territory you're treading on when passing through. But he's not the master I serve." Guerin never flinched. He stood there, his expression stoic. "You keep berating me to admit I'm his informant." His gaze narrowed. "Yet why do I get the feeling it's the last thing you want to hear?"

Eve started to open her mouth and slam him with a harsh retort, but realized at the last second that she didn't have a clue how to respond. He couldn't read her that well— could he? She hadn't even admitted it to herself. He didn't know a damn thing about her or what she wanted.

"You don't have a clue—" A loud crash from above cut off her remaining words. She spun and ran for the stairs.

"What is it?" Guerin called out behind her.

She was about to find out and didn't have time for twenty questions. Eve's home was located directly behind her club and outside the city limits. The property was somewhat isolated, which was exactly how she liked it. Any unexpected noise or disturbance in her house meant one thing only: trouble.

Taking the stairs in a burst of preternatural speed, Eve made it to the top of the thirty wooden treads faster than a human could have taken two. And came to an abrupt halt.

Smoke.

The scent was unmistakable. Laughter and the sound of multiple voices penetrated the walls, followed by more shattering glass and the clatter of objects slamming onto the floor.

Seth's team had found her, and the bastards were

attempting to burn her out.

Adrenaline flooded her veins, jolting her heart rate and body into action. Eve bolted back down the stairs. How had this happened? Her head spun over possible scenarios as she scrambled for her keys to the small aboveground escape door. She had to get them out of there.

Them?

Eve froze, her fingers white-knuckling the key chain. Was she really going to save Guerin? If so, where would she take him? For all she knew, he'd led her pursuers here.

"What's going on, Eve?" Guerin's calm and smooth baritone voice washed over her. "I smell the smoke and your panic." Eve snatched the ring from the hook on the wall and swung around, the metal jingling with her momentum. Guerin stood there, fisted hands at his side, watching. "Am I a part of your exit plan?"

"It appears I've been found, and they plan to either expose or fry me," she stated, not bothering to hide the pissed-off edge to her voice. Eve marched over to the cage. "Did you have anything to do with this?"

His glare said "Fuck you."

"Answer me! Before we both end up a pile of ashes before our time."

"I've *been* telling you the truth." He cocked his head to the side. "Why would you believe a damn thing I say now?"

"Dammit!" She shoved her hands in her hair, tempted to pull it out by the roots. "Why can't you give me a straight answer?" He was driving her mad.

"If I were one of your enemies, do you think I'd let them barbecue me?"

Her head and chest hurt from all the conflicting emotions

swimming around inside. But he had a damn good point. Smoke thickened the air, reminding her she was out of time.

Eve located the correct key and shoved it in the lock. A moment later, Guerin stepped through the door. Eve swallowed hard and sent out a quick, silent prayer that her instincts weren't letting her down.

"This way." She darted toward the rear of the basement and the hidden narrow door. It was their one chance for survival. On the way, she grabbed the coat Guerin had been wearing when she'd abducted him. She tossed it to him since the male was still in his underwear.

"Thanks," he muttered, and slipped it on.

"Humans in service to Seth will be waiting for us out there." At the door, Eve stopped and glanced back at Guerin. "I take it at your age you can withstand a brief run through sunlight?" She cocked one brow in his direction. There was no mistaking the vibration of power rolling off the male. Power that said he'd seen more than two centuries. But even the eldest of vampires still couldn't phase through full sunlight. Their molecules would incinerate from the UV exposure.

"Did you just call me an old man?" He flashed her a smirk.

Eve had to resist the urge to roll her eyes. "So I can presume that's a yes?"

"Yes," he replied with the same cocky grin.

"Good."

"What about you?"

"What about me?" She shrugged.

"The sun…"

"Don't worry about me. I can take care of myself. All

you need to do is focus on following my lead. When I open the door, we head left toward my car—a black Mercedes." Eve turned away as a whispered "yes, ma'am" reached her ears. She closed her eyes and breathed deeply. Why was she saving this asshole? Eve opened her eyes and unlocked the heavy steel bolt securing the five-by-two slab of oak. She looked back, ready to give him the signal to haul ass, when all the air punched from her lungs.

Naked.

It was the only word her stunned mind could form. Eve spun in place, and her rear bumped against the door. Guerin stood there, completely nude, with his briefs and coat in his grip.

"W-wh-what are you doing?" Dear God, she was stuttering like a young girl who'd never seen "boy parts" before. Unbidden, her gaze slid down his body, over sculpted abs, and lower still to the impressive package between his legs. Granted, these were no ordinary boy parts. Oh, no. This was the full-grown kind of male appendage that made a woman's heart pound, her palms damp, and other areas of her body even wetter.

"It's been a while since I last fed, and I'll endure the sun better if I shift."

"Oh…right." Eve whipped back around and bit back a groan. *Pull it together, woman.* Shifting wasn't a talent Eve had inherited, and she hadn't considered the option. She needed her head on straight if they were both to make it out of there. "On three." She yanked the door wide. "One, two, three."

Eve darted into the bright sunlight, then hung a left toward the secondary vehicle she kept fueled and ready—

just in case. She squinted against the intense rays, but behind her, Eve could hear the soft thumps of Guerin's four paws on the grass. He wouldn't last long out there, but her half-human DNA gave Eve a longer window of tolerance. Which was exactly why Seth's men were flushing her out at this time of day. They knew if she truly were the rumored hybrid, the sun wouldn't cook her like an overdone Pop-Tart.

A flash of movement out of the corner of her eye had Eve swerving to her right at the same moment a broad silver-laced net fell to the ground, missing her. Small doses of silver didn't bother Eve. The shit stung, but nothing she couldn't handle. Yet a large net would feel like a thousand wasps burrowing their stingers into her skin, immobilizing her.

A loud snarl unleashed behind her, followed by a shout for help, halted Eve in her tracks. Guerin, in wolf form, had a large bald man down, his canines pinning the human's neck to the ground. Dark mahogany-colored fur shone in the sun's rays. Powerful muscles flexed underneath the thick coat with the incredible strength it took to hold the hulk of a man in place.

For her.

Guerin was protecting her.

And it was provocative as hell.

Her heart pounded and her chest heaved. From exertion, fear, or the sight of the fierce beast in front of her? She wasn't sure.

"Looks as if Seth will be very pleased."

Eve spun in the direction of the voice. Then another human emerged from her right—then another opposite him. Until six men came at her from all angles.

Slowly, they closed in, forcing Eve to pivot on her heels, keeping each one in sight. The man on the ground was no longer a threat, judging by the limp state of his body. The wolf backed away and stalked toward the gathering posse with his crimson-stained muzzle drawn back, exposing his long canines. A wicked growl rumbled from his throat.

What was he doing?

They were here for her, not him.

He swung his head in her direction, anger and resolve shimmering in his eyes. Her gaze met his, then caught something else. Smoke—but this time it wasn't coming from the wood and shingles of the home burning before them.

Oh shit. Guerin. White tendrils trailed upward from his fur.

"Get out of here!" Eve's fangs dropped into place, and she bared them at the wolf.

Guerin's large muzzle lifted in defiance a half second before he lunged at another one of the men. He was insane. The crazy beast was going to fry himself. One of Seth's henchmen launched himself toward the scattered net as the others tightened the circle around her. Damn, it would be so easy to just phase out of there.

Except…

Her gaze darted to the animal ripping into one assassin's leg. If she disappeared while Guerin was in his current state, Eve would end up leaving him behind. Phasing wasn't an option for the shifted vampire.

"Come on, Eve," a large, dark-haired man wearing torn jeans and a black turtleneck piped up as he crept forward. "We know it's you." He nodded. "Why not make this easy on everyone? No pain. No blood." His dark eyes narrowed to thin slits. "Let us take you to Seth."

"Fuck you," she spat.

Turtleneck guy's mellow expression morphed into a lethal frown.

Adrenaline ran thick in Eve's blood. Her arms and legs trembled from the hormone's effects. Eve eased one foot back, her gaze swinging among Guerin, turtleneck, netting guy...she pivoted and faced the three men behind her. *Surrounded.* And Guerin was less than five minutes from going up in flames—just like her house.

There was only one way out.

If she failed, they were both dead. But if she didn't try, the outcome would be no different.

Eve stretched her arms out at her sides, tossed her head back, closed her eyes, and sucked in a deep breath. She'd never attempted to take out so many at once and had no idea what state the effort would leave her in. But she was out of options. This *had* to work.

One by one, she curled her fingers into tight fists as if she were gathering the energy around her and concentrating it into the palms of her hands. Hundreds of small lightning bolts of energy zinged along her arms, up her legs, coalescing in the center of her chest. She squeezed her fists, nails biting into her flesh. The ball of heat grew into a raging inferno behind her sternum. Eve gasped for air. *More.* She rocked on her heels. Her head fell forward and she opened her eyes. The men were on her now, but a hazy wave of energy encompassed her, keeping them on the other side. Puzzled looks that said *What the hell is she up to?* tossed among them. Seth's minions had to be thinking, "Do we run and risk death by Seth's hands, or stay and see if we can outlast whatever she's doing?" Oh, she was about to give them the answer they were waiting for.

The blaze behind her sternum licked at her spine with its fiery tongue.

One more second.

Eve dug her fangs into her lip, and the metallic taste of her own blood washed over her taste buds. Sweat dripped off her forehead, stinging her eyes. Her vision blurred. Images warped.

It was as if the world around her pulsed at a different beat…and pain was its metronome.

Now.

With a rapid spreading of her fingers, Eve released her store of energy. It erupted from her chest, taking out the men in front of her. She spun, sending the wave out like a fan, knocking the others from their feet. The blast would disrupt their brain waves and temporarily—if they were lucky—turn off their lights.

It was over.

She slumped to the ground. Or had the ground reached up to her? Who knew? God, her brain was short-circuited. The earth tilted beneath her palms, and her stomach lurched. *Pull yourself together, Eve. You're the only chance you and Guerin have.*

Guerin!

Hidden beneath the smell of the last four years of her life going up in flames, the musky scent of singed fur invaded her nostrils, jolting her limbs into action. Eve pushed to her feet and staggered toward the limp, smoldering body that was Guerin's wolf form. Thank God, in his unconscious state he hadn't reverted back to his human state yet, or he would have been in even worse shape as he lay in the afternoon sun.

Eve yanked her shirt over her head and draped it over what she could of his head and flank. She had to find him shelter. Her arms trembled as she slid her hands under his front legs. Eve half dragged, half carried his dead weight toward her car. Air sawed in and out of her lungs, partly out of fear, the other part—exhaustion. She was stronger than any human woman, thanks to her hybrid DNA, but damn... he was huge, and she'd overexerted herself knocking out six men.

At the car, Eve pulled her keys from her pocket and popped the trunk of the Mercedes. They were in the country with no other dwellings for at least ten miles, so this was their best immediate solution besides digging a hole and burying themselves. She hoisted his upper body up over the lip of the trunk, then gripped his lower half and repeated the process. He tumbled into the dark pit with a dull *thump*. As if his flesh somehow recognized the safety of the darkness, he reverted back to his human appearance.

The cramped interior didn't allow for his long limbs to extend and relax, so he remained on his side, nude and in somewhat of a fetal position. Eve grabbed the wool blanket she kept stored for emergencies from behind him and spread it over his large, curved frame. His dark hair, singed on the ends, lay matted against his damp cheek. She had no idea why he'd risked his life for her. He could have run and saved his own neck. What had possessed him to stay behind in an attempt to protect her?

Who was he...really? And why the hell had he sought her out?

She leaned in, and with a trembling hand, smoothed the strands away from his face. The shadowed interior swayed, and she staggered into the bumper. Eve gripped the rim, steadying herself. *Shit.* She had to get them out of there before she passed out and fell in the trunk along with him.

Thanks to her mother's paranoia she was always prepared for the worst-case scenario, so Eve had a backup plan. The vampire in her trunk would have to deal with his cramped quarters for a few hours.

Chapter Six

Arran's jaw tightened, his molars grinding under the pressure as he watched the Enclave's master force-feed their reluctant ex-warrior prisoner. Markus released Kenric's wrist with a gasp and fell backward onto his cot. Kenric swiped a hand over his face. The sheen of perspiration was visible even from the distance Arran stood from the silver-lined cage. The drain of forcing Markus to feed every forty-eight hours had to be exhausting, not only from the mental strain, but physically as well. Markus rolled onto his side, coughing.

"Get the hell out, you son of a bitch," the prisoner managed to wheeze after catching his breath.

Kenric didn't flinch; instead, he closed the wound at his wrist, then unrolled the sleeve of his black sweater. "I'm not letting you die. Whether you fucking like it or not," the master growled.

Markus slowly lifted his head. Dark eyes filled with resentment narrowed on Kenric and chilled the air. "Someone needs to find you a new toy...Master," he spat. "Because while you're in here giving me all this love and attention, your precious Enclave warriors are screwing with your life." A deep laugh erupted from his chest. "You don't see what's right under your nose, do you?" Markus flopped onto his back, chuckling like a child who'd just cheated at a game and won.

The master of the Enclave stared at the former warrior in silence, then shook his head in what appeared to be pure frustration and turned on his heel. Arran stepped from the exterior doorway and headed toward the cage entrance. With a gloved hand to shield him from the silver's caustic effect, he swung the door open for Kenric to pass through. Arran's gaze shifted to the frail-looking warrior moving into a sitting position on the side of his cot. Markus's cold stare locked with Arran's. One side of the former warrior's lips lifted in a sly, knowing grin.

"How is sweet Gabrielle?" Markus cocked his head. "Is my newest fledgling treating you well, Warrior?" Arran's grip tightened on the bar of the cage door. "What?" Markus shrugged. "You seem pissed. I would think you'd appreciate my turning her into a vampire for you. Because now"—Markus reached between his legs and slid a palm over his crotch—"you get to fuck her for an eternity."

"You have truly morphed into an insane bastard." Arran slammed the door and twisted the key, securing the bolt. "And to think, I once thought of you not only as my partner, but my friend." He could have sworn a flicker of something other than malice surfaced in Markus's expression. But before it could take hold, the look was gone. Wishful thinking.

"Awww... Now be nice, Arran, or I might have to spill

our little secret."

Arran jammed the palm of his gloved hand into the bars, rattling the hinges before whirling away from the enclosure. A wicked burst of laughter rolled from the cage as Arran exited the holding area. Sick SOB. This had to end soon—all the subtle omission of details to Kenric, lies about where exactly Guerin had gone and what his second-in-command planned to do while there—or he was going to end up killing Markus.

He should have never agreed to be a co-conspirator in Guerin's plan. He was lying not only to Kenric, but to Gabrielle as well. And he hated it.

Keeping this secret from his mate was slowly eating away at him from the inside out. But Guerin didn't want the information about Kenric's possible daughter going any further than the two of them. According to Guerin, if Gabrielle knew, there would be no way she'd keep this from Emily, Kenric's mate.

Hell, he was probably right.

Hiding this from Kenric was hard enough on Arran, but he could only imagine how the covert knowledge would have plagued Gabrielle.

The fact that Markus loomed in the center of this fucked-up ménage only made matters worse. But they needed Markus. The former warrior had been with Marguerite for the past two years and held the intelligence they needed to locate Eve. Before she came looking for her father—and the Enclave. Arran had to completely agree with Guerin on one point. If she turned out to be as vindictive as her mother claimed, Eve would have to be stopped.

Arran took the stairs two at a time to the first floor,

following Kenric's path. At the top, he exited into the open expanse of the hallway that led to a kitchen on his left and the den farther down on his right. Arran's boots thumped against the hard maple floors as he marched forward.

"So what do you think Markus meant when he said the Enclave's warriors are screwing with my life?"

Kenric's deep voice ricocheted off the walls and froze Arran in his path. Arran glanced over his shoulder and found the Enclave's master standing with his back against the wall off to the side of the basement door. A dagger twirled in one gloved palm, the pearl handle shimmering as it whirled end over end.

Damn, he was good.

When Arran came from below, he hadn't sensed even the smallest trace of the vampire's presence waiting for him there. Arran turned and faced Kenric.

"He's insane." Arran shrugged. "That's what I think. Marguerite broke him, and he wants to get inside your head and take you down with him. Finish the job Marguerite was never able to."

Kenric nodded and pushed away from the wall. "Maybe," he said as he drew closer to Arran. "You know, it's not the first time Markus has insinuated he knew something about my team that I didn't." He halted, leaving less than a foot of distance between them. "Why do think he wants me to believe such a thing?"

"Like I said, he's mad. Crazy mad."

"I agree. He is." Kenric reached down and slid the blade back into his thigh sheath, then glanced back at Arran. "But the way Guerin walked away from the Enclave without a word about where he was going or when he would return?

Leaving you to tell me he needed some time away, because he couldn't tolerate watching me rehabilitate Markus after what he'd done to our mates and the Enclave…" Kenric shook his head. "This isn't like Guerin." He nailed Arran with a glare. "And it's starting to reek. Has Guerin been in contact with you?"

"I haven't heard from him." At least that part was the truth. The bastard hadn't returned any of his messages since they'd spoken last night.

"I see." Kenric nodded once more but never released his gaze. "Two days, Arran." Kenric's eyelids narrowed. "Out of respect for your loyalty and service to the Enclave, I'll give you a little more time. But by the time my ass has to return to Markus…I want answers." Kenric brushed past him.

Arran released the air that had become trapped in his lungs. "Dammit," he mumbled under his breath. This had gone to shit faster than he'd anticipated. Whatever Guerin had planned, he'd better move fast. Because in two days, there was about to be one large, pissed-off master vampire crawling all over his ass.

Chapter Seven

Anticipation hummed hrough Seth's veins like a snake that had licked the air and detected its prey mere inches away. On the stairway's landing, he gripped the polished brass knob of the corner banister and breathed deep. Tonight he hovered one step closer to having it all. *Yes.* He could almost taste the victory.

It was decadent, sweet, and all his. Well…it would be soon.

He reached low and repositioned his swollen cock before continuing down the steps. The flavor of a conquest always made him want to fuck. That was something else he'd have to take care of before much longer.

On the main level, Seth made his way to the basement door and headed below. His calyx had informed him earlier that the expedition posse sent to verify Eve's identity and retrieve her had returned. He crossed the expanse of the room, his boot heels releasing a distinct click off the lower level's concrete floor.

Near his receiving area, Seth spotted only three of the six men who'd comprised the group waiting.

And no female.

What the hell was this all about? He sucked in a breath and his gut rebelled. The stench of failure permeated the air.

Seth eased onto the seat of his royal-blue velvet armchair, his in-house security flanking him, and met the lowered gazes of the trembling trio. His jaw ached from the effort it took not to kill them before hearing their sob story. Because he knew that was exactly what they were about to spill. It required every ounce of his control not to rip their throats open and allow their incompetent blood to fill the sewers.

"Out with it," Seth snarled. "What have you learned and where are the others?" He steepled his fingers and braced himself for the play-by-play. The apparent spokesman of the group painted a shaky and pathetic tale of how one female and a vampire in wolf form took out six men and escaped. They were the only ones to have regained consciousness after her attack and had disposed of the others before reporting in.

But it was her.

There was no doubt.

She'd fought them in daylight and her power… His pulse leaped, and the muscles in his forearms twitched in restraint. So fucking close. Seth didn't know whether to roar with rage at their feeble attempt to snare her, or feast on their hearts in celebration.

He had to know what made the female tick. Sample her DNA. How did she balance the power of a vampire along with her sensitivity as a human? So many unanswered questions about her existence. How did the vampire antigen live in balance with her human cells without consuming them?

Could her tolerance to sunlight be replicated? Was it possible to vaccinate a vampire with her particular human genetic traits and acquire her abilities? He had to find out. Seth swallowed back the growl of frustration clawing its way up his throat. One thing was for sure—they would die tonight for losing her.

He would have to start again. But at least he knew where to focus his search: the Rose's Thorn. Eve wouldn't show herself again, but someone there had to possess knowledge of where she would hide.

"Seth."

The unexpected mental call yanked his attention from the situation at hand. Shit. She was early.

"Yes, Mistress," he replied silently.

"I'm waiting for you in your quarters. I do hope you have good news to share with me this evening."

Seth cringed. Her games were a tedious but necessary evil. He suppressed the chuckle at the pun. Evil. An understatement for what lay beneath the gentle purr of the female upstairs.

Without a glance at either of the males bracketing his chair, Seth spouted his command and rose. "Dispose of them however you see fit." Abrupt inhales resonated from the trio, mixed with a barrage of desperate cries for mercy. It would do them no good. About as much use to them as his pleas would be when he shared the latest failure to produce Eve. At least their pain came with an end in sight. His, on the other hand… He sighed and began his trek upstairs.

"I'm afraid the news will not be to your liking, Mistress," he mentally transmitted. A shriek pierced his head, sending an icy chill of dread down his spine.

Chapter Eight

Hunger.

Two syllables.

One simple word.

But for a vampire, those six letters possessed the power to bend the mind of even the eldest creature of the night to its will. Guerin's fangs bore into his lower lip. The copper taste of his own blood did little to sate the ravenous beast in his gut.

"Good. You're coming around."

Eve. On instinct, he inhaled deeply, drawing in her unique duo of fragrances—cinnamon vanilla. Mmm… Delicious and unsettling. They possessed the power to flip the switch on his hunger and divert his attention toward a desire of another kind: lust.

The ache in his fangs eased, and his incisors receded to a more tolerable position. He swallowed hard, working to find a hint of moisture in the desert he called a mouth.

Judging from the strength and clarity of Eve's voice, she'd fared better than he had.

He cracked one eye open, then another, and peered at his surroundings. Gray paneling encircled the room. Pale-yellow lighting glowed from a table at his right. A few feet away another small round table and two chairs sat beneath a heavily draped window.

Definitely not the Ritz, but at least he was silver cage–free, and getting out of here would prove much simpler. Because if he didn't, it wouldn't be long before the need to feed would haul his ass to the edge of his sanity.

Guerin rubbed a palm over his face, the stubble there way beyond a five o'clock shadow, and hoisted his aching and starved body in the direction of Eve's voice. He blinked, and his heart stuttered even in its weakened state at the vision in front of him. Another lamp shone behind Eve, haloing a band of golden light around her raven hair.

An angel born from the womb of darkness? Was it even possible?

"Impressive," she added from the wooden chair she'd placed near his bed. "I thought it would have taken much longer for you to recover from that amount of UV exposure."

"What can I say?" Guerin drawled. "I'm an overachiever." He nodded at the room around him. "Where are we?"

"Always the wise guy." Eve glanced around the small quarters. "This is my backup place." She settled her gaze on him. "A girl can never be over-prepared." Eve threaded her fingers through her hair, pushing it away from her face. "Are you ever serious about anything?"

Guerin smirked. "Beautiful… Seriously, I would think that you'd like this side of me a hell of a lot better. It's prettier."

"What?" She tilted her head and tossed him a smug grin. "You don't think I can handle the *real* Guerino Lombardi? The one who stays hidden behind the smart-ass remarks and charming smiles?"

A snort escaped his throat. "Handle it?" Guerin rolled onto his back and draped an arm over his eyes. "I'm sure Eve Devonshire can handle whatever is thrown at her." After witnessing her talents for the past few days, psychic shock waves, walking in daylight, abilities he'd never seen even Kenric, a master vampire, wield, left no doubt the woman could handle whatever came her way. The genetic combination of a master vampire's DNA crossed with an abnormally strong female vampire such as Marguerite had resulted in producing a hybrid offspring who could go toe-to-toe, and then some, with any vamp. And it was one mother of a turn-on. He sighed.

"You didn't answer my question."

"Which was?"

"The real Guerino? Who is he?"

"That wasn't the question." He slid his forearm away and turned his head toward her. "You asked if I thought you couldn't handle it. And you got your answer."

Eve's expression cooled, right before she stood and nailed him with a hard glare. "No more games. Who the hell are you and what do you want with me?"

Guerin swung his legs over the side of the bed and launched himself to his feet. A loose gray pair of sweats dipped low around his hips. Well, thank Christ for small favors. At least his bare behind was finally covered. He ground his molars, searching for patience. For the strength to handle this the right way.

Fuck it. Guerin curled his fingers into a tight fist. She wanted to know why he was here, he'd give her all the damn info she begged for. Including the part where he'd helped to kill her mother… The world tilted on its axis. *Whoa.*

His stomach roiled.

He stumbled back, jamming his calves against the mattress frame to keep from falling on his ass. Reaching behind, he fumbled for something solid to keep him horizontal. The room dimmed, and Guerin plopped onto the mattress, his pulse thumping hard in his ears. *Yeah.* He'd tell her as soon as he got a handle on his lights. Guerin blinked, attempting to clear his vision. Eve was in his face. Her lips moved, but the steady drumbeat in his head garbled her words.

"Feed… Blood."

Blood. She said something about blood. *Yes.* His fangs shoved through his upper gums to full extension at the same moment hot pain arrowed through his gut, ricocheting off his spine.

"Oh, fuck," Guerin moaned, clutched his abdomen, and rolled backward. He'd pushed the hunger aside for too long. *Out.* He had to get out.

Guerin lunged for the other side of the bed. Cold sweat rolled down the side of his face and dripped into his eyes. He swiped at it with a trembling hand and forced himself to his feet once more.

"Get your ass back on the bed, vampire!" Eve appeared in front of him again, her fangs bared.

"Move," he snarled. "Or I'll do it for you." In his current state, he didn't trust being alone with her for one more second.

Instead of stepping aside, Guerin watched—mesmerized—as Eve lifted her wrist to her mouth and bit. A crimson stream bubbled up around the perfect curve of her lips, staining her flesh and evoking a cold shiver over his own.

His mouth watered.

Fangs throbbed.

Air scorched a path into his lungs.

He'd never wanted—craved—anything more in his life. And no way in hell did he have the patience or inclination to analyze which of the visions in front of him he desired more: Eve or the scarlet fluid escaping her vein.

Then she was there, without having to ask, her essence flowing onto his tongue.

And it was ambrosia.

He rocked on his heels, but Eve stretched her other arm across his lower back, steadying him. The assault of her flavor over his taste buds, the heat of her blood mingling with his, was unlike anything he'd ever experienced over the centuries. His cock surged to life. He groaned and gently sank his fangs, needing more. Eve mumbled something in response, then the warmth of her body enveloped him. She pressed into him, breasts to his chest, hip to hip, her heat seeping under his skin as her blood heated his veins. The roar of her heartbeat filled his head to near bursting. Eve was everywhere. Her essence went cell-deep, sparking off his neurons and marking his soul. But the crazy shit was, at that moment, he didn't give a damn.

She was pure indulgence. Hot, liquid sin. That last piece of delectable chocolate cake you knew you should walk away from, but if you didn't have at least one more taste, life wouldn't be worth living.

He glanced at the swell of her breasts against his chest, and it took every remaining fiber of his control not to take her down, bury his face, and continue to drink between what had to be nirvana.

"Enough," she commanded. "Enough for now." Eve brushed her fingers up his spine.

Guerin swirled his tongue over the wound, closing it, then kissed the evidence of his feeding. He followed the soft inside of her arm upward with his lips. *Damn.* Every inch of her was sweet. The rigid length of his erection pulsed behind the thin cotton of his pants. If the taste of her blood and the feel of her skin next to his had him this crazed, he could only imagine what the flavor of her arousal would to do his mind. And he would surely die if he didn't find out soon.

At her neck, he teased the bounding pulse with his tongue, then lifted his head. Pale-blue eyes, glowing with desire, met his.

"Beautiful," he breathed. Guerin cupped her face, holding her gaze, and brought her mouth to within a hairbreadth of his own.

"Guerin...," she whispered. "I—"

He brushed his lips over hers, stealing the small gasp of air she'd released, then pulled back. "Need you." Before she could respond, Guerin wrapped his arms around her, spun, and lowered her onto the bed. Their mouths, tongues, intertwined in a kiss that threatened to consume him. Before Guerin was ready to let go, Eve broke away, and he found their positions quickly reversed.

"Let's get one thing straight, Lombardi," she stated, straddling Guerin's hips. "I'm not one of your weak human conquests." Without warning, Eve snatched his arms from the bed, spread them wide, and pinned him to the mattress. Not unusual for a female vamp, except with Eve, the maneuver had been performed by her mind.

He was so fucking hard.

One touch. *Shit.* One damn touch from her and he'd blow.

Guerin gritted his teeth for strength. Eve reached for the hemline of her T-shirt. Then with a move he never knew could be so seductive, she tugged it over her head. Long midnight tresses fell free and skated over her skin. Full creamy white breasts, their nipples taut and a deep rose color, rocked inches from his chin. Even if he'd wanted to, Guerin couldn't have contained the groan emanating from his throat.

Eve leaned forward, braced her upper body with one hand against his pec, and gripped his chin with her other. The look she nailed him with had his balls drawn taut. She licked her lips, then added, "*I* decide when—or if—I'm topped."

Christ. His eyelids shuttered under the assault on his senses. She was dominant lust personified. He sucked in a stabilizing breath.

His former Mistress had pushed his boundaries—his love—to the breaking point. She'd been so eager to see how far he would go to please her. Guerin had learned too late that she had only been about the game of manipulation. After his years with Daniela, Guerin had shut himself down with a vow: he would never repeat the same mistake twice. Never again would he risk falling for a female vampire. Especially one with a taste for domination and sadism.

Yet here he was with Eve and on the verge of unleashing the animal he'd long since locked down inside his mind. But God help him, he didn't possess the strength to push her away. He'd promised himself he'd never submit again, but right now, he'd die if he didn't have her. And he wouldn't have her any other way.

"Yes," he whispered. "You decide."

"Yes. I do," she purred. Eve moved lower, taking Guerin's sweats down his thighs. His erection sprang free from its confines, arching up to rest on his lower abdomen. The cool night air inside the room did little to subdue the hot need in his shaft. Not when the vision fueling his lust was now naked, and her warm body slid up his. Like a panther stalking its prey, she was grace in motion, shifting and stroking every inch of him, as if she were leaving her scent, her mark, on his flesh in her wake.

Finally, Eve straddled his waist, the heat of her pussy branding him. Guerin tossed his head back. His biceps strained against her hold. *Holy hell.* She was going to kill him before he ever got the chance to love her.

Whoa. Love *her*?

He squeezed his eyes shut and shook his head. Where had that come from? The residual traces of hunger must be messing with his mind. Lust and sex. That's what this was. She knew it, and he knew it. Besides, he'd long since learned that love had no business in the middle of a good fuck.

Guerin opened his eyes. "Come to me," he uttered, his voice low and gravelly in his ears. "Let me taste you"—he narrowed his gaze—"pleasure you."

A shuddering breath escaped her, and she scooted forward. Eve tilted her upper body toward him, grasped the headboard, and teased the hard pebble of her nipple over his lips.

"Take it," she breathed.

Damn. He didn't have to be told twice. Guerin sucked it in and gently scraped his teeth across the sensitive tip. Eve hissed.

"Oh, God." She slipped her fingers into his hair, nails biting into his scalp. Fuck yeah. Guerin opened wider, taking the entire dark areola into his mouth. So soft. Sweet. He circled the hard nub with his tongue before flicking it over the end. She pressed him closer, urging him on with a moan. He sucked hard, then pulsed on the engorged nipple. "Guerin...," she cried out. "I need..."

Guerin broke his hold. "Let me give you what you need." Eve glanced down, and in the soft room light, her cheeks were flushed with arousal. Her gaze flickered toward either of his arms and the pressure holding them in place vanished. Guerin didn't waste another second questioning her motives or her reason for releasing him. Instinct had him gripping her hips and pulling her forward until her bare sex rested over his face. He darted his tongue out, sinking it between her folds and stroking upward to her swollen clit. Eve arched in response and rocked her hips as if searching for more. Guerin slid his palms down and cupped her ass, holding her in place. Right where he wanted her. So damn delicious. He worked up and down, back and forth, sucking, licking, pushing her to the edge, then reeling her back. At the apex of her swollen, pulsing core, Guerin drew lazy circles. Everything about her from the way she tasted, her scent—hell—even the feel of her pussy on his tongue drove him wild. He didn't care if he never came up for air.

"Guerin...," she gasped, a hard quake rocking her body. "I need to come... Now."

His cock twitched, and he glanced up. "Once more."

"What?" Eve dropped her gaze to his.

"Beg." Guerin lifted a brow. "So fucking hot."

"Never," she growled. "I don't beg." Her voice dropped to a sexy purr, and her almond-shaped eyes narrowed on him.

Tucking his chin, Guerin sent a hot puff of air over her clit. Her breath hitched, and the headboard jerked in her grasp.

"Oh God. I swear, Lombardi, I'm going to…" She shook her head.

"Don't tease, beautiful." Guerin slowly shifted one hand, allowing the tip of his finger to ease inside her slick core. Eve's head lolled between her shoulders.

"More. Yes…" Her hips flexed, beckoning. And he obliged, sinking deeper. *Christ.* She was so hot, wet, her muscles tightening around him. He squeezed his eyes shut. How in the hell would he survive with his shaft buried inside her? His heart slammed against his chest at the thought. In and out he pumped. Panting hard, Eve rocked in time with him. Guerin slid a second digit inside and flicked his tongue over her engorged nub.

"Not enough," she groaned. "Dammit, Guerin… Do it!"

Guerin wrapped his lips around the swollen bundle of nerves and sucked. As if lightning had reached through the plaster ceiling and arrowed down her spine, Eve jolted and cried out. Guerin continued working her clit. Hot arousal flowed over his hand, her sweet flavor making its way inside his mouth and coating his tongue. He groaned.

Eve released her hold on the headboard and melted backward onto the mattress. But he didn't let go. Not yet. Guerin rose, following her.

"No more," she uttered on a groan. Tiny tremors shook her thighs with each gentle pull he gave to her clit. Guerin made one more pass from where his fingers still stroked inside her to her sensitive bud, taking in every drop, then moved to the throbbing pulse at her groin. He nuzzled her there. The heat of the fast-moving blood beneath warmed his cheeks, his lips. His fangs burst from his gums, and he dragged the pointed tips over her soft flesh. As if on their own accord, her legs spread wider in response. "Oh my God…," Eve called out, her tone desperate with need. "Yes. Christ, yes."

He struck. Hot blood filled his mouth as his name filled the room. Guerin held her in place with one hand as another orgasm erupted along her arms and legs. He swallowed hard, reveling in the strength and potency of her blood. But it wasn't enough.

Inside. With everything in his being, he needed to be inside her, feel the silken walls of her pussy grip his cock. Guerin sealed her wound with his tongue and slipped his fingers free.

"Come to me, beautiful." He slid his forearms under her shoulders, taking her into a sitting position before lifting her slightly from the mattress and easing her toward him. "Take me," he growled. Eve placed her legs over his thighs and hovered over the head of his pulsing erection. She wrapped her arms around his neck and leaned in, balancing herself over his cock.

"You want to fuck me?" she whispered in his ear.

Electricity zigzagged down his back. He arched and thrust his hands into the hair at her nape. "Christ!" He pressed her down in the direction of his aching rod, but she wouldn't be moved. *Holy mother of...* She was so damn close. The hot trickle of her arousal trailed down the backside of his cock.

"Answer me, Guerino." She yanked a handful of hair at the back of his head, sending a jolt straight to his shaft. He sucked in a lungful of air through his teeth. "Do you want to fuck me?" This time, her tongue followed her words, the tip tracing the curve of his ear.

"Yes." He tightened his hold around her body, pressing her into his chest. God, he loved the way she felt in his arms. The way her curves molded to his frame. The full swell of her breasts next to his heart—a perfect fit. *Shit.* Lust had damn near fried his brain cells.

"Yes, what?"

A groan rolled from his throat. "Please allow me to fuck you."

She plunged onto his shaft, the heat and clasp of her body short-circuiting what was left of his brain cells.

"Eve," he cried out.

Again she surged up, then drove herself onto him once more. His balls tightened, and the pressure of his release pulsed at the base of his cock. No way would he last. Christ. It was too good. Guerin reached for her hips, working her up and down his length. Eve teased his lips with her own, and Guerin hungrily opened, welcoming her inside. Their tongues mimicked the lust-filled dance their bodies performed. The pounding of his heart beat a deafening staccato in his ears.

He could barely breathe.

So good.

Guerin broke away and buried his face in the curve of her neck, the sweet smell of her skin and sweat a heady feast to his senses. *Have to focus. Don't want to let go.*

Need to come.

No. Fuck. No.

Need to hold on.

Just one more minute. So good.

So damn good.

Eve's nails raked down his back, leaving a trail of fire in their wake and catching him off guard. Guerin's neck arched at the same moment his fragile control snapped. He cried out in pain—in ecstasy—and the head of his cock erupted. On and on his release pumped, and Guerin rocked his hips in time to the waves of his orgasm. His eyelids shuttered under the pleasure, and on the other side of the lids, a dazzling swirl of stars swam. It was as if he was on some kind of mind-altering drug trip—and he never wanted the high to end.

Eve shuddered in his arms, his name on her lips snatching him back to reality. He held her until the last tremor rolled through her body. Guerin collapsed onto the mattress, taking her with him. Except for the sound of their heavy breathing, they lay in silence, Eve on his chest with his cock still buried inside.

Chapter Nine

"Shit!" Arran slung his cell across the room. The device landed with a soft *thump* in the center of the king-size bed he shared with Gabrielle. *Voice mail again.* Arran's forty-eight-hour reprieve was up, and unless Guerin contacted him soon with news, he was going to have to face Kenric with the truth.

He'd never felt so torn in his life.

Torn between his loyalty to Kenric, and the promises he'd made to Guerin. They were ripping him in two.

But the lack of contact from Guerin had already tripped the switch in his head that said their second-in-command was in trouble. So in reality, he didn't have a choice.

"Dammit." Arran crossed the room, plopped on the edge of the bed, and grabbed his boots. He just hated that it had to be him tasked with laying this bombshell on Kenric.

"When are you going to tell me what's wrong?"

Arran glanced up at the sweet sound of his mate's voice.

Gabrielle stood in the bathroom doorway. A large white towel wrapped her torso, while she worked the dampness from her dark locks with another. God, she was breathtaking. He'd never understand how he could deserve such a treasure in his life.

"What do you mean?" Arran shot his gaze down to the black leather and rubber in his hands. "Nothing's wrong."

"Yeah. Right." The soft brush of her feet over the carpeted surface said his mate drew closer. But he didn't need his ears for confirmation. The tingle under his skin that ran straight to his cock always alerted him to her presence.

"Have you forgotten we're connected, mate?" Gabrielle pressed her way between his thighs, forcing him to release his grip on the boots. But that was fine with him; he'd much rather have his hands wrapped around his woman.

Arran slid his palms over the exposed section of creamy flesh along her legs, then up and over the curve of her hip. "Now how could I forget something like that?" He leaned forward, and using the long, sharp tips of his fangs, bit into the cotton hiding her curves and pulled it free. The towel dropped to the floor. "Mmm…that's more like it." Arran flicked his tongue over one hard pink nipple. A gasp escaped her lips right before she wiggled, breaking free of his hold.

"That's not going to work this time, vampire." She wagged a lone finger. "I've tried to give you time and ignored the walls you've put up, blocking me from some of your thoughts. But I don't like the effect this…this problem is having on you." Gabrielle moved back between his legs, her warm palms going to his cheeks, embracing him. Arran closed his eyes, soaking in the serenity she brought to his soul. "I'm worried about you," she whispered. Arran lifted his eyelids. He hated the sound of those four words on her tongue. "I'm your mate—your other half. You don't have to carry whatever this is alone."

No one else on the planet could get inside his heart like Gabrielle. Get inside and melt the damn thing down. He pressed his hands to hers.

"I know," he breathed. "I know you're there for me." Arran nodded. "But the issue I've been dealing with is something that deserves to be revealed to someone else, before I have the right to share it—even with my mate."

Gabrielle slid her palms free. "Fair enough." She dipped low, pulled the towel from the floor, and wrapped it back around herself. "Is this...issue something you plan to, or are able to, reveal soon?"

Arran finished tying the laces of his second boot and stood. "I don't have a choice. The truth has to come out—and now." He grasped Gabrielle by the arms and tugged her to his chest, slamming his lips to hers as if the taste of her mouth—her love—would give him the strength he needed to do what had to be done tonight. "Need you," he mumbled against her soft flesh, driving his fingers through her damp hair. "So much."

"You have me. Forever."

A groan escaped his throat, and he pressed her backward, biting, sucking, their tongues dueling for more. He'd had every intention of walking out the door the moment he stood. But then he was in Gabrielle's arms, and at that second, nothing else mattered more than being inside her. God yes, she was his other half, and before all hell broke loose, he wanted her one more time. Just like this.

Gabrielle's back bumped the wall, and Arran jerked her

towel. *Raw.*

Her chest heaved with each breath. *Wild.*

He spun her, placing her face against the wall. "Open for me," he commanded.

Mine.

She spread her legs, and a moan bubbled up from his chest at the sight. His cock throbbed in response. Arran unbuttoned his jeans and lowered his fly; the slight tremble racing over his mate's flesh at the sound did not escape his attention. He closed the gap between them, pressing his hard shaft between the folds of her ass.

"Oh, God...," she cried.

Dampness greeted the head of his erection, sending a shiver of pleasure over his skin. So wet.

"You ready, Kitten?" He slid the hard length of his rod back and forth, brushing the opening to her core with each pass. Gabrielle pressed back into him.

"Yes! Christ, Arran. Take me." She tossed her head to the side, exposing the pulse pounding at her neck. Arran hissed.

Then dove.

His fangs sank into her flesh as he thrust his cock into her heat. Arran roared inside his head from the pleasure burning a path along his nerve endings. *Oh, fuck!* The truth would have to wait just a few more minutes.

· · ·

Thirty minutes later, Arran stood outside the door leading to Markus's basement holding area. Most mature vamps could go longer than two days between feedings, but with

Markus ingesting so little blood in spite of Kenric's attempts to basically force the fluid down his throat, their commander was down there every other day.

Tonight was no different.

The wood swung open and the tall dark figure of the Enclave's master strode through. Arran pushed away from the same spot Kenric had stood the other night and fell in step behind the commander.

"Something you've come to tell me?" Kenric continued on toward his office, never glancing back. Arran followed. Once inside, Kenric rotated and leaned against the front of his desk, waiting for Arran to cross the threshold. "Close the door," he directed as Arran joined him in the privacy of the room.

Arran scrubbed the palms of his hands back and forth together, finding it hard to remain still. *Dammit.* He glanced up at Kenric sitting there with his arms crossed, and the job of looking the other male in the eye became increasingly difficult.

"You want to sit down?" Kenric pointed to a chair.

"No." Arran shook his head. "Rather stand." He shoved his hands in his jeans pockets. "Thanks," he tossed out in afterthought.

"Arran…" The Enclave master's voice dipped low. "Either you spill what the hell is going on with you and Guerin, or so help me I'm about to rip—"

"Guerin went to Germany. He's looking for your daughter." Kenric froze.

Oh shit. What the hell was I thinking? Arran had pulled the pin and dropped the info on Kenric like a grenade.

The master of the Enclave straightened to his full

height. His six-foot-four frame suddenly loomed a hell of a lot larger, but Arran stood his ground. It was time Kenric knew the whole story, and he had every reason in the world to be mad as hell.

"What did you just say?" Kenric bellowed. "Because either you've lost your *fucking* mind, or I'm hearing things."

"Guerin is in Nuremberg trying to find Eve."

Kenric shook his head. "You're not making any damn sense." He reached up and sliced his fingers through his dark hair. "Who the hell is Eve? And don't give me some bullshit again that she's my daughter." A scowl registered on his face. "You've been a vampire way too long not to know that our kind are sterile." He turned and marched around his desk, yanked his chair out, and shoved himself into the seat, facing Arran. "Who told you this crazy-ass story?"

Arran moved to the front of Kenric's desk. The commander swiveled in his seat, adjusting to hold his gaze. Arran leaned in, dropping his hands onto the wooden surface.

"Marguerite made the claim. Right before she died."

Kenric's jaw ticked as if he were chewing on the revelation, then a snarl formed. "No. Way. In. Hell," he bit out, each word carefully enunciated as if the bold declaration alone could make it a fact. Kenric launched from his seat, putting them face-to-face. "Marguerite would say anything—do anything—especially with her last breath—to make sure she fucked me over as much as possible." He scoffed and backed away.

"We're not the only ones she's told this story to, Kenric."

His gaze narrowed. "Who? Markus?"

Arran nodded.

"So he's your source for the truth?" Kenric rolled his

eyes and knocked his chair away with the back of his legs, hurtling it into the wall with a *bang*. "Dammit. That's all you've got?"

Before Arran could form his next word, Kenric rounded his desk and was in Arran's face. "I want Guerin back here. Now!" He retreated an inch. "I assume you can reach him, since I'm sure you're aware he's not answering my calls."

"That's why I'm here tonight. I haven't been able to reach Guerin for two days."

"Son of a…" Kenric swiped a hand over his face and turned away. "Explain," he growled. "All of it." He pivoted, hitting Arran with a hard glare. "From the beginning. Every word. Every detail."

Arran slumped into the nearest chair. The air he hadn't realized was trapped in his chest came rushing out along with the events he'd kept hidden over the last thirty days. He began with Marguerite's confession along with her declaration that his prodigy would be coming for the Enclave.

Next, Arran revealed their decision to keep the revelation from Kenric until Guerin could gain positive proof of Marguerite's claim. Then he told of Markus's validation of Marguerite's statement before her death and of Eve's last known whereabouts: Nuremberg, Germany. Lastly, he filled Kenric in on what few conversations he'd had with Guerin since his departure.

Through it all, Kenric remained silent and unmoving. Even during the details of Arran's last contact with Guerin. The one were Guerin had supposed confirmation of Eve's existence from Markus's source, and a lead to the girl's whereabouts.

Silence. Arran propped his elbows on this thighs and

rubbed his bare palms together. He stared at the floor. Damn, the quiet was unnerving. He could only imagine the turmoil spinning with hurricane force inside Kenric's head.

"Whatever you need me to do, I'll do it." Arran swung his gaze up from the hardwood planks toward Kenric. "Say the word, and it's done."

"How is it possible?" Kenric whispered, glaring at some distant point beyond Arran.

"We don't know. Markus didn't know. Marguerite never told him. At least that's what he said."

Kenric whirled and headed in the direction of the office door.

"Where are you going?" Arran sprang from his seat.

With his palm wrapped around the doorknob, Kenric glanced over his shoulder at Arran. "Nuremberg."

Chapter Ten

Eve hadn't moved since her last orgasm. In fact, she'd lost track of time and couldn't remember when she'd ever stayed in a man's arms after sex. Damn, when had she ever lain with anyone? Her past encounters had been all about reaching a satisfying ending, then parting ways. That was it.

Clean and simple.

She lifted her lashes and peered up at the strong features of her lover. An odd fluttering sensation quivered in her chest, then settled in her gut. Eve bit her lip, stifling a groan. Nothing about Guerino Lombardi was either clean or simple. The man was complex, provocative, and after spending the last few hours with him—*oh, yes*—deliciously dirty.

"Time for answers, Lombardi." She pushed back into a sitting position, not at all happy with the warm and fuzzy feelings swimming around in her stomach. *Ridiculous*. Warm and fuzzy she was not.

"Well, that didn't last long." Guerin lifted his head from

the bed, then braced his upper body on his elbows.

"What?" She shrugged, and then brushed her fingers through her hair, giving him her best cool and collected face.

"Our sexually induced truce." He quirked a smile

She scoffed. "We scratched an itch, Lombardi." Eve pulled the bedsheet up and over her breasts. She searched the room, needing anything but those dark-brown eyes of his to focus on, and added, "What gave you the idea there was a truce?"

"Maybe it was when you shoved your vein in my face?" he snapped. "Or perhaps when you asked me to fuck you?"

Eve swung her gaze back to him, heat scorching her face. "I believe those UV rays may have fried some of that gray matter of yours." She let the words linger, allowing the venom they contained to sink deep. "I wasn't the one do-ing the begging…" Eve snatched the sheet and scrambled from the bed, wrapping it around her torso. "You've had a hard-on since we met. I'm surprised you've stayed coher-ent considering the massive blood loss." Silence filled the room—the uneasy kind of stillness that surrounds someone when they were the butt of a joke but somehow the last one to know. Eve whipped around.

A grin sat on Guerin's face, one that said someone's ego had not only been stroked but perhaps licked in the process. With one hand clasped to the bed linen, Eve flung the other up and wagged a finger at his expression. "What are you smiling about?"

"Massive, huh?"

Air rushed from her lungs, as if his question were a needle piercing the bubble containing her anger. *So not fair!* How did he do that? She wanted to be mad.

Pissed as hell.

But just like that, he'd tipped the scale, throwing her off-balance. Infuriating—and exhilarating all at the same time. She'd always been the one in control. If there was one thing her mother had taught her, and taught her well, it was to never allow a man to get the upper hand. But this submissive, who soaked up pain and domination with a thirst that left her dry and panting, put other alphas to shame. And the combination…intoxicating.

"You are so…" She shook her head.

"What?" He cocked his head, the motion and spark in his eyes daring her to say something to encourage him even more. Shit. She had to keep her head. Her life depended on it.

"I need a shower." Eve gathered the sheet around her and marched toward the bathroom.

"Leaving me alone?"

Eve stopped in her tracks.

"You're not worried I'll bolt without a cage to hold me?" His words skated down her spine. The challenge in them, unmistakable. He'd moved and stood behind her. She didn't need to look. The heat of his body—his presence—vibrated under her skin.

With her spine straight and her chin up, Eve pivoted. "Do I *need* to place you behind bars, vampire?" She lifted her gaze to his. "Or perhaps shackle you to the floor with silver manacles?"

His eyes narrowed, igniting a flicker of red around the pupil. But whether it was a result of anger or arousal, she wasn't sure. The air separating their bodies sparked, the hairs on her arms standing on end. Eve swallowed hard, her throat suddenly parched. If only containing this male were as simple as a lock and key. "No…," she added. "I don't think either will be necessary, because you won't be going anywhere. Not till I'm ready for you to leave." Eve lifted a brow, knowing she'd stabbed a virtual hot poker into the testosterone-filled beast. "We're not finished here." What the hell? Guerin had come looking for her and had yet to give her any answers. Granted, he'd proved he wasn't part of Seth's colony. But what was his agenda, really?

"No." His voice dipped to a deep, rusty tone. "We're not." Guerin closed the gap between them. The fist holding the sheet at her chest was the only thing keeping her nipples from grazing his chest. She didn't know whether to be grateful or curse her rotten luck. "And I'm not going anywhere." One strong arm snaked around her back and yanked her into his pelvis, taking her breath in the process. "But only because it's what *I* want. Don't mistake it for anything else." Guerin's other hand gripped her nape, his fingers threading into her hair, holding her steady. "Only in bed do I follow your orders."

A shiver raced over her flesh, triggering a rush of hot arousal from her core. The warm trickle dampened her thighs. Guerin's nostrils flared along with the flame swirling his irises.

"Maybe that's where I should keep you, then?" Eve lifted her hand, allowing her nails to follow the dips and ridges of his abdomen and upward toward his sternum. "Chained to my bed. Your every move at my command."

A rumble vibrated off his chest, and his cock flexed against her hip. Her womb clenched. "I think you like the idea, vampire." She trailed an index finger around his areola, then scraped the hardened bud before capturing the tip between her fingers and squeezing tight.

Guerin hissed.

Eve released her sheet and placed his other nipple in the same hold. His head fell back between his shoulder blades on a groan.

"Oh, shit." Guerin pulled her in, his hips working the length of his erection against her. She dropped her hands and retreated, breaking free from his grip. Guerin's head snapped forward and he growled in disapproval.

"Shower." Eve allowed a slight smile to play on her lips, then she turned and continued into the bathroom. After pulling back the white plastic curtain and adjusting the lever, she had the water at the perfect temperature. Eve stepped under the spray, her back to the door. "Join me." Nothing about her tone suggested the words were a request.

Strong hands glided up her back inch by inch as if savoring every centimeter of her skin. Her eyelids lowered, his touch pulling her breath deeper into her lungs. So good.

Don't get lost in this, Eve. In him… The words rang inside her head, snapping her back in control. She pivoted away, grabbed the soap, then passed it over her shoulder to Guerin. With her hands braced on the tile, Eve faced the wall and eased her legs apart. The invitation and command needed no explanation.

The wet and slippery sound of lather generating inside his large hands echoed in the confined space. Her nipples pebbled into hard points, but it wasn't the chill in the air drawing them tight. Anticipation of his roughened palms on her flesh hummed through her veins. Her fingers curled, nails searching out the small lip where ceramic met the grout for a hold.

Then he went still. The pelting sound of the water beating porcelain was the only thing left moving in the room. Not even the air dared to escape her lungs. What was he doing? *Touch me. God, please touch me.* She bit back a groan.

"Guer—"

Two broad palms, wet, hot, and hard, landed below her buttocks, jamming the rest of the word in her throat. Her fangs shot from her gums at the sensation—the claiming. She wanted to cry out, but instead, Eve bit down, jamming the sharp points into her lower lip. He rubbed the tissue there, then slid north over her cheeks. Slowly he worked the globes of her ass, teasing her. Straying close to the crease but never slipping inside. Then up her back he moved, the soapy warmth of his hands heating her blood along the way. At her shoulders, he somehow found every ounce of tension and kneaded it away. The soft lavender scent of the soap filled her nostrils, and her head lolled.

"Very nice…," she crooned.

"I'm glad you're pleased," he replied, his voice low and deep.

One of his hands fell away, only to return seconds later with the oval shape of the bar under his palm. Down and over her shoulder he roamed, using the soap as if it were a massaging stone. Guerin trailed beneath her arm and around her side, then up until his loosely closed fist rested under her breast. Using matching movements, he followed the same path on her opposite side. His arms surrounded her, and he cupped both breasts as if testing their size.

"Perfect," he murmured into her hair.

Guerin's chest pressed into her back. *So easy.* It would

be so easy to let go. Let him take her weight. All of her. Just for the next few minutes. But to do so would mean letting her guard down—trust. A simple five-letter word, yet it held the power of life and death in her world. Plus, wasn't it a two-way street?

The vampire's slippery palms encompassed her nipples, moving in tight circles over the sensitive buds. The firmness of the bar inside his hand heightened the little explosions of electricity arrowing straight to her clit. And it proved her undoing. Eve whimpered and her knees buckled. If it weren't for his body wrapped around hers, she would have crumbled.

Crumbled.

The very idea of that verb happening to her in regards to a man seemed foreign. She rocked her head. Yet her body conformed to his, humming like a finely tuned instrument that he played like a master.

But to a melody *she* controlled.

Exquisite.

Eve reached up, arched her spine, and laced her fingers through his damp strands. His cock, a hard and incessant rod, nudged the crease of her ass.

"Let me touch you." His words were hoarse at her ear as his hands drifted away from her breasts.

"Yes." The answer tumbled from her lips on primal instinct.

The soap fell to the porcelain with a *thud*, and his hands dipped low. His fingertips speared the slickened folds, skating over the quivering nub at the apex of her pussy. Eve gasped and went to her tiptoes, settling the ridge of his cock between her cheeks.

"Oh, God," she groaned. Guerin answered with a rumble of his own and rocked into her. One of his hands left her sex, followed by a shift of his hips, then the thick ridge of his erection slid between her buttocks. Back and forth with subtle thrusts, he buried his cock a little deeper, a little farther. The long fingers of his other hand caressed the sides of her clitoris, ratcheting her higher and higher, but not quite enough.

"You feel so damn good." In and out, he pistoned. Her core ached for the hard length that only teased the mouth of her pussy. Eve moaned.

"Guerin…" Her thighs trembled. "Make me come." Was she begging or commanding? She didn't know anymore.

"My pleasure," he breathed. His hand darted forward, sinking a finger into her core. Her channel clenched and she cried out, soaring straight to the precipice of her orgasm. But then the hard presence was gone before she could take flight. She gasped, released her grip on his hair, and slapped the tile with both palms.

"What are you doing?" she groaned.

He stroked her swollen bundle of nerves once, then twice. *Yes.* Her breath hitched. Then he was inside her. The firm presence of his shaft penetrating her sex… Eve unraveled.

"Guerin…!" Hard tremors rocked her body.

"That's it," he whispered in her ear. "Come for me, beautiful."

Lightning raced across her nerve endings. Endless sparks of pleasure took her up, up… *Don't stop. Please, don't stop.* Had the words left her lips or had she spoken them inside her head?

But Guerin didn't stop. His thrusts quickened, in her core and between her folds. Guerin's arm tightened around her waist. The sound of his breathing was reduced to hard pants. He was close.

Her tremors slowed to gentle quakes, and the thought of his imminent orgasm pulled her back to the present. *Not yet, you don't, vampire.*

Eve twisted free of his hold, spun, and knocked him back under the spray. A harsh gasp of air burst from his lungs. Before he had time to spring forward from the deluge of water, Eve dropped to her knees.

"What the hell was that for?" he growled, swiping a hand over his face and eyes, pushing a mass of wet locks back over his forehead in the process.

She encircled her fist around the base of his thick erection, her fingertips not quite meeting. The flutter in her stomach intensified at the sight. Eve looked up through her lashes. The dark and brooding male met her gaze with a stare that sent another wave of tremors through her core. The leash she'd held over her beast was about to break.

"You come when I say so; that's what this is about. Understand?" She narrowed her gaze and tightened her grip on his cock. Guerin hissed, slamming one palm onto the checkered tile with a *smack,* grabbing the shower curtain rod with the other. "Do you understand?" Eve filled her other palm with the tight sac beneath the base of his shaft and tugged for emphasis. Guerin tossed his head back and growled. The corded and bulging veins mapping the sides of his neck pulsed.

"Yes."

"Yes, what?" Eve gave a slight twist to the jewels. His

head snapped forward, fangs glistening from beneath his upper lip. Water sluiced over his shoulders and rolled down over the dips and hollows of his abs. His bronzed skin gleamed. Damn. The male was a powerful presence who made her want to remain on her knees in worship to his divine anatomy.

"I understand," he said, each word slow and deliberate. "I come when you say."

The affirmation of his submission surged through her. A transfer of power that compared to nothing else.

"Good." Eve lifted his shaft, leaned in, and applied a moist and heated trail with her tongue from her fist to the tip. Once there, she traced the crown's ridge before dipping in for a taste of the beaded precum rising from the slit. A pleasure-filled utterance of approval rolled from Guerin's throat, and a hint of a smile curled the corners of her mouth at the sound. She opened wide and sank over the large head, taking him as deep as possible. A shiver raced through Guerin, vibrating through his shaft. Eve worked the length up and down with her lips and tongue, making sure to apply enough pressure at the base as a reminder of who controlled his release.

"Fuck, Eve…" Guerin dropped his hands to her head and sank his fingers into her hair. Using her tresses for leverage, he held her steady and pumped his hips, sending his cock deeper into her mouth.

Eve grabbed his hands with her own, jerked free, and fell back onto her palms. She glared up at the stunned male, who stared back at her as if she'd lost her mind. "You forget your place. And for that"—she stood and pulled back the curtain—"game over." Eve stepped from the tub, snagged two towels, wrapped one around her torso, and headed for the bedroom.

Plopping on the edge of the bed, she dragged in a deep breath and began the process of drying her hair. The mindless act helped to calm her down. And God knew she needed to get herself under control. She'd never experienced such chemistry with a man. She barely knew him, and mere days ago, she'd suspected he was part of Seth's crazy scheme to abduct and dissect her like a lab rat.

Trust was something she'd given to only one person in her life: her mother. She'd been the only person who had ever been there for her, since her father hadn't cared enough to stick around. So why did it mean so damn much for Guerin to give her his? She hadn't failed to notice the word "Mistress" seemed to be absent from his vocabulary. Either he didn't trust her enough to lower his walls completely, allow her to be in complete control — to be his Mistress — or he was hiding something.

The latter was what scared her.

Movement in her peripheral vision caught her attention. Eve turned her head and found Guerin standing a couple of feet away in the bathroom doorway. Well, more like filling the doorway with his more-than-six-foot frame. A white towel draped low on his hips but failed miserably to conceal his lingering hard-on. With his arms spread wide, he held the molding in his hands as if it were his lifeline. His Adam's apple bobbed on a hard swallow, then he spoke.

"I haven't done this…" He closed his eyes, and Eve could almost see the wheels inside his mind spinning, searching for what he was attempting to say. He opened his eyes. "This." Guerin released the frame with one hand and motioned back and forth, indicating the two of them. "Sexual submission to a female." The words exited on a rush of air, as if he'd lose his nerve if he didn't spout them as quickly as possible. "In a very, very long time."

"So was your fetish history part of the reason you were chosen to find me? Let me see if I've got it right about how this was all supposed to go down…" Eve held up her hand, checking off her mental list with a lift of a finger. "You lure me in. I give you a taste of what you've missed. You get to fuck me, and then what?"

His dark gaze captured hers, and time slowed to a crawl. She had no idea how long they remained like that: connected. But when the moment came to disrupt what they'd created, an odd sense of what Eve could define only as sorrow washed over her. As if deep down, she knew once everything was out in the open they could never go back.

"This wasn't part of the plan."

"Then tell me what we're doing here. Why are you in my life, Guerino, and exactly what do you want from me?"

Chapter Eleven

Arran stepped from the Enclave's rented Jag, pulling the dark shades from his face. He squinted at the red neon sign mounted a few feet away over the club's dark dungeon-esque door. A fallen red rose glared off its black backdrop with a prominent single thorn pointing north. A drop of blood hung from its spiked tip.

"This was Guerin's location the last time you spoke to him?" Kenric joined Arran and glanced up at the club's logo. Arran nodded.

"The informant told Guerin that Eve's last known location was here at the Rose's Thorn."

Kenric's nostrils flared. "Smells like there was a fire close by and not too long ago." The master vampire's gaze swept his surroundings.

"Yeah. I agree." The scent of charred wood singed his nostrils. Reflex had Arran passing a hand over his face as if he could wipe the odor away.

"All right." Kenric worked the leather between his gloved fingers. "Let's get inside and piece together something that'll point us to our missing second-in-command—so I can kill him before somebody else gets the chance." He sauntered in the direction of the door, his boot heels crunching on the gravel parking lot.

Arran smoothed his palm over the stubble on his lower jaw, chewing on the impact of Kenric's last statement. He shook his head. *Nah, he wouldn't.* Arran slid his hand to the back of his neck, working the knot building at the base of his skull. No doubt Kenric probably felt like killing the vampire, but he knew the master of the Enclave, and honor would never allow him to act on emotion alone.

For the entire flight, Kenric had barely said a word, uttering only what was necessary. Arran almost wished their mates had joined them. Emily's company might have been a calming presence for the other vampire. But there was no way either warrior would have put them at risk by bringing them on this mission. Besides, someone had to stay behind with Michael to make sure Markus was kept secure and alive. Not an easy task since he ate only by force, and the only one able to achieve that would be two thousand miles away in Germany. Neither option was a perfect one. But Markus was locked away, in a weakened condition, and no threat to their mates. Kenric had made sure to get an extra meal into the wasting vampire prior to their departure. If all went well, they'd be back in the States before Markus required another feeding.

He followed Kenric into the dimly lit club. The chest-vibrating beat took him back nearly a year ago to Fairfield, South Carolina, and Wicked Ways, the Goth club where he'd stumbled into Gabrielle after he'd left the Enclave. His cock twitched at the memory. *Damn.* He'd never get enough of her. Didn't want to. Arran wanted to savor every second, touch, and pleasure that was Gabrielle. Forever.

"The bar." Kenric tapped his shoulder, yanking him back to the present.

"What?"

Kenric leaned in closer and shouted over the music near Arran's ear. "The bar." He nodded in the direction of the massive piece of architecture and added, "Let's see what the bartender can tell us."

After passing through a few dozen gyrating bodies, they snagged a couple of empty stools. The crack of a whip sizzled through the air. Arran turned toward the origin of the sound. At the back of the club, a couple of halogen spotlights glared off a St. Andrew's cross in the corner of the room. A bound, nude woman swiveled to the dance of the whip at her thighs and buttocks. A small group had gathered around the display, enthralled in the action. Arran's gaze fell to the vampire at his side.

"Nice place," he mumbled.

"Interesting," Kenric added with a quirk of his lips.

"Was möchten Sie?"

Both men turned their heads in the direction of the bartender's voice. Wearing only a pair of cutoff jeans and twin piercings in his nipples, he stood with his hands braced on the edge of the wood, waiting for their order. Kenric held up two gloved fingers. "Vodka, *bitte.*"

The man nodded, then went to work on their shots. Arran leaned toward Kenric. "You actually think this guy's going to tell us anything about what goes down here?"

Kenric cocked his head. "Absolutely not," he scoffed.

"What I figured." Arran straightened as the bartender returned with their drinks. He fisted his and tossed it to the back of his throat.

"Excuse me," Kenric called out to their hovering bartender as Arran plopped the shot glass back onto the bar's high-gloss surface. The man moved in the elder vampire's direction, capturing the open bottle of Stoli in the process. He glanced at Kenric, then to Arran, and lifted the liquor to offer another round. Arran covered the glass with his palm and shook his head. The one shot had been for the sake of appearances. He nodded and returned his attention to Kenric.

Kenric crooked his finger, drawing the other guy closer. *"Sprechen sie English?"*

"Einwenig." He cleared his throat. "I know a little."

"Excellent." Kenric placed both elbows on the wood, bringing them face-to-face. "Then I need you to listen very closely." The other man's gaze met the master vampire's, then glazed.

Bam.

He had him.

A vampire as old and powerful as Kenric required only a mere second to grab a human's mind. Arran glanced around the room, keeping an eye out for anyone paying too much attention. A few uninterrupted moments was all they needed for Kenric to find out if the bartender had seen Guerin. He swung his head back to the mind-melded duo. Under the beam of halogen lightening, a fine sheen of sweat glistened on Kenric's brow. He was pushing hard and fast to get in and out of the bartender's mind quickly.

Arran swung his attention once more to the dance floor. A petite, young brunette wiggled her hips and pivoted around at the same time, flashing him a drunken smile. *Shit.* He jerked his gaze to his partner and the human.

The two hadn't moved. Arran groaned, then swiveled on the stool.

Damn, but *she* had.

Her head swayed from Arran, then to the brain-locked pair. Party girl's mouth fell open, and she slurred some version of a question in German that sounded like "what was up with them?" *Oh, hell no.*

He wasn't doing this.

Arran slammed a wave of compulsion into the mind of the sloshed twenty-something. With the language barrier, he was limited to giving her only a sense of urgency to turn and leave. It would have to do. Her eyelids shuttered and she staggered. Arran jumped from the stool, steadied her, then guided her in the opposite direction. *Off you go.* She hesitated for a split second as if mulling over what she'd been doing there, then proceeded back into the crowd.

Kenric tapped his shoulder. The bartender had moved away and now stood at the sink, wiping his face with a damp paper towel. He looked as if he'd eaten something bad, but the effects should wear off in an hour or so.

"Let's talk." Kenric nodded toward a vacant booth, then headed in that direction. A couple of heartbeats later, Arran slid onto the leather seat across from the other vampire.

"So what did you learn?"

"Guerin was here." He nodded. "I got a good image of him at the bar. At one point in the night, a female, blonde, lots of black latex, handed him a note to give to Guerin."

"Any idea what it said?" Arran shifted in his seat.

"Yeah. Luckily, the guy couldn't resist taking a look." Kenric swiped a hand through his hair. "Someone wanted him to meet them behind the club if he wanted more info about Eve."

"Shit." Arran growled deep in his throat. "That must have been what Guerin was up to the last time we spoke. Going to meet whoever sent him the little invite." Frustration brewed like a storm in the other vampire's eyes, clouding the blue. Kenric shoved away from the table, rocking the back of the bench with his sudden movement.

"*Entschuldigen sie bitte.*" Both men swiveled their heads in the direction of the tall raven-haired server, wearing a red corset and not much else but a smile. She stood at their table, empty tray in hand. "Beer, wine?" She continued, propping her hands and tray on the table, her breasts nearly spilling from the confines of her top.

"*Nein,*" Kenric shook his head. "No. No, thank you."

The server stepped away, and Arran returned his attention to Kenric. *Wait a minute. This might not be a dead end after all.*

"You said a blonde in latex gave the bar guy the note, right?"

"That's right…"

"From what you saw, do you think you would recognize her again?"

Kenric appeared to study the remembered image in his mind for a moment, then nodded. "Yeah, I probably would."

"Ten bucks says she works here." Arran glanced around the room, placed his elbows on the table, and laced his fingers. "Give me ten minutes with her and—"

"We'll find out who wanted some alone time with Guerin." A slow grin formed on Kenric's face.

"Let's find our courier." Arran slid from the seat.

With the amount of leather each warrior had draped himself in this evening, they had no trouble blending in with the fetish crowd. They maneuvered around the perimeter of the room, scoping out the residents of high-backed booths and the grinding couples under the black lights on the floor.

Near the front entrance, Arran turned to check on Kenric's progress when a familiar scent—one that wasn't his master's—jerked him to a halt. A glimpse at Kenric's expression said he'd caught a whiff too. *Vampire.* Both did a three-sixty, attempting to get a bead on the other bloodsucker who'd joined them in the room. But as quickly as the molecules had appeared in the air, they were gone.

Dammit.

Kenric snagged his arm, pulling him in. "Let's find the girl, get what we came for, then blow this place before we bring any more attention to ourselves," he said, his voice low and gruff. "The last thing we need is lost time soothing a bruised ego of the master of the colony here, since I didn't announce our intended arrival."

Arran nodded. "I hear you."

"Wait..." Kenric's gaze darted toward the crowd. "There." He indicated with a tilt of his head a full-figured blonde wrapped in tight pink latex, making her way across the floor. "That may be who we're looking for." Kenric slipped through the crowd and Arran stayed close, following his lead. A few feet away, she pivoted, facing them. Kenric glanced back and announced, "That's her."

Arran tapped him on the shoulder in confirmation,

before brushing past him. "My turn." He sauntered over, painting his best grin on his face. The blonde didn't miss his approach, beaming a smile of her own back at him. He didn't like having to lead the woman on. He had all the female he needed at home, but this was for Guerin, for Kenric, and for the Enclave. The information she held inside her head could save not just one warrior's life but all of theirs.

"Hi there," Arran said, slowing to a stop in front of her.

"Hallo." Her matching pink smile broadened.

He reached out and trailed his fingertips down her arm, then leaned in at her ear. *"Sprechen sie English?"*

"Ja—yes." She nodded. "I speak English."

"Excellent." Arran straightened, then lifted her chin with his thumb and forefinger, bringing her gaze to his. "I need you to take us somewhere private. Do you understand?"

Her smile faded right before her lips parted as if on the verge of a question, then her eyes clouded. "I understand." The statement tumbled from her instead.

"Good girl," Arran replied, releasing his hold on her. "What's your name?"

"Ingrid."

"Take me somewhere quiet, okay, Ingrid?" Arran brushed a stray hair behind her ear. To onlookers it would appear like flirtation, a hookup for the next few minutes. "Everything is going to be fine."

Ingrid blinked, then sauntered toward a small, dimly lit corridor. Arran kept close, but glimpsed Kenric in his peripheral vision, keeping them in sight.

Arran watched as Ingrid retreated farther down the hall, pausing at the second door on her right. She pulled a set of keys suspended on a chain from her cleavage, then slipped one of them in the lock. Kenric stood leaning against the wall at the entryway, staring out at the crowd. But Arran knew the other vampire was aware of their every move.

The door opened and she stepped inside. Arran eased over the threshold and surveyed the room: an office. Except for a small wooden desk and a couple of chairs, the room was empty. He returned to the door, glanced down the hall, and gave Kenric the all-clear signal for him to join them.

With her back to the desk, Ingrid waited for her next instruction. "Very good, Ingrid." Arran drew closer and her chin lifted, keeping her gaze locked with his. "This is perfect." The door clicked behind him, signaling Kenric's arrival, followed by the clunk of the deadbolt. The master vampire's presence moved in beside him.

Being the younger of the two vampires in the room, Arran possessed the mental strength to grasp flashes of images from a human's mind. But to search their memories for more, Arran needed assistance to go deeper—blood. It had been years since he'd pushed that far. But it wasn't as if he was some damn new trans. He was more than capable of getting the job done.

"I need you to relax for me, Ingrid. Can you do that?" She tilted her head, and her eyes narrowed. Her expression told the story of the battle playing out between human will and the compulsion laced in his words. "Relax, Ingrid," he whispered the words again, then cupped her face. She leaned into his caress and the lines of worry in her face softened. "That's it." Arran brushed the loose strands of hair away from her throat, exposing her pulse. "Close your eyes now." Her lashes lowered, the tension visibly leaving her body. Arran flicked his gaze at Kenric, and the master nodded his go-ahead.

The room blurred around Arran with the speed of his strike. Ingrid released a whimper, and hot blood rushed over his tongue. Her fingers threaded through his hair, tugging him closer. Arran reached up and stilled Ingrid's advances, backing his hips away from hers. This wasn't about pleasure. The only purpose this feeding served was to save a fellow warrior—and friend.

His pulse raced under the influence of her life-giving essence, and with it, his connection to her mind strengthened. Arran dislodged his fangs and licked the wound, sealing her vein. Her flesh had already taken on the darkened color of a bruise in formation. Good. The mark would help with the hookup cover story he intended to plant in her mind when they were finished.

The whimper that had begun earlier from Ingrid had evolved into a moan. The human was extremely susceptible to the compulsion he'd used to induce pleasure, not pain, with his bite. A good thing, since her mind was like putty in his hands. Bad, since the putty existed with a single-minded purpose: sex. Arran moved from her throat, and her head lolled. He clasped her cheeks in his palms, steadying her.

"Ingrid." With a receptive mind, compulsion worked beautifully on direct questions. But there were times when it was more beneficial to *see* what the other person had experienced. And this was one of those times. Ingrid could have witnessed something significant and had no idea.

"Hmm?" she replied in a throaty groan.

"It's time to open your eyes."

"No, no, no, no." She shook her head against his hold. "Don't stop," she breathed, and clasped at his shirt for him to return.

"Don't worry. I'm not going to stop." He wrapped his hands around hers. "But I need you to open your eyes first. Then we'll have a real good time." At least it's what she'd leave believing.

Ingrid's eyelids fluttered open, and Arran latched onto her gaze. He reached inside, curling his mind around hers, tightening his hold. A small gasp escaped her lips. With the added connection of her blood mingling with his, Arran should be able to get a clear picture of whom and what Ingrid had interacted with over the last forty-eight to seventy-two hours.

Layer by layer, Arran pushed through the protective fibers defending the source of her memories. Then without warning, it shattered. The barricade holding back the tidal wave of synaptic data unleashed. Garbled voices and images sped through his head like a movie reel on fast-forward. The room swam under the onslaught. His ears rang.

Had to…slow it down.

He staggered, losing his grip on her hands. Then a strong arm at his back stabilized him—Kenric.

"Control it, Arran," the master's deep voice whispered in his ear. "You're in charge. Filter what you don't need."

Arran drew in a deep breath and clenched his fists. The stolen memories tumbling through his neurons slowed. All he needed was a second or two to screen whether or not they were relevant to his search. Multiple scenes of club life floated past. Night-to-night operations of the establishment taking place between Ingrid and a redhead: Mistress Fallon… The name, spoken more than once by the blonde, echoed in his head.

"We're running out of time." From a distance, Kenric's voice worked its way into his consciousness. Arran managed a nod, continuing to sift through the fragments of the last few nights of Ingrid's life. Damn, the woman spent a lot of time at the Rose's Thorn.

"Whoa…" Arran slammed on the mental brakes inside his head.

"What is it?" Within his vision, the large dark form of the other vampire drew closer to his side.

"Guerin. He's at the bar, asking to speak to the owner. This is the right night." Arran's heart pounded.

"The redhead, the one she calls Mistress Fallon, is agreeing to meet with him."

Come on, let's see who gives you the note. Mentally, Arran whisked through the next few frames inside her mind.

Show me…show me. Damn! He was so close. Then… His breath hitched.

Got you!

"Mistress Fallon."

"What?"

"She's the one who gave the note to Ingrid." Arran risked a glance at Kenric. One corner of the master's lip curled.

"Good work."

Arran returned back to his source of information. "Ingrid, you still with me?"

"Yes," she softly uttered.

"Very good." He reached out, slipped one of his palms in hers, and squeezed. "Ingrid, have you spoken to or seen Mistress Fallon today?"

She shook her head. "No."

"Yesterday?"

"Yes."

"Where is she?"

"She didn't say. Mistress called to let me know she wasn't injured in the fire."

His gaze darted to Kenric, then back to Ingrid. "What fire?"

"The fire that destroyed her home behind the club. She called to say she was okay but didn't know when she'd be back to work. She would be staying out of town for a while."

"Interesting…," Kenric added. "Her home burns the day after she plans to meet with my second-in-command." A charged moment of silence passed between them. "Unusual timing, don't you agree?"

"Oh, yeah. Some coincidence."

"See what other images you can gather from her memories of the other night. What happened after she gave the bartender the note?"

Arran once again pushed into her mind, fast-forwarding back to the night. *What else did you see, Ingrid?* Interactions with club guests. Mistress Fallon in her office, then Ingrid watching her boss from the rear of the club. Fallon is meeting with Guerin, but—wait. *Well, who do we have here?* Same clothes as Mistress Fallon, but not the same hair. And the look on Guerin's face… *Could it be? Lucky for us you're a bad, bad girl, Ingrid, spying on your boss.* If she would only move close enough to hear what they were saying… But before he could learn more, Ingrid turned, and moved back toward the club door.

"Damn!"

"Well…?" Kenric demanded, impatience ringing in his voice.

"Your instincts were right." Arran glanced at the other vampire. "Ingrid saw more. She'd followed Mistress Fallon when she met with Guerin." Kenric's brows lifted. "And based on Guerin's expression when Fallon showed up and had suddenly gone from a redhead to a brunette…" Arran pivoted on his heels, facing Kenric.

"Fallon is Eve."

"We found her," Kenric said. "Son of a…" He shook his head as if the knowledge that his supposed daughter was within reach had rattled his brain cells.

Arran backed away from a soundly sleeping Ingrid. She lay with her head on the armrest of the office's black leather love seat. The memories of their time together neatly altered to reflect an intimate encounter with a man whose description he didn't match. Satisfied that all the loose ends were tied up, he turned toward Kenric.

"So logic dictates that if we find Eve, aka Fallon, we find Guerin."

"I agree." Kenric sauntered closer and peered down at the pink-wrapped female. "She mentioned that Fallon had called yesterday."

"That's right." Arran pivoted on his heel and faced him.

"That would mean"—Kenric tossed him a sideways glance—"Eve left her calling card on Ingrid's phone."

"Damn. That's right." Not wasting another second, Arran leaned over, and after mumbling a quick apology, checked the pockets practically molded to Ingrid's backside. The first one was a bust, but the second… A hard rectangular object formed a ridge under the latex. Arran slipped his fingers inside. "Got it." He straightened and held up the slender rhinestone-encased iPhone between his thumb and forefinger.

"Excellent."

Arran slid the pad of his finger across the lock bar and went straight for her recent call log. After a quick scroll, the name "Fallon," showed up on two calls from yesterday afternoon. One incoming—one outgoing. His gut tightened.

We're one more step closer, Guerin. Hang on.

"Found it." Arran handed the display over to Kenric.

The other warrior gripped the phone, his gaze hovering over the screen, then, "Let's get out of here," he said without looking Arran's way, his voice gruff. The sound of frustration laced with pain couldn't be missed in the other vampire's words. Arran didn't know how Kenric had kept from taking his head off for partnering with Guerin on this plan. Kenric turned and led the way. After easing the door open and checking the hallway, they slipped through the corridor and made a beeline for the exit.

At the XJL, Kenric handed over the cell, then rounded the rear of the car toward the driver's side. "I'll drive."

Arran took the passenger seat, the smell of leather and wood enveloping him. Kenric settled in behind the wheel and pressed start. The engine roared to life. The dark warrior wrapped his hand around the wheel, the leather encased inside his palms releasing a squeak under the pressure of his grip.

"I want you to get Gabrielle on this," Kenric commanded, his gaze directed at the windshield. "See what she can do to get a GPS location on Eve with her cell number." After a moment, he shifted and faced Arran. "With any luck, she's left her damn phone on, and it'll lead us straight to Guerin."

"We'll find him." Arran nodded. "We'll find Guerin and

your daughter."

Kenric jerked his head back to the wheel, shifted the car into reverse, and accelerated out of the parking lot. The crunch of gravel scattering under the wide tread filled the cabin, then the car dipped, and they were back out on the main road.

"We don't know she's my daughter," Kenric spat. "And I refuse to buy in to Marguerite's attempt to cleanse her soul on her deathbed. I need more proof."

"I get it. It blew my mind when I heard it, too. I can only imagine what Emily thought of this last-ditch effort of Marguerite's."

When Kenric didn't respond, Arran glanced over. The other male's throat bobbed, then he added, "She doesn't know about Eve."

Oh, fuck.

"She went through so much hell with Marguerite. I just couldn't bring myself to tell her about this preposterous claim without some damn proof." Kenric released the wheel long enough to slam his palm back onto it.

"You don't have to convince me. I understand." Arran released a long sigh. "You don't want to hurt her."

"How the hell do you think she's going to handle hearing about a daughter I gave to a woman as evil as Marguerite—a woman who tried to kill us both? A child, because of me, Emily will never carry. One that we'll never share." A groan rose from his chest. "How do I tell her that?" His gaze flickered toward Arran. "Tell me, Arran. If this is true, how do I do that to her?"

Arran's chest constricted. He braced his elbow on the door and rubbed his hand over the lower half of his face.

The rough feel of the late day's growth of beard scratched his palm. "Son of a bitch," he cursed through his fingers. "I don't know, man." Arran shook his head. "But for what it's worth, and in case you're wondering—" Arran turned and stared out the passenger window at the dark countryside. "I haven't told Gabrielle everything. I didn't feel it was my place to tell her until you knew more and were ready. So she won't divulge any info about Eve to Emily."

"Thanks." The soft-spoken response pulled Arran's gaze back to Kenric.

"I'll get Gabrielle working on this now." Arran pulled his cell from his jacket.

• • •

A low-frequency vibration emanated from the dark-burgundy jacket Seth had tossed onto the chaise in front of the bedroom window. He gave his mind a gentle shake and did his best to focus his attention on the clitoris of his Mistress and forget the cell phone's beckoning. He knew better than to neglect his immediate duty: bringing her to yet another orgasm. The stripes on his back were still healing from the previous night when he'd failed to bring her Eve.

"For God's sake, answer your damn phone," she growled and shoved at his head, knocking him away from her pussy. "You're no good to me distracted."

Seth slunk away from the bed and onto the floor, crawling on his hands and knees toward the buzz. He bit back a growl of his own. *Too many years of this shit.* He'd been her puppet, her slave, for more years than he cared to remember. Granted, there was a bit of love and hate to their...

relationship. He'd always had a fondness for S&M, and she was a master at pain. It was what had drawn him to her. But the female took her desire to dominate and humiliate too far. He'd stayed this long because her money and colony had given him the means he'd needed to get close to Eve, but once he had that bitch...Christ. He was going to enjoy watching his current Mistress bleed, beg—his cock twitched under the weight of the thick metal ring twisted around his shaft and balls.

"You may stand."

"Thank you, Mistress," he replied, using his well-rehearsed tone of submission. Seth stood, strode the remaining few feet to the chaise, and retrieved his cell. "Speak."

"Sir, there's been an interesting development I felt you should be aware of." Seth recognized the voice: one of his minions who'd been watching the Rose's Thorn since the burnout. At some point, Eve or someone on her behalf would come back, and they'd be waiting.

"Well, don't make me have to pull it out of you," Seth bit out.

"Two vampires entered the club tonight. Never seen them before. One very old. He reeked of power. Possibly a master. He and the other male spoke with the bartender, and then met with the club's manager in back."

Fuck me! There would be only one reason a master vampire would risk entering another's territory—unannounced—and showing his face at the Rose's Thorn: Eve. Too much of a coincidence for there to be any other explanation. Someone else was after her. His pulse throbbed in his temples. She was *his*.

"Don't let them out of your sight," Seth ordered.

"Already taken care of. I'm following them as we speak."

"Good. I want to know their every move." If they found her, excellent. But they'd die before they laid claim. Seth tapped end call and tossed the device back onto his jacket. His fists curled of their own accord, the blood boiling in his veins. He would have Eve. He'd endured too much not to have her. Rage festered in his gut. His vision hazed to red.

"Seth. Don't make me wait." Her voice wrapped itself around his throat like a noose. Instinct had him reaching up and clawing at the unseen stricture choking his neck. Seth roared.

"Get off me!" He twisted and leaped into the air toward her, fangs and claws bared. She shrieked and threw her arms up in defense. He landed on top, straddling her flailing body. Animal against animal. Beast versus beast, they fought for dominance. She was a much older vampire, but he was a male, stronger and faster. And his submission had been by choice, not force.

"You want a taste of my blood, slave?" Her nails dug into the sides of his face. The searing pain only drove him harder. "Want to hurt me?" she growled.

He couldn't think past the vicious need to feel her flesh under his claws, drink from her throat. Pain. The desire to inflict or receive it had blurred in his mind. At this point, he didn't care anymore.

The room spun, and suddenly Seth faced the ceiling. "No!" he cried out, arched his spine, and rolled. He straddled her hips, pinning her arms to the mattress, and…she laughed. Fucking laughed. Air sawed from his chest.

"I love it," she purred and licked the traces of blood from her lips. "Haven't had a good fight in years." Doors at his left and right swung open with a *crash*, and a pair of her personal bodyguards blurred inside. Seth jerked at the same moment a set of silver manacles slammed onto his wrists with a loud click. His flesh sizzled under the weight and toxic effect of the metal. He bit back a groan.

A cool palm stroked his blood-slicked cheek. "Aww, my sweet Seth. You are such a delight. Almost as entertaining as…" Her coy expression morphed into an icy stare. The guards yanked his naked body back by his shoulders, allowing her to rise from the bed. She pivoted and tossed her blond tresses from her shoulders before leaning over and fisting a handful of his dark strands. As much as he hated to admit it, the sting went straight to his balls. How messed up was that? "Just imagine the fun we'll have tonight with your punishment."

Chapter Twelve

Just how far was Guerin prepared to go with Eve?

How much should he—or could he—reveal?

She really was Kenric's daughter. He had no doubt. Not after everything he'd witnessed. How would Kenric feel when he learned he'd already slept with her? Guerin's head spun with the implications. He stifled a groan, watching her watching him. Waiting for him to spill his guts about what he was doing there, why he was searching for her.

Fucking her.

Eve was so damn beautiful. He dug his nails into the soft pine.

Damp midnight locks hung halfway down her back as her pale-blue gaze raked him where he stood. His cock throbbed from the relentless hard-on she'd left him with. God, the things she did to him. The things he *wanted* her to do to him. Shouldn't that be wrong? She was his best friend's daughter...

But nothing had ever felt so good and so right.

I'm so screwed.

Guerin released his hold on the doorjamb and strode toward her. He eased onto the side of the bed, Eve at the foot, their backs to each other. Maybe what he had to say would be easier if he didn't have to look into her eyes? Because something told him Eve had no idea her mother was dead. She seemed more like a woman trying to survive than one seeking vengeance for her mother's murder.

"Talk to me, Guerin. Why were you looking for me?" As if sensing he needed the distance to speak, she didn't move.

"I heard about you from...someone who knew your mother back in the States."

"What do you know about my mother?"

Wait for it. Don't tell her more than she needs to know... yet. Guerin had to play this very carefully, filling in the blanks as they went along. At this point, instinct said she wasn't a sadistic bitch like her mother, but he hadn't spent enough time with her to know for sure. He had no idea how much she knew about Kenric, the Enclave, or her mother's current state. Nor did he know how she'd react when she learned who he was, and the role he'd played in her dear mother's demise. She'd either thank him, hate him, kill him—or all three.

But ten bucks said the latter would be her favored approach.

"She was Marguerite Devonshire. Correct?"

"Unbelievable..."

"So you don't deny it?"

As if she'd never heard the question, Eve babbled on. "My worthless father left us before I was born and tried to erase us from his memory. Not that it meant *Mother* ever forget about him. I'm all she has. She wouldn't risk letting my existence get out to someone other than her closet circle of allies. And she'd left most of them behind when she went to America searching for my father again." A guttural sound of frustration left her.

And there it was. The information Guerin had been waiting for. Marguerite had lied to her all these years. She believed Kenric knew about her and had abandoned them. His fingers curled into tight fists on top of his thighs. *Shit, shit, shit.*

"Who was it she told?" The tone turned urgent.

After a deep breath, Guerin added, "The male had been a trusted lover of hers. I wouldn't have believed it, but I didn't see a motive for him to lie."

The bed rocked, and he looked up. Eve was on her feet, standing in front of him. "She will kill him for betraying her." As with her father, anger transformed her tropical-blue irises into a brilliant display of fire and ice. "He gave you his head when he divulged this information. Why would he tell you and risk forfeiting his life? What did you have on him?"

"Nothing."

She scoffed. "Try again."

He sighed and dropped his gaze back to his hands.

"Wait. You've referred to her twice in the past tense. What aren't you telling me?"

The match had been lit, and the fuse burned on the TNT between them. Nothing he could do now other than let it blow. He braced himself and continued. "My informer wasn't worried about your mother's retaliation, because …" Guerin glanced up.

"Because what?" Eve braced her hands on her hips.

"Marguerite is dead."

Her hands fell away from the gentle curves of her body, and the fire vanished from her gaze as if doused by the flood of tears welling in her eyes. Eve blinked, as if fighting their mere presence.

"You don't know this for sure," she stated matter-of-factly, her voice tight.

"It's true."

"You don't know that!" Eve lunged forward, slamming her palms into his chest and rocking him back. Guerin latched onto her wrists and steadied her, locking his gaze with hers.

"It's true," he whispered.

"Stop saying that," she snapped with added venom, but the choked sound to her voice gave away her pain. Eve jerked, trying to free herself from his hold, but Guerin clamped down on his grip. "Let me go!"

"No."

"No?" She yanked again.

"No."

Eve straightened, nailing him with what had to be her best intimidating glare. "Who the hell do you think you are?"

"The man who just told you your mother is dead, and the one who's going to fucking hold you for as long as you need me to."

"You son of a—"

Whatever else she'd been on the verge of saying lodged in her throat as if her mind had suddenly registered what he'd meant. A solitary tear crested and trailed unchecked down her cheek. *Oh, hell.* At that moment, he'd give his life to take away the pain in her eyes. Her knees wobbled.

"Come here." He made the request, but she didn't move. And it took every last drop of patience he could muster not to drag her into him by force. But Eve was not a damsel in distress who needed a hero to save her.

Not that she'd admit, anyway.

This would have to be on her terms.

She swallowed, then chewed her lower lip.

"Come here." He lifted his arms, still holding on to hers. "Please..." She fell into his chest, her body trembling. Guerin wrapped himself around her, wishing like hell his body would act as a sponge and wick the sorrow from her heart. He smoothed a palm over her dark tresses. "I've got you," he whispered into her hair.

She grieves for Marguerite.

The concept of someone actually *not* wanting Marguerite dead rolled around inside his head like an oversize pinball going nowhere. It didn't fit. Yet to Eve, the evil bitch had apparently been the only person she had in the world.

That was about to change.

More than his next breath, he wanted to tell her she'd never have to be alone. His jaw ached under the restraint. She had a father who Guerin knew without a shadow of a doubt would want her in his life. *Shit. He* wanted her in his life.

What? He gave his brain a mental shake. *Back it up.*

He couldn't believe the thought had even crossed his mind. Guerin Lombardi didn't do relationships. Besides, how the hell would that work? She was Kenric's daughter, for Christ's sake. The man was going to fucking hate him for keeping her a secret for two seconds, much less for the last five weeks. Add the fact that he'd slept with her in the process of hunting her down to possibly kill her...

Oh yeah. Prizewinning son-in-law material there.

Eve squirmed under his tight hold, then shoved out of his arms and spun, giving him her back. "Sorry," she mumbled, quickly swiping her fingers over her cheeks, removing the evidence of her tears.

"I'm not."

Her spine straightened, and she went perfectly still.

"You needed someone, and I'm glad I was here."

"I don't *need* anyone," she gritted out through clenched teeth, marched toward the end of the bed, and snatched up the towel she'd used to dry her hair.

"Bullshit."

She snapped her head in his direction. "Fuck you!" she spit back.

"Anytime."

The white terry cloth fluttered to the floor at the same moment Eve sped around the mattress. A blur of pale flesh told him her palm was up and headed straight for the right side of his face. Guerin leaped to his feet and snagged her wrist midair, bringing her swing to a halt. She hissed, fangs bared.

"We're not fucking...yet," he deadpanned. "So no hitting allowed, beautiful."

"Damn you." She growled, curled her fingers into a fist, and yanked her arm free before retreating a few steps. Eve edged toward the other side of the room, her gaze never straying far from his. Her fingertips grazed the sheets along the way. Guerin followed her progress. Their stance was opposing, but her stare didn't quite touch his eyes. It fell somewhere behind him, unfocused.

"I've sensed that something was wrong for a while now," she began. "I just didn't want to admit what the feeling meant." Eve lowered her gaze and placed her hand to her chest, absently rubbing a lazy circle. "There's been this… empty ache behind my breastbone that wouldn't go away," she whispered. "It's like I've been grieving, but I didn't know why or who, for weeks now." Her fingers curled into her towel, bunching the fabric. She shook her head. "I didn't want to believe it was my mother." She lifted her eyelids. "But deep down, I already knew," she added hoarsely.

"I'm truly sorry for your loss." Her pain touched him more than he expected, and for hurting her, he *was* sorry. But he'd never apologize for being a part of removing Marguerite from the world of the living. An uneasy silence fell between them. He grabbed his sweats from the floor, waiting for what was coming next.

"A part of me doesn't want to go here, but I don't think I can live not knowing."

Guerin braced himself. *Don't ask me this. Don't ask me…*

"How did she die, Guerin?"

"Does that really matter?"

"Yes, it matters," she bit out. "She was my mother, and I want to know what happened to her. I deserve to know."

Damn, damn, damn. Guerin studied the gray article of clothing in his hands. As a creature of the night, he'd lived teetering on the line between truth and deception for three centuries. So why the hell did he find it so damn hard to lie to the woman standing on the other side of the bed?

"What do you know about her death? Please, Guerino… tell me what you can."

The sound of her plea tugged his head up. The lost look in her eyes plucked at every guilty fiber in his being, slowly unraveling him. He swallowed against the hard lump closing up his throat. Eve was right. She did deserve the truth. Yet he couldn't tell her he'd played a part in taking Marguerite down. With the current skewed version of who and what her mother was impregnated in her mind, there was no fucking way she would understand. At some point, he would tell her the whole story. But not now.

"All I can tell you is that there was a big battle: Marguerite and her minions, against a small group of vampires called the Enclave." That much was true.

"The Enclave..." The name fell from her lips as if she were testing the feel of the words. A warm sensation spread through Guerin's chest as she caressed the name on her tongue. Surprise filled him at how much he wished he could open up, and she'd embrace his reality. Then the expression on Eve's face turned dark, chilling his veins. "That was the name of the group Mother once said Kenric St. James had formed—my father. Oh my God..." Eve speared her fingers through her hair. "He killed her!" She shook her head.

"How do you know he was the one who did it?" The conversation had taken a turn down a slippery slope toward hell.

"Oh, please," she replied. "It's his Enclave. Whether he drove the stake in himself or not, doesn't matter. He's hated her for as long as I can remember. Mother always said he never wanted either of us."

"Why? I don't understand why you think he hated you both so much."

"Kenric resented the hell out of my mother for creating

him and conceiving me. Even though by siring him, she'd saved his life. He'd been a warrior even back in his time. My mother rescued him from the field and turned him before he died from his battle wounds. Yet she told me that he always hated being a vampire."

"So he left your mother before you were born, and you never knew him."

"That's the gist of it. A real winner in the daddy department, huh?" A laugh bubbled up and out of her that had nothing to do with humor. "So ironic, I have a whole colony on the hunt for a small piece of me, but my own father would rather I had never existed," she stated, her tone weary. "Why you?" Eve tossed out, breaking the tension. She raised her chin a little higher, the cool air of control settling back in to place.

"Why me, what?" He shrugged, feigning a nonchalant attitude he didn't come close to feeling.

"You never answered my initial question. When you learned about the existence of Marguerite's child, why did *you* have to find me? I understand why the others are tracking me — what they're after. What's in it for you, Lombardi?"

"You intrigued me." He tossed a smile in for good measure.

"As you so politely put it earlier: bullshit."

He laughed. "Touché."

"Try again."

"I'm more than three centuries old, my dear." Guerin plopped back down on the bed. "Very little surprises me anymore. The information Marguerite's lover shared with me about you…let's just say you captured my attention." He eased back until his shoulders rested on the headboard, one leg up on the mattress and bent at the knee. "I couldn't resist finding out if you were real."

"I see." Eve moved onto the bed, facing him on her knees. "And now that your curiosity has been satisfied, what's next?"

Guerin leaned forward, bringing them closer. "I would say that's up to you, beautiful." He trailed a finger down her cheek. "But I think you, or should I say *we*, have a more pressing matter to deal with. Like who has us on the run?" God knew, a new conflict added to the already-tenuous situation Guerin had gotten himself into wasn't something he needed. But with the vampire's attempt on Kenric's daughter, a female he was growing to care about, whether he liked it or not, a new enemy was exactly what Guerin *had* acquired.

"True." She settled onto her backside and sighed. "Seth Keller. He's been after me for a few years, but I've managed to stay out of his grasp and I thought I'd finally given him the slip this time. So I opened the Rose's Thorn. That was around the time I learned my mother had left for the States. Everything was under control…and then you showed up." Eve's gaze fell to the towel snugly wrapped around her, and she played with the frayed hem. "My senses went on high alert. A vampire appearing at my door and looking for Eve…" She glanced at him from under her lashes. "What else was I to think? You had to be working for Seth. One of his minions."

"I'm no one's minion," he stated. "Never going to happen. Not after— How's that saying go? Fool me once, shame on you, fool me twice…"

"Someone took advantage of your trust." Her tone

made it a statement, not a question. She knew exactly where he was coming from.

"You could say that." Compassion stared back at him in her clear blue eyes, and the realization floored him. Every fiber in him screamed: Marguerite may have raised her, but this woman possessed more of Kenric's heart than her mother's.

"That's part of the reason why you said it had been a very, very long time since…"

"Yeah." He sighed, then uttered, "Daniela De Santis." Her name left a nasty taste in his mouth. "My creator, or sire, whatever you want to call it," he bit out and swiped a palm over the lower half of his face as if he could wipe away the bitter aftereffects of talking about her.

"Did she turn you against your will?" she asked, her voice gentle. Eve joined him against the headboard, both facing the opposing wall.

"Oh, no." He laughed, but not a damn thing was funny. "I was all for it. Dying for her to turn me, in fact." He glimpsed the dark-haired beauty at his side. "I would have done anything for her at the time. And I nearly did…" Guerin sucked in a deep, stabilizing breath. He couldn't believe he was telling her this shit. Not even Kenric knew the extent of what he'd endured for Daniela, but truth be told, it was a major part of why he'd connected with the master vampire years ago. And it was why Guerin felt so strongly about Marguerite that he had wanted to do whatever it took to help his best friend stop the pain once and for all.

"How did you two meet?"

"When I was in my late twenties, I met Daniela just outside of Rome. She'd come for a late-night visit to the home of a wealthy businessman where I was working as one of the stable hands. Up until that point, I'd had to fight for everything I'd ever had in my life.

"When I was a little more than a year old, my parents died in a fire. I was told that my father had saved me, and then went back inside for my mother. But neither ever came out."

"I'm so sorry." Eve smoothed her palm over his arm.

"It's okay. It was a very long time ago." Guerin stared at the chipped paint on the far wall, doing his best to detach his emotions from the hellish trip down memory lane.

Guerin's mind wandered back to the moment Daniela had stepped from her carriage. Her blond hair had hung in long ringlets over the shimmering green silk of her tight bodice. Holding the door, waiting for her exit, Guerin had forgotten to breathe. The night had been so cold, and a fine mist had hovered in the air. Chills raced down his arms at the memory. It was as if he'd seen his sire for the first time last week, instead of more than two hundred and fifty years ago.

But when Daniela had turned her head, capturing Guerin with her dark gaze, he'd heated to near combustion.

"So, after years of struggling to survive on a daily basis, garnering the attention of a beautiful, wealthy woman was one heady trip. She opened my eyes to a world I never knew existed—and for many years, I was completely enamored."

"She must have hurt you pretty damn bad."

"Yes," he whispered. "And I wanted every bit of it."

"She was your first Mistress?"

He nodded. "My first, and only." He risked a glance in Eve's direction. "Daniela had homed in on something about me I hadn't realized myself: how much I enjoyed pain and domination when it came to sex." He closed his eyes. Images flickered behind his eyelids: blood, chains, and crops. Sounds echoed inside his head: the crack of whips, agonized groans of ecstasy. "She became an addiction I would have done anything for, just to have another taste." Guerin's head fell back with a *thud* against the wood. "For a long time, it disgusted me to realize how far I'd let it go. How far I'd let *her* go. She took me to a place inside my head where I didn't even know who I was anymore. I thought I was in love." He scoffed and opened his eyes, facing Eve. "I didn't have a clue what love was."

"You were young, Guerin. And it sounds like she was a manipulative bitch who knew exactly what she was doing."

The corner of his mouth curled at the curse. "Perfect word to describe her." He pivoted his head and focused on a dull gray picture of some unnamed coastline with waves crashing onto the rocks. The words came easier when he didn't have to look directly into Eve's eyes. "When Daniela discovered the high tolerance I had for her games, she became feverish with the idea of seeing how far she could push me. And like a moth to a flame, I'd come back for more — and more." He rubbed his palms over his thighs and curled his fingers into the fabric. "I really thought there had been much more between us than the show I provided. But after twenty-five years of providing her entertainment — bleeding for her…" He dragged his attention from the painting to Eve. "The light dawned on how messed up our 'relationship' was when she asked me to kill for her."

Unbidden, his mind went there — as if sucked back more than two centuries with the force of a dark vortex.

"Kill her?" Guerin tugged on the metal that held his wrists against the St. Andrew's cross. The human female lay on the floor, her eyes wide with horror, a gag stuffed between her lips, and her arms bound.

Daniela plucked the key to his shackles from the table beside him, and with a click, released one of his cuffs, then the other, followed by his ankles.

"You said you'd do anything for me…" She straightened and pouted, her eyelashes fluttering. His gut twisted. She was a master of manipulation. "I know you're hungry." Daniela's nostrils flared. "Doesn't she smell divine?"

And that she did. Like ripe berries on a summer morning. He closed his eyes, but the human's racing pulse drew him like a foghorn in the night.

"Feed, my pet," Daniela demanded. "Then destroy her before you drain her dry. I want to watch, marvel in the strength and power of my beautiful creation." Daniela stroked his face, and he opened his eyes. Her fingers fell away before she ripped the nipple clamps from his chest. Pain arced, then shot down his spine, carving a path straight to his shaft. He wasn't prepared for the exquisite onslaught of sensation.

And it was too much.

Guerin's legs buckled, and his orgasm erupted. "Oh, fuck…," he groaned, and his knees slammed onto the wood planks. His cock pulsed, adding more insult from the cock ring with each wave as he emptied. A hard shiver rocked him.

Gasping, he glanced up through the damp strands of his hair at his Mistress. She no doubt would be pissed.

"You disappoint me." Daniela shook her head, scowling. "Do you plan to compound your failure and deprive me of the pleasure of watching you take down the prey I've so

graciously provided?"

He swallowed hard and turned his gaze to the trembling female. Hunger surged, a clawing beast under his skin and inside his mind. The animal cursed the lingering particles of his humanity that hesitated. Feeding was a necessity. For the last quarter century, at his Mistress's side, Guerin had sunk his fangs into human flesh more times than he could remember. But killing…?

He'd done and been many things to survive before he'd met Daniela. Some he was more proud of than others. A young orphan on the streets had to be clever and possess a strong stomach if he wanted to survive. And he'd managed to make it when others had succumbed. Yet a murder was something he'd never considered adding to his list of accomplishments.

Daniela's nails dug into Guerin's cheeks, and she yanked his head up. "I thought you said you loved me—would do anything for me? Did you lie?"

Panic seized him like an invisible net, freezing his limbs. "No. I would never lie to you."

"Then kill *her," she demanded, fire flashing behind her irises.*

The vampire inside him roared to life, driven by hunger and the primal need to please its Mistress. Guerin lunged. The room blurred, and he was at the human girl's throat. Fangs extended, he struck. The female's spine arched under the impact, and her essence burst down his throat. Guerin drank her down. Swallow after greedy swallow, he indulged until the room tilted under the rush.

He reared back from the girl's neck on a growl, his vision red and his veins on fire. "Kill her!" *Daniela's command rang inside his mind. Claws extended, Guerin lifted his hand, ready to rip away his prey's throat and fulfill his Mistress's wish. The human's head lolled, her doe eyes locking with Guerin's in one last soul-filled plea for mercy from the monster prepared to destroy her. Something clicked inside his brain.*

What the hell have I become?

Guerin dropped his arm. Frantic, he scurried away from her body.

Laughter ricocheted off the walls. "Pathetic!" Daniela cried out, and her palm impacted his cheek with a piercing crack, jarring the bones in his face. "Secure him," she ordered her minions. "Use the silver this time. I want to make sure he hangs around to see how the girl dies because he didn't have the balls to finish the job."

"Hey…Guerin…" Eve squeezed his fingers, pulling him back into the present. "Where'd you go?" she whispered.

He forced a thin smile. "A place better left buried in the past." Guerin swiped a hand over his mouth and chin. "Anyway…I escaped and never looked back." He shook his head. "When I walked away from Daniela, I did the same with the lifestyle—a hard and clean break from it all. So to let someone in like that again…and allow her to see what makes me tick…" He looked over at Eve. "I made a vow to never get sucked back in to trigger those needs. Ever.

"Been there. Done that. And I didn't like the T-shirt."

"I see… Are you saying that's it, then? You won't let down your walls for anyone?"

A low grumble rolled from his throat, and he fisted a handful of her hair, but not enough to pull at her roots. He held her gaze, her blue irises darkening into a midnight storm. "You drive me crazy, beautiful. Make me contemplate things I swore I'd never do again…"

The pink tip of her tongue appeared, and she moistened her lips. So inviting. And he couldn't resist. But Eve met him halfway, their mouths colliding, melding in a fusion of desire. She opened and he swept inside. Searching, tasting, jonesing to sample every inch she'd allow.

Eve reared back, leaving a burst of cool air where the warmth of her body had once been. "Stop," she commanded.

"What's wrong?"

"There's an earlier matter that's been left unfinished. One you never asked my forgiveness for."

"I see…," he drawled and sat back against the headboard.

"You see? What?" Before he could form his next word, Eve straddled his hips and held his chin in her hand. As if it had a mind of its own, his cock surged upward, rock hard, seeking the heat she provided.

"I see I haven't made sufficient amends for my lack of control earlier." He reached high and curled his fingers around a spindle in the headboard.

Eve drew closer, her mouth centimeters from his lips. Cinnamon and vanilla. Damn, they were now officially his two favorite scents on the planet. Guerin swallowed, forcing the groan back down his esophagus. The warm and wet tip of her tongue stroked his lips. *Fuck. Me.* He lifted his hips, driving the covered hard ridge of his shaft into her center. Eve hissed and pulled away.

"You move when I tell you to…" She lifted a brow. "Or this is over. You have to trust me enough not to take you somewhere you don't want to go. Can you do that?"

Guerin inhaled, slow and deep, forcing his body into compliance. Maybe it was who she was—or wasn't. He closed his eyes. Whatever. He was now thinking: *to hell with the promise he'd made. For now.* This would never last anyway. He knew it—and shit, she had to know as well. So how risky could it be? If he made sure to hold on tight, give her exactly what she asked, nothing more, maybe he could do this. Just one more time. Savor the pain. The pleasure. And not lose a piece of himself along the way.

He opened his eyes. "Yes." Eve lowered his arms to the mattress.

"Very good." A seductive smile tugged at the corners of her mouth. Eve lifted her hips from his body and maneuvered from the bed. Her movements fluid, effortless. She stood beside the mattress and allowed the cotton around her to drop to the floor. His head swam. *Damn.* Every ounce of blood pounding inside his veins must have surged to his groin.

"Three hundred years old..." She let the statement hang, reached down, and tugged at the edge of the towel, loosening it from around him. The cotton fibers scratched at the sensitized flesh, then fell away, allowing his thick erection to spring up. "To make it to such an impressive age you would have to possess a great deal of self-control," Eve went on to say. "Don't you think?"

Guerin narrowed his gaze in her direction. "I'd like to believe so."

"Yet earlier..." She started toward the end of the bed.

"A momentary lapse. I—"

Eve came to a halt and snapped her head in his direction. "You speak when I give you permission."

Gripping the sheet at his side, he conceded. "Yes."

Apparently satisfied, she continued the short journey to the other side of the bed. Eve climbed back on, settling on her knees next to him. Her full breasts jutted forward topped by the most delicious rose-colored nipples that had ever graced a female. His mouth watered for their flavor. Unable to resist the urge, his gaze raked her. Guerin's palms itched to stroke her soft curves. Her bare pussy beckoned him. The scent of her arousal had his fangs barreling from his gums. Had he ever been more hungry for a female?

"Eyes up, vampire!" Guerin swung his gaze to her face. "Show me that control. I want you to show me what kind of leash you have over the animal inside. The beast that wants to take what it craves." Eve reached over and fisted his cock. Guerin's breath shuddered from his lungs at the sensation. "Longs to give in to the unyielding desire." She stroked up to his crown and spread the large drop of precum leaking from his slit over the head before retreating." A low groan resonated in his throat. "Give me your hand," she demanded.

Guerin extended his arm.

"Take your cock." She released him, and he did as instructed.

Eve smoothed her palm down his thigh, spreading his legs farther apart in the process. "Stroke it, vampire," she said, her voice firm and unwavering. "Let me see what you would do if I wasn't here. What takes you to the edge when you're all alone, aching for release?"

Slowly he slid his palm up and worked the sweet spot at the base of the head before moving back down the shaft.

"There's just one thing...," she added, then leaned forward and wrapped her lips around the tip of his erection.

"Ah, fuck!" He hissed.

She lowered her mouth over him until she bumped his fist at the base, then pulled back. "You don't come until I give you permission."

Oh, shit. He growled and squeezed his eyes shut.

"Do you understand?"

"Yes," he stated.

"Yes…" Her palm slid under his scrotum, warming the back side of his sac. She cupped him, and then her grip tightened on his balls. A zing of electricity ripped up his spine, and his cock jerked hard against his grip. It was all he could do to remain still under her hold. *Christ.* Guerin opened his eyes and lowered his glare to hers.

"These are mine," Eve declared. "I say when they get to release. Are we clear?"

"Yes," he bit out between hard pants. Blood pulsed in his cock, a constant throb under his hand.

"Good." She released his sac.

His balls ached with each beat of his heart, and the engorged veins in his shaft stood out in sharp relief. He didn't dare move his hand. *Oh, hell.* A couple of hard strokes, and he was going to blow. *No. No. No.* Guerin inhaled deep.

"Come on, Guerino." She parted his legs wider, then situated herself between them. "Work it for me." Eve placed one hand on each of his thighs and leaned over his groin. Her breasts with their pink hard tips nearly brushed the back side of his hand.

He dragged his fist up his cock, milking another drop of precum from the tip. As if waiting for the bead to appear, Eve leaned in and swiped it away with her tongue.

"Oh God!" he groaned and froze mid-stroke.

"Don't you come," she nearly growled. "Keep going."

Again he worked his pulsing length. Up and down. Over and over. His balls were beyond tight. He clenched his buttocks against the incessant pounding of the cum at the base of his shaft.

"Have to stop." He panted and dropped his hand away. A prolonged ache swelled in his sac and radiated up his cock. "Oh shit," he groaned. "Fucking hurts." He tossed his head back.

"I didn't say stop." Eve slinked her palm over his engorged erection.

His hips surged up at the sensation. "Oh shit! Don't!" Guerin seized the bedsheets at his side. "Gonna come…"

Eve's fist clamped onto the base of his shaft, creating a physical barrier between his cum and its intended destination. The effect radiated like a hard punch into his balls, then up into his gut. Guerin squirmed under her vise grip, and a rash of cold sweat popped from his pores.

"Gorgeous." Her soft praises glided over his flesh and into his mind, calming him. "Did you know that the most delectable blood can be found right here?" Eve trailed the index finger from her other hand over one of the distended vessels on top of his shaft. "And the longer the male delays his orgasm, the sweeter the flavor?" She glanced up from his hard length. A shiver ran over his body, lifting every hair.

"Oh God, beautiful," he moaned. "You'll have to hold me back." He shook his head. "There's no way in hell I'm not going to come if you…"

"Trust me," she whispered. Before he had time to process her request, Eve had half his cock in her mouth, and a slice of pain radiated up his dick. Guerin arched.

"Fuck! Eve…"

The fist she'd wrapped around the base of his erection constricted even further, refusing to allow his orgasm passage. His pulse slammed against the barrier between his cock and balls.

Then she sucked, feeding off the engorged vein running the length of his shaft.

Pleasure and pain blurred. Endorphins flooded his system, and his mind took flight.

The room tilted on its axis. A hard tremor rocked him, and the bed creaked under the force.

Stop! Too much.

Oh God… No. Shit, shit… He tossed his head from side to side. "Don't…don't stop." His jaw hung open. Guerin had no idea if the words had only occurred inside his head or exited his mouth. Air sawed in and out of his lungs, charring a dry path down this throat.

Eve slid her lips from the head of his cock with a sucking *pop*. "You are so delicious." Her movements stilled at his groin, but her grip stayed firm at the base of his shaft. "Let me know when you feel I can release you."

Without the added stimulation of her mouth, the ache in his balls had tempered for the moment. "You can let go…" Guerin choked back the word "Mistress." He couldn't go there. Give her all the power. He wasn't ready. Didn't know when, or if, he would be.

"Why can I let go, vampire?"

Guerin met her stare. "Because I'm not going to come until you give me permission."

She quirked a smile, then pushed away and stood. "On your knees."

The idea of moving at the moment had Guerin's nerves on edge. Any brush against his cock would only add more pressure behind the cork. And dammit if the head of his dick didn't already feel like Mount Vesuvius waiting to blow. But he managed to make it up and onto his knees, his rigid shaft standing at attention, red and pulsing. Eve slid a chair up to the side of the bed, sat on the edge of the wooden seat, and faced him. Perfectly at ease in her nudity. She placed one long leg over the other, providing a brief glimpse of the pink lips of her pussy. His cock jerked. *Tease.* Guerin's eyelids shuttered.

"Open your eyes."

He lifted his lids.

"Look at me." Guerin stared into her blue depths. "Spread your thighs." He complied, and shuffled his legs a few inches apart. "Good. I want to see all of you." Slowly her gaze drifted low. His pulsed leaped, as if her inspection were an actual caress to his body.

Eve looked up from her perusal. "Where would you have me touch you, Lombardi?"

Everywhere.

"Show me what you'd have me do." She lifted her hand and placed her fingertips to one of her own taut peaks. Her lashes fluttered at the contact, but her gaze never wavered.

"You are wicked, beautiful."

"And you love it," she purred.

Yeah. I do. Maybe too much.

Guerin brushed his palms over his own nipples and rubbed the roughened texture over the hardened tips. Twinges of pleasure skated along his nerve endings. Then he dropped low, past his erection, and cupped his balls. Using the pads of his fingers, he massaged the flesh behind them. The pressure sent a pulse of sweet sensation up his shaft. His breath hitched and he groaned. Guerin closed his eyes, allowing his head to fall back between his shoulders. Unbidden, his hips rocked with each gentle stroke of his hand.

"Open your eyes." Eve's command yanked his attention forward. "Look at me." Guerin bore his gaze into hers. "That's my hand touching you," she whispered. "Tell me how it feels."

"Too good."

"You want to come?"

"God, yes," he groaned.

"Before I let you come...what are you holding back from me? Show me what else you'd have me do. Take me there."

He swallowed hard, and never leaving the hold of her gaze, Guerin shifted one hand behind him. Then gently, he moved the other up to his shaft. Preum slicked the hard flesh, making his engorged cock even more sensitized. He jammed his fangs into his lower lip at the onslaught of his slight touch.

"Tell me, what am I doing to you there?"

"You're stroking me. Here." Guerin swiped his middle finger around the tight ring of his ass. "And here." He pumped his shaft, milking more of the clear fluid from the crown. Eve straightened from her chair and closed the distance between them.

"You like what I'm doing?"

"Yes," he forced out.

"Harder. Faster... I want to make you crazy."

Sweat rolled down his temples and stung his eyes, but he held them on Eve. Guerin bore down on the tissue near his swollen prostrate and pumped his cock. "Need to...," he muttered, his voice hoarse. "Now. Shit! Too much."

"Remove your hands." Eve yanked his fist away from his shaft and his arm from behind him. Guerin choked out a grunt of disapproval, but then her fingers replaced Guerin's around his cock.

"Oh, fuck!"

"Come for me." The dark clouds of desire in her eyes shifted into a raging storm. "Now!" she shouted, then took his rod down her throat.

Cum exploded up his balls and out his shaft. The room dimmed, and someone cried out. It had to be him, but he didn't recognize the sound. On and on, his orgasm jetted.

And Eve… Oh hell, Eve. Guerin threaded his fingers into her hair. She hung on, taking everything he had and more.

The feeling in his legs had turned to nothing more than pins and needles by the time the last drop left his balls. Guerin was about to pull back when a sharp stab of pain radiated up his lingering erection.

"Shit!" Guerin jerked, but Eve held him in place. "What are you…?"

Then she sucked.

"Oh my God. I can't…" Slowly he rocked between her swollen lips, and Eve responded, drawing harder on the pricked vein. His cock thickened, and a familiar tingle grew again at the base of his spine.

Eve gasped and fell away, catching herself with her palms. "I want you." Her gaze bore into his, the need and emotion raw, slicing into his soul. No way in hell he could deny her.

A growl tore from his throat.

She was in his arms, up against the wall, her legs wrapped

around him.

When had he moved?

But the outcome couldn't have been more perfect. Guerin dug his fingers into her midnight locks and tugged, lifting her chin. He studied every centimeter of her face, from the way the little wisps of hair curled around her cheekbones to the pale curve of her neck. Enrapturing. The sound of her rapid pulse beat inside his head like an ancient spell, as if she were trying to draw him into her snare. And damn, if it wasn't working like a charm.

"Are you going to fuck me, Lombardi, or stand there and stare at me the rest of the night?"

"What?" Her question snatched him back, and he chuckled. Damn, the woman was one of a kind. He thrust his hips, placing the head of his cock inside her entrance. Her lips parted, and her breath hitched. "Oh yes, beautiful. I'm going to fuck you."

Chapter Thirteen

Arran pulled the Jag alongside the curb, then killed the engine along with the lights. The dashboard clock read 7:00 p.m. He released a lungful of air, trying to eradicate the itch to jump out of the car, explode into the small apartment at the end of the block, and drag his fellow warrior out. Gabrielle had called them in the wee hours of the morning after she had narrowed down the coordinates of the number they'd given her from the cell phone. Waiting through another round of sunshine and sunset before they could leave had been hell.

He glanced over at his commander. The strain of the last two days was evident in the lines around Kenric's eyes. The uncertainty of how this would all play out was driving Arran crazy, but he could only imagine what torment Kenric was enduring.

"How do you want this to go down?"

Kenric rolled the pearl handle of one of his daggers inside his palm and stared out into the empty, dark street.

"Take them by surprise." The elder vampire faced Arran. "We won't get another chance. We move in hard and fast and get Guerin the hell out of there." He looked away. "What's left of him."

"Guerin is not Markus." Arran squeezed the wood of the steering wheel. God knew he needed something to ground him. "He's stronger than that. You've known him longer than any of us, but from what I've seen during the years I've been in service to you, Guerin, and the Enclave, it would take a hell of a lot more than a week with a female for him to snap." Kenric closed his fist around the hilt of his weapon. "You survived her mother, and Guerin will survive her daughter."

Kenric sheathed the blade, the metal sliding into the sleeve without a sound.

"You're right." Kenric glanced his way. "So let's go have a little family reunion and retrieve my second-in-command."

Arran reached for the door handle, but his cell vibrated against his chest, bringing him to a stop. "Hold up." Kenric settled back into his seat as Arran reached for his phone. Gabrielle's name lit the screen, and his heart rate kicked up a notch at the sight. He swiped the red answer bar and placed the device to his ear. "Hey there. What's going on?"

"I know this is probably a really bad time…"

"That's okay," Arran said. "What's going on?"

Kenric turned in his seat, the glare from the male saying Arran had his full attention.

"Tell Kenric I tried to stop her." The pleading tone in Gabrielle's voice coiled itself like a noose around his heart.

"Who? Emily?"

"Yes."

"Stop her from what, love?"

"Give me the phone," Kenric demanded and shoved his hand in front of Arran's face.

"Hang on, Gabrielle. Kenric wants to talk to you." Arran passed his cell to the other male.

"Talk to me, Elle," Kenric began. "What's wrong with Emily?"

Arran watched as the expression on Kenric's face morphed from concern to rage.

"Dammit!" Kenric shouted and slammed his fist onto the car's dashboard.

Oh, fuck. Arran groaned inside his head. This was not good.

"I know it's not your fault," Kenric added. "I don't blame you." He glanced at Arran before leaning back onto the headrest. "Please do me the courtesy of informing Markus that I will kill him when I get back." He paused and Arran heard Gabrielle's soft voice responding and then, "Thanks for letting me know," Kenric said, and passed the phone back, his gaze focused elsewhere.

"You okay?" Arran shifted in his seat, more and more anxious to grab Guerin and get his ass back stateside.

"Yeah. I'm fine. It's Emily I'm worried about." Dread settled like an anchor in Arran's gut. Both of their mates somehow knew what was going on in Germany. And Arran realized how they'd found out. Markus. He turned his gaze toward the Enclave's master. The other male's expression seemed about one match strike away from exploding all over someone's ass.

Arran replaced the cell to his ear. "Hey, Gabrielle. I'm here."

"I'm sure you have to get off the phone. Kenric will fill you in."

"Okay." Arran studied the fist he still had wrapped around the steering wheel. "Yeah."

"I love you." Her soft words drifted through the cell and brushed his heart, bringing the edge of a smile to his lips despite the gloom in the air. "Come home to me soon. You hear me?"

"You can count on it. I love you, too." Arran tapped end call and slipped the phone back into his jacket. Arran's gut twisted. What a fucked-up week. When did the world decide that he got to be the messenger of bad news to one of the deadliest vampires on the planet?

"So what happened?" he asked his companion.

"That son of a bitch Markus decided he was ready to spill his guts. He sent word through Michael for Elle and Emily to pay him a visit. He had something important to tell them." Kenric grabbed the door handle and pulled. "I need some air."

Arran exited the vehicle too, moved to the front, and leaned against the hood next to Kenric. "How is Emily?"

"She's on her way here."

Arran cringed. This was not going to go down well.

"Shit!" Kenric swung away from the car, tossed his head back, and growled, then pivoted on his heels and faced Arran. "Elle said Emily wouldn't talk to her after she'd learned why we were here. The last thing she said to Elle was for her to tell us she was on her way." He shook his head. "What does she think she's doing?" Kenric swung his arms up as if he were surrendering to an invisible foe.

"Coming for her mate," Arran said.

The other male's gaze narrowed on him, and he stilled.

"She needs you, and you need her right now, whether you realize it or not." Arran couldn't believe what was coming out of his own mouth. Before Gabrielle, he'd never been the sentimental type, but this mating stuff had apparently opened another side to him. Opened his heart. Kenric shook his head again and sighed.

"So let's get in there" — Arran motioned toward the end of the street with his chin — "grab Guerin, and find out what we're dealing with so your mate will be safe."

Kenric nodded.

Both males moved down the street, their heels gliding over the cobblestone streets in silence. Shadowed predators on the hunt.

Blinds were drawn in the two visible windows of the small apartment, making it difficult to tell if anyone was home or awake. Hopefully Eve and Guerin were inside. The sun had barely dipped below the horizon, and with any luck, the timing would catch her still sleeping. But with Eve the odds were fifty-fifty if that would even be the case. There was no way of knowing the extent of her capabilities.

"If this is a studio apartment, we'll be walking right into the center of her den and bedroom. There won't be anywhere to hide." Kenric glanced his way, then back to a door at the top of the steps. "For anyone."

"I'm ready when you are." Arran pulled a short blade from the sheath at his thigh. With a nod from Kenric, they made their way up the five steps to the stoop. Kenric held up three gloved fingers then counted them down, one by one to zero. He reared back, then raised a booted foot and slammed it into the wood. The door busted away from the frame with a loud *crack* and banged into the wall behind it. The Enclave's master was anything but subtle.

Both charged into the room—Kenric going right, Arran left.

Movement from a bed positioned across from the door snagged Arran's attention. Guerin shot forward, then onto his feet as a blur of color bolted from the mattress and across the room.

"Damn! Kenric!" His gaze swung to him. "Arran." Guerin dragged both hands through his hair and over his head. "You could have knocked, you know?" He stood there gawking at them in nothing more than a pair of sweats as if they were his parents and had interrupted his date.

"What the fuck, man?" Arran shook his head.

"Kenric?" A female voice called out from the other side of the room, catching Arran's attention. But based on the intense stare Kenric already had pinned on her, he'd tracked her from the moment they'd entered the apartment. "Kenric St. James?" A beautiful woman with long dark hair wearing a pair of loose cotton pants and white snug-fitting T-shirt eased forward. "Master of the infamous Enclave?" Kenric gave her an almost indiscernible nod, but it was there nonetheless.

And then he spoke, one name barely uttered above a whisper. "Eve?"

"What? You don't recognize the daughter you left behind?" The question wafted across the room like a pebble tossed into calm waters. But in the next second, a storm surge raged on its heels.

Eve cried out and went airborne. *What the hell?* Her arm reared up and back, sending a flash of light glimmering off a blade.

Kenric! Reflex launched Arran into action. He lunged toward the other male, his only thought to protect the Enclave's master. But before his boots landed, Eve stood between them.

"Eve!" Guerin called out and was already over the bed and beside Arran.

Kenric swung his arm wide, deflecting her first strike from his chest. "Don't touch her!" he bellowed as the blade jabbed through his leather jacket. Arran watched as Eve carved a path down Kenric's biceps, ripping the material and his flesh wide. The metallic scent of blood filled the air. Eve yanked the knife free and froze, her chest heaving. Each labored breath she released felt like a second ticking off the timer of a bomb ready to ignite.

But Kenric stood there. Silent. Motionless.

What the hell was he doing?

"Come on!" she cried, breaking the eerie stillness. "Fight me."

"I'm not going to fight you."

"Yes, you are," she growled and tossed her hair back. "You've wanted me and my mother out of your life for centuries." Eve scoffed. "Well, one down and only one more to go." She pulled the blade a little higher, a crimson stain still glistening on the tip. "But I'm not going down quite that easily."

"Dear God...Eve!" Guerin surged forward, but Arran turned and blocked him. "Get out of my way," he growled into Arran's face, shoving against the hold he had on Guerin's upper body. Guerin glanced over his shoulder toward the pair. "Don't do this, Eve," he added. His voice descended to more of a plea.

"I have no intention of fighting you. Tonight or ever." Kenric's tone was calm, unwavering, picking up where they'd left off. "You're hurt. Confused. I barely know you. Why would I want you dead?"

"Damn you!" Eve cried out right before a loud crash ricocheted off the walls. Arran spun. Eve had Kenric's back against the wall, her blade at his throat. Both men surged forward, prepared to peel her off their commander.

"Hands off," Kenric barked the command, aiming it directly toward Arran and Guerin.

"That's right," Eve hissed, pressing the edge of the blade deep enough beneath Kenric's chin that a thin trickle of blood seeped over his Adam's apple. "You don't know me. How could you?" She shrugged. "You were so disgusted with the mere thought of my conception you didn't stick around long enough."

"You only know what you've been told." Kenric gave a slight shake of his head, but not enough to dig the knife in any deeper. "Oh my God. You look so much like her. Marguerite's hair—the shape of your face. But you have my eyes and mouth." Eve stood frozen as if his assessment fascinated her. "You're really my daughter." He shook his head once more. "I don't need a DNA test. I can't explain why. I just feel it. It's true." His throat worked. "Christ. I didn't know about you. "

"You son of a bitch!" Eve rammed him against the wall once more, sending the seascape crashing to the floor. She cried out, then flailed at his body, ripping the leather and cotton of his clothing away. "Fight back, you bastard!"

The commander stood frozen—his expression one of

compassion, not anger. *Damn.* Arran could barely stand there and watch while the commander allowed her to vent her contempt and frustration on his body. Over and over, she slashed at his torso until nothing remained but flesh that looked like a wild animal had gone apeshit on his ass. But to Arran's surprise, none of the wounds Eve delivered were even close to life-threatening. *Shit.* Maybe a molecule of Kenric's genes had survived after all, and she wasn't completely affected — or infected — by Marguerite.

As if the battery fueling her rage were running out of juice, Eve's movements slowed. For the first time, Kenric lifted his arms and gently circled his fingers around her wrists, bringing them to his blood-splattered chest.

"Eve," he whispered.

"Shut up." She shook her head, her dark hair whipping back and forth like a black fan deflecting his words. "I don't want to hear your explanations or your damned excuses." Eve swung her head back and her arms free. "It's nothing but bull—"

She stood there, deflated, as if something had sucked the air from her lungs. Arran followed the direction of her stare. Her focus had zeroed in on the Enclave symbol tattooed on Kenric's arm.

"Eve...please," Guerin called out, but Eve didn't budge. "Let me talk to you. Let me explain." Pain creased the warrior's face, flattening his mouth into a grim line. Guerin didn't look like a man in agony from a stay in hell. He resembled one whose visit was about to begin.

Chapter Fourteen

Oh my God... It's exactly the same. Eve couldn't pull her gaze away from the scarlet-stained black ink. Whatever she was about to say had lodged in the back of her throat. The image before her eyes had shut down her ability to speak. Her heart rate sputtered, then kicked back into gear as if it had hit a speed bump. A wave of nausea swelled in her gut. She swallowed back the bitter taste of bile.

She'd been so stupid.

From the moment she'd watched Guerin swagger across her club's floor, she'd been an idiot. The matching ink could mean only one thing: not only did Guerin know her father, but *he* was one of his damn Enclave.

Too much for one night.

Betrayed at every turn. She sucked in a deep breath, pushing past the knot of pain in her chest threatening to take her down. *Oh, hell no.* Her so-called father may have defeated her mother, but he wouldn't see her crumble. She wouldn't be erased from his world that easily. Eve reversed her step, putting the other two vampires plus Kenric in her sight. She'd been so blinded by the surprise meet-and-greet with dear old dad, Eve couldn't believe she'd turned her back on the other male.

"You lying bastard." The insult clawed its way out of her throat, the rage-filled words directed toward the male she'd allowed inside her heart, not the one who shared her DNA. She was beyond infuriated.

"Eve, I…" Guerin took a step toward her.

"Stop!" Clutching the hilt of her dagger, she reared her arm back. "Don't you come near me, or I swear it'll be the last move you make."

"Please." Guerin lifted his palms as if in surrender. "Give me a chance to—"

Eve laughed. "To what? Explain?" She shook her head. "Oh, yeah. I'm hanging around for that story, so you can tell me this wasn't all a setup to take out the last ugly reminder for your boss." An odd mix of what looked like hurt and regret flashed in Guerin's eyes. But what would she know about those emotions? She'd made sure to never get close enough to anyone to recognize them. "Did you draw the lucky straw, Guerin, and get to be the one to bait the trap? Must be pretty damn proud of yourself. You even got to get your rocks off more than once before your team arrived to try to finish me off."

Guerin's gaze darted to Kenric, then back to Eve.

"Oh, I'm sorry." Eve gave him her best "oops" expression, including the hand to mouth, then added, "Did you not want Dad to know his prize warrior had slept with his daughter—the target?"

She glimpsed the man in question. The large vampire with irises that mirrored her own looked torn between which person in the room to pounce on: her or Guerin. But who the hell knew what was going on inside his head? And she didn't have time to waste figuring him out. As if she cared anyway. Eve was outnumbered, and not by weak human minions sent by Seth. These were seasoned vampires and judging by the power rolling off the one who was her mother's sperm donor, he was a master. She might be able to take out two of them with a mental blow, but not Kenric. She had to get out of here.

Eve bolted for the door, digging deep for every bit of vampire speed she could muster. Cool fresh air blasted through the thin layer of her clothes. *Yes.* The element of surprise had gotten her through without a snag. At the end of the drive, she slowed long enough to phase. Away.

She coalesced and landed with a *thump* on the roof of a two-story home across the street and three houses down. The hard, cold surface of the roof tiles slamming against her bare feet had her gasping for breath. Eve crouched and gripped the molded clay for balance.

"Eve…" It was Guerin's voice inside her head.

He wasn't yelling. His words were soft and gentle, brushing her mind. She turned toward the apartment from where she'd fled. He stood in the drive, facing her general direction. The hour stretched well past midnight, but her excellent night vision painted him picture perfect.

They'd fed on so much of each other's blood over the last two days, sharing a telepathic conversation or picking up her trail would be a simple feat for vampires their age. Yet instead of pursuing, he stood there, staring into the night. A dull ache blossomed behind her sternum. *Oh my God.* Her head lolled between her shoulder blades, and she stared up at the stars. *You have so lost your mind, Devonshire. You* cannot *be feeling disappointed that he's not coming after you.*

"*I know you can hear me,*" he went on to say. "*You're still close. I can feel you. Don't leave like this. I told Kenric and Arran to stay inside. Let me talk to you alone. I promise I'm not going to chase you, because I don't want to push you farther away. No one wants to hurt you.*" He rubbed both palms over his face, then dropped them with a sigh. "*I know…poor choice of words. Because I already did hurt you. Fuck! Eve… I don't know how to fix this. I screwed up.*"

Eve turned away and her vision blurred behind the pool of tears. She blinked, and the dam broke, releasing the waterworks. "Shit," she mumbled, and quickly brushed them away with the back of her hand.

"*I just know—I just know it can't end like this.*" A heavy sigh left his lungs. She could hear it. Could feel his desperation. "Come back, Eve." The deep timbre of his voice slid over her skin, caressing her, beckoning her.

She shook her head.

No, no, no.

Stop it! Eve bit her tongue to keep from crying out the words. He'd lied. Played her for a fool. And she didn't need a round two to learn her lesson. She'd have to be the stupidest female on the planet to get sucked back in. Kenric hated her as much as he had her mother. And where did that get Marguerite? Dead.

Their matching tattoos said it all. Guerin was one of them. His loyalty was to the Enclave. His pretty words had been just that, words. Like the rest of them, he'd had an agenda, and it had almost gotten her killed.

"Come back to —" A litany of guttural sounds followed. Eve whipped back around.

Oh shit! Her heart raced.

She phased in closer, nails scratching into the baked surface of the next house. Two vamps had appeared on either side of Guerin.

Seth's DEAD minions.

They must have followed Kenric and the other male here.

A silver chain, based on the pained expression on Guerin's face, formed a thick noose around his neck. He clawed in strangled silence at the constrictor with both hands. Fangs bared and teeth clenched.

"Her scent clings to you like a fucking second skin," one of the minions growled into Guerin's ear, his voice low, but the snarl on his lips as he mouthed the words made them easy to read. "If I can't drag Eve's ass back to Seth, you'll have to be the next best thing." He tossed a grin at his partner, then back to Guerin. "Bet she'll come for lover boy here." The filthy bloodsucker yanked hard on the chain in emphasis, bowing Guerin's neck into an angle that would have snapped a lesser male's spine.

Bastards! Eve surged to her feet, closed her eyes, and reached inside for her power to phase once more. Then stopped. What was she doing? She lifted her eyelids and watched the scene unfold below. One of the vampires pulled something from his pocket with a gloved hand, jerked the end covering off with his teeth, and then jabbed it into the exposed part of Guerin's neck.

They were drugging him.

Within seconds, Guerin's knees buckled. Each vampire held his slumping body up by an arm. Judging from the strained look on their faces, the dead weight of the powerful male was almost more than the two bloodsuckers could handle.

Her gut twisted at the sight. She should help him. Shouldn't she? Her fingers curled into a fist. But didn't he deserve exactly what was happening to him? He'd sold her out. Led her father and his crew right to her doorstep. And they were still inside. If she stuck around, there was a chance the DEADs collecting Guerin would take her, too, or her father and his partner would have her head.

The threesome phased, then reappeared down the street beside a van parked beneath a busted streetlight. Like a large bag of garbage ready for the local dump, they tossed him into the vehicle. After folding his legs into the cabin, they pulled the sliding door closed with a *snap*, scrambled toward the front and piled inside.

Payback is hell.

Eve clutched the fabric covering her chest. So why did it feel as though she was the one who'd just lost a piece of heaven?

"Where is he?" Kenric's deep voice yanked Eve back from her little pity party. She dropped back down into a crouch. The Enclave's master stood in the drive of her apartment along with the one called Arran, blades in hand. "Guerin," he called out, but keeping his voice reserved. The blond beside him lifted his head and appeared to take a big whiff of the air.

"We may be in Germany," he drawled. "But damn, the DEADs smell exactly the same."

"True," Kenric chimed in. "It doesn't matter which side of the Atlantic they're on. The stink is unmistakable."

The scent of Seth's minions must have drawn them outside, expecting to join Guerin in a battle. Eve watched as both males lifted their daggers a little higher. The silver-plated blades glinted in the full moonlight, triggering the memory of the story her mother had told her before she'd left for America about her father's Enclave. How Kenric had banded a group of warriors in South Carolina to keep the Death Euphoria Addicts or DEADs—vampires who became addicted to the head rush they achieved by feeding until they drained every last drop from their victims—in check.

How very *noble* of his commitment to protect the humans. The knot in her stomach twisted a little tighter. *Hypocrite.* Playing hero to everyone else, yet he'd walked out on his only child.

Tires screeched, signaling the minions' exit with Guerin. The males whirled in the direction of the vehicle.

"Son of a..." Kenric muttered. In unison, they bolted toward the van. "They must have Guerin."

"What the hell is going on?" The van had a head start on them and was already making a left on the next street. The two males slowed. "Why take him and not kill him?"

"Good question." Kenric pointed to another vehicle, and they crossed the street in a blur. The lights flashed on a Jaguar parked along the curb. "One that I'm about to beat the answer to out of them," he added and folded himself into the driver's side of the automobile.

The car made a dizzying U-turn and hauled ass in the same direction the van had taken. Eve leaped from the roof and landed with a soft *whoosh* on the grass below. Time to make haste into her apartment while they went after Guerin, grab what she needed, and disappear—from everyone.

Inside, Eve snatched up her wallet, keys, cell, and what few clothes she'd kept stashed there for emergencies. She'd have to find yet another city and start over with a new identity. God, she was so sick of living like a hunted animal. She couldn't imagine how it must feel to have a place to call home, a family, trust. A fantasy—a longing—she'd keep hidden deep within her heart. Something she'd never allowed herself to dream or dwell on too much, because the two would never be her reality. Yet for a split second when she and Guerin had played lovers, Eve had almost allowed herself to believe he'd cared. She'd dropped her walls and had even trusted him enough to let him see her cry. And he'd held her, promised to continue doing so as long as she needed him. For the first time in maybe never, someone had made her feel cherished, loved. Marguerite may not have been the hugs-and-kisses type of mother, but Eve had never doubted she'd cared for her and had done her best to keep her safe. But what Guerin had made her feel was different. The kind of deep connection a man possessed for a woman. The till-death-do-you-part kind. A laugh bubbled up and out, but she clasped a hand to her mouth, stifling the noise. Damn, she sounded crazy. Trust and love. She sniffed and ran her fingers through her hair. Those two words did not apply to her. Not in her world.

Chapter Fifteen

The pounding inside Guerin's head threatened to split his temples and competed for his attention with the burn at his wrists and ankles. He dragged his eyelids apart and blinked, trying to focus in the direction of the pain in his extremities. Shit, how long had he been out? A single bright light beamed from above and glinted off the silver manacles holding his arms up and out at his sides. Since he'd arrived in Germany, he'd been knocked out and either tied up or caged three times.

Damn, this was starting to get on his nerves.

Guerin's skull bumped off the stone wall behind him. If he didn't already know he was a badass, this getting kidnapped shit would be giving him a complex.

A flurry of movement in his peripheral vision had him swinging his head in its direction. The intensity of the hovering spotlight made it difficult to see details in the darker room, especially for his kind. A vampire's sight was designed for moonlight, not the sun. But of course, whoever had brought him here understood that fact and had used it to his advantage. Constant harsh light would not only make for a miserable prisoner, it would partially blind him as well. But his heightened sense of smell wasn't impaired, and it told him that at least three DEADs had been, or were, in the room.

Guerin breathed deep, sampling the air for identifying markers. Another distinct aroma lurked beneath the stench of the trio. He recognized a familiar scent mingling with the bolder one. A chill raced over his flesh, forcing his spine rigid. *Not here... She couldn't be here.* Unbidden, he inhaled once more.

It was gone.

He was imagining things. The drug in his system had his senses all fucked up. The lingering stronger scent conveyed a vampire of a bit more age than the strung-out males who'd caught him off guard. That little fact still chapped his ass. He'd been too distracted dealing with the emotions after Eve had exploded from the room. He hadn't even sensed the DEADs' proximity until they'd appeared right under his nose.

A damn rookie mistake.

Guerin closed his eyes, giving his retinas a momentary break. They'd left him alone for the time being, and he needed the temporary solitude to shake off the effects of whatever they'd dosed him with—fast.

"Ah, I see our guest is finally awake." And there he was. *That didn't take long.* A male voice penetrated Guerin's too-brief moment of recovery. No doubt the elder leader of the freak show that surrounded him.

Guerin lifted his eyelids. The proximity of the blood-sucker allowed him to make out the details of his features.

Bright-green eyes stared back at him from a face that could have been carved in stone: an aristocratic nose and high cheekbones were finished off with a square chin. Hair so blond it was nearly white brushed his shoulders. He'd rolled the long sleeves of a blue shirt up to his elbows, exposing more of the pale skin. The male held his arms across his chest, twisting the oversize face of his watch back and forth over a thin left wrist. The vampire narrowed his gaze, studying Guerin, worrying his timepiece as if the action somehow gave him clarity.

"Seth Keller, I presume," Guerin drawled.

A grin, or perhaps it was more of a sneer, lifted one side of his mouth. "I see my reputation has preceded me."

"You could say that," Guerin tossed back, with no attempt at trying to hide the venom laced in his tone.

"Since we're playing the 'get to know each other' game, what's your name?"

"Why the hell do you care?"

Seth *tsk*ed. "My, my… Someone's grumpy." Seth's gaze raked him, then lingered on his right pec and the Enclave symbol. One pale brow arched before he narrowed the gap between them. Their difference in height placed his nose about an inch beneath Guerin's. The other male tilted his head and leaned in toward Guerin's throat. In reflex, Guerin clenched his fists, not sure if blondie intended to bite or give him a damn hickey. Either option had his stomach contents ready to rebel. Instead, Seth inhaled deeply along the length of his pulse. Afterward, the other male's head lolled with his eyes closed as if he were in some sort of euphoric state. *What the hell?*

"So unique…simply divine." Seth licked his lips, and his

eyelids popped open. "What was it like, fucking the hybrid, Guerino?" His pupils had dilated, erasing the green of his irises and leaving a barely visible line of white at the perimeter.

Guerin's fangs burst through his gums. Adrenaline surged, tightening his biceps, once again testing the strength of the shackles and rattling the chains. He snarled. "Go to hell."

The blond growled in response as his palm impacted Guerin's face with an ear-popping *whack*. The warm, copper flavor of blood seeped onto Guerin's tongue. He straightened his head, slinging strands of hair that had fallen into his eyes back over his forehead. How the hell did the bastard know who he was? *Markus?* But how?

"Too late." Seth grabbed Guerin's chin, locking their gazes. "We're already there," he whispered, his elongated fangs glinting in the harsh beams. Guerin twisted free of his grip. Seth laughed and reversed his step. "Oh, but Eve will soon change everything."

"You're no closer to getting your hands on her than yesterday, you crazy son of a bitch. What the hell makes you think holding me changes anything for you?" Guerin knew the amount of blood they'd exchanged would keep them connected for several days at least. But that didn't mean she'd try to find him. He'd betrayed her, and he wouldn't blame Eve for allowing him to rot and die at Seth's hand.

A loud *crack* inside his skull was the only indication that Seth had moved. A half second later, Guerin realized it had been the sound of his head meeting the rock wall behind him. The force of Seth's grip on Guerin's jaw held him there.

"Never underestimate me or take me for a fool, Lombardi." A low growl followed his warning. "Her scent covers you like a provocative cloak. You reek of sex. And judging by the number of bite marks"—Seth yanked Guerin's head to the left, then right—"she's filled her gut on your blood." He released his hold and reversed his step.

"You are a fool if you think she'll give herself over to you because of me," Guerin scoffed.

A sick grin formed on Seth's face, and he shook his head. "You know what they say about those who doth protest too much."

"I was nothing to her, Keller. You're wasting your time." Sadly, Guerin knew he was right.

"Perhaps." He shrugged. "But I have a feeling I'm going to enjoy every second of trying to get her attention, anyway."

. . .

Eve punched the mound of foam under her head, then collapsed back down onto the lumpy excuse for a pillow. *Sleep. Please.* God, why couldn't she pass out and forget about the last ten hours? Forget about the pained looked in the blue eyes that bore a striking resemblance to her own. Forget about the pleading sound in Guerin's voice as he'd called out to her...

"Stop it!" Eve cried out into darkened expanse of her rented room. "Let it go. It was all a plan to trap and destroy you, Eve Devonshire. Lies. All of it. Don't you forget." She rolled to her side and sighed. More than likely the males from the Enclave had caught up with Seth's minions, retrieved Guerin, and they were all in their beds sound asleep.

Unlike her.

Last night hadn't been her proudest moment, watching them drug Guerin and take him away. Her stomach roiled at the memory. But two of Seth's DEADs had circled Guerin on the outside, and the Enclave duo had huddled on the inside. What other option had there been for her other than to run?

Kenric wanted her dead. Except it hadn't made any sense since he'd refused to fight her, attack her, when she'd done everything she could to taunt him into doing so.

He'd killed her mother, so why else had he come to find his long-lost child other than to take her down as well? Eve worried her lip, her mind spinning with scenarios. Perhaps he hadn't fought her because he'd wanted to lure her into lowering her guard. Yet he was a master vampire. If he'd wanted her dead, he could have crushed any resistance against him she could have mustered, especially with two of his team at his side. What did Kenric want from her? Because he couldn't possibly want his daughter in his life now.

Her heart pounded in her throat—every beat feeling as if it were larger than the last. She gasped and sprang up, clutching the scratchy cotton sheet to her chest.

Get a grip. She pulled in a deep breath past the constriction. *Get a grip.*

She'd known her whole life that her father hadn't wanted her. So why should today be any different? Eve flopped back onto the mattress and stared up at the small stream of daylight flickering across the dingy ceiling tiles. Her mother would have never lied to her on such an epic scale. Right? That would have been too cruel—on so many levels. She rubbed her eyes. Why did she suddenly doubt the few things she knew to be the truth?

You know why.

Guerin's face loomed to the forefront of her mind. His warm, dark gaze melting her as he'd offered to hold her as long as she'd needed him to. Eve groaned. *No.* She'd be a fool to begin questioning her life because of the touch and feel of a man she'd known for less than a week, and the words of another man—a stranger—who'd abandoned her before she'd been born.

Unbidden, her eyelids drifted closed. Images of multiple dark skylines speckled with diamonds zoomed by in her mind. Faces of strangers, too numerous to count, shuttled past as if on fast-forward.

So many places.

But not a single connection to anyone.

Exactly the way her mother said it had to be to keep her baby alive. The all-too-familiar ache swelled in her stomach. The one she'd carried with her for as long as she could remember. Years later, she'd learned the pain had a name: loneliness.

"Stay in here, Eve," her mother demanded in a hushed voice as she shoved the little girl inside the tiny bedroom. "No one can ever know you exist. Listen to me, and if you want to live, you'll keep your mouth shut." Marguerite backed away and the door released with a soft click, *as a key rattled in the lock,* clunk.

Eve's lip trembled, but she didn't dare cry. It hadn't taken long to learn that tears never helped. They only clogged her nose.

Voices approached outside her door. Eve scurried closer to the wood and crouched, placing her ear to the surface. Mother would be so mad if she knew Eve listened to her with her guests sometimes. But there was no way she'd ever find out. It was usually hours before she'd return, and Eve was always fast asleep by then. Mother would stroke her hair, waking her for a moment, then whisper in her ear, "Mommy's secret treasure. Sweet dreams."

Their murmurings grew more distant as their footsteps trailed down the hall. Eve pressed her ear closer to the door. Her mother treated her more like a human, coddling her as if she would break. But Eve's hearing was better than Marguerite knew. Some things Eve had learned were best kept to herself.

"This is Andre, Marguerite."

"A pleasure...madam," the deep male responded, his words sounding slurred. Was he drunk?

"Mmm. Indeed," her mother cooed. "What brings you both here tonight, Ana? I wasn't expecting you."

"I want him, Marguerite."

Her mother chuckled. "Well, dear...I am not keeping you from him. Have him."

"No. I mean I want him how you took Kenric."

"Shhh!" Her mother nearly screeched, "Do not speak of this again. Or am I to regret ever divulging my deepest secret to you?"

"I've never betrayed you, nor do I plan to."

"Very wise."

"But it's not fair, Marguerite. You keep this secret of how you conceived only to yourself."

"No!" Marguerite bellowed, and a loud crash rang out. "She's mine! I am her creator, and like my daughter, that knowledge is mine alone."

"It's cruel, Marguerite. I'm your one and only confidant. I deserve this. Give me the chance to try. I've honored your wishes, and I've told no one. For God's sake, you trusted me over her own father. It takes two to create a child. You didn't create her by yourself, and he doesn't even know she exists!"

Eve gasped and jumped away from the wood, knocking over the small table by the door with a bang *in the process.*

Her heart raced. He doesn't know?

A loud smack *of flesh against flesh ricocheted through the air. "You fool!"*

Seconds later, the key rattled inside the lock to Eve's bedroom door. Eve picked herself up and hurried to her bed. She jumped onto her quilt as her mother entered. Her heart was in the back of her throat, making it hard to swallow.

"Eve, darling." Her mother lifted her skirts and glided across the wood floor to Eve's bedside. "You were listening at the door, weren't you?"

A lie was on the tip of Eve's tongue, but when she looked up into her mother's green eyes, there was no use trying to dodge the truth.

"Yes." Eve nodded and drew her legs under her night-gown. The bed dipped with her mother's added weight, and Marguerite lifted Eve's chin, holding their gazes locked.

"That was very naughty, Eve." She sighed. "And you're going to have to forget everything you heard." A ring of fire swirled around her mother's pupils.

Eve's eyelids sprang open and she shot forward in bed. Her chest was too tight as if there was no room for the air to squeeze past the pain inside. She darted from the mattress and rushed to the dingy bathroom. Eve hit the light switch, twisted on the cold water, leaned over the sink, and splashed a handful into her face. The chilled liquid wrung a gasp from her throat, jarring her lungs into action.

She snatched a towel from the shelf over the toilet and stared at her reflection in the mirror. Blue eyes instead of her mother's green glared backed at her. Except for the irises, she was her mother's spitting image. Her stomach rebelled, bile eroding the tissue at the back of her throat.

"Nearly three centuries," she whispered into the empty space. "All these years…was there ever a moment when anything you told me was the truth, Mother?" Eve rammed her fist into the glass, shattering the large rectangle into tiny fragments. Shards hit the laminated counter and showered the basin in reflective confetti.

Violated.

Eve stabbed her fingers into hair, holding on to her head. Her mother had manipulated her mind. Altered her memories to reflect her own version of reality.

No, no, no! It was a dream. She was falling apart for nothing. It had to be her mind playing tricks on her.

Kenric couldn't have been telling the truth. Tears welled, blurring her vision. Eve stumbled from the bathroom and made her way to the end of her bed. She plopped onto the edge of the mattress. If what he'd said was true, then her whole life had been a lie. All her mother had fed her for as long as she could remember were lies.

"Oh, God," she groaned. How did one digest something like that and move on? But deep inside, Eve had a feeling she was about to learn.

Her so-called "dream" hadn't felt like a mismatch of images constructed from her imagination. No. The event had unraveled inside her head as if someone had pulled a string from the fabric holding together a veil of memories her mother had tried to keep hidden.

Too real.

"What do I do now?" she whispered. So much damage lay between her and her father, a river of deceit Eve had no idea how to cross.

Chapter Sixteen

It was another long night for the record books.

Pulling back the heavy drapes in the hotel suite, Arran took in the city of Nuremberg, its lights awakening in the setting sun. Guerin was out there—somewhere. But this time, Arran didn't have a damn clue where to begin their search.

Eve had escaped only moments before the DEADs had arrived. She couldn't have had time to arrange his abduction. So who the hell in Germany wanted the Enclave's second-in-command?

"You ready to go?"

"Yeah." Arran pivoted, grabbed his daggers from the end of the bed, and stowed them, one in his boot, the other in the sleeve strapped to his thigh. Kenric tossed him his coat, then slid his own over his shoulders.

"The sun should be well below the horizon by the time we reach the airport," Kenric said on the way out the door. "According to the text, Emily's jet arrives in an hour."

"So you haven't spoken to her yet?"

"No." Kenric hit the down button to call the elevator. A bell dinged and the doors slid open. Both men stepped into the empty box and rode the seven stories down to the garage level. Neither spoke. The tension in the air did all the talking. Other than Emily, Guerin was the closest thing Kenric had to family. And even though Arran and Guerin had broken Kenric's trust with the Eve situation, nothing had changed. They wouldn't stop until Guerin was found.

At their rented Jag, Arran slipped in behind the wheel, shut the door, and pressed the start button.

"After we pick up Emily, what's our next move to find Guerin?" Arran shot a glance toward the master vampire in the passenger seat.

"We find Eve."

Shit. How in the hell were they supposed to convince her to give them a hand?

"Based on the bites on their necks, Eve and Guerin have shared each other's blood. She's our best chance at getting him back. Besides that, my gut says she's the reason he was taken in the first place. Somebody wants my daughter." Kenric's head cranked in Arran's direction. "But they're going to have to come through me first."

After a forty-five-minute drive, Arran maneuvered the vehicle within a few feet of the G450. Their timing had been perfect. According to the text message Kenric had received a few seconds ago from Emily, the Enclave's jet had arrived only moments before.

Minutes later, Emily appeared at the top of the steps and Kenric exited the Jag. Kenric's female was a beautiful woman with long dark-auburn hair, hazel eyes, and full curves. At the bottom of the stairs, Kenric placed a protective arm around his mate's shoulder and guided her toward their ride. Emily was a little shorter than his Gabrielle. But Arran had a preference for women closer to his height. Arran smiled, his mind pulling up the image of his own female. Gabrielle fit him perfectly. In every way.

The rear door opened, and Emily slid inside, followed by the larger vampire. Since Emily had come into Kenric's life, he'd never seen the Enclave's master happier—content. Hopefully, the appearance of a daughter Kenric hadn't known existed wouldn't shatter their world.

"Hello, Emily." Arran caught her reflection in the rearview mirror. "How was your flight?"

Emily glanced up. "Long and confining. Like being trapped in a coffin for ten hours at thirty-five thousand feet."

Arran nodded. "I couldn't agree more. Not a fan of small spaces myself."

"Get us back to the hotel, Arran," Kenric said. "We all need some time alone to feed…" Kenric's gaze slid to his mate's. "And talk. Then we need to formulate the next step in our strategy."

"I'm on it," Arran replied, made a one-eighty, and pointed their vehicle toward the Autobahn.

"I've missed you." Kenric's words drifted into the forward compartment. Arran did his best to tune the other male out and focus on the road.

"Me too," Emily whispered. "We definitely need to talk—among other things—when we get to our room."

The leather squeaked, and the car rocked. Out of the corner of his eye, Arran caught Kenric's image in the mirror, his large frame covering Emily's, their mouths locked.

Shit. Arran repositioned in his seat. This was going to be one long-ass ride.

"Christ, wildflower…," Kenric growled. "You smell delicious, and I'm damn hungry."

Arran's fangs surged through his gums at the sound. "All right, you guys. Hang on. Don't forget you've got company up here with really good hearing."

A throaty chuckle exited Kenric, and he rolled back onto his side of the car. "Point taken."

"Yes. Besides…" Emily readjusted her clothing. "You and I"—she looked pointedly at Kenric—"still need to have a long talk." Arran had never been more happy to not have an invite to that particular conversation.

They made it back to the hotel in record time. *Thank God.* Being the only male on this side of the Atlantic without his mate was growing more difficult by the minute.

Inside their suite, Kenric and Emily excused themselves and headed to their room on the opposite side of the living space. Arran aimed for his private space. But it wasn't quite far enough. Even with the distance between them and two sets of walls, Arran couldn't help but overhear some of their heated exchange. Emily couldn't understand why Kenric had left the country without sharing what he'd learned with his mate. She'd never felt more hurt. He'd left her out of the loop on something that was going to affect both their lives.

The shit was gut-wrenching, and Arran couldn't take the pain in Emily's voice another minute. He grabbed the remote and turned on the TV for some noise cancellation. After shooting Gabrielle a text message informing her Emily had arrived and sending her his love, Arran opened the patio doors to his room and stepped outside. He needed the air to clear his head.

Finding Eve was next on the agenda. If they found her, they were one step closer to locating Guerin. But where the hell to start looking? She could be anywhere in Europe. His cell buzzed in his hand with Gabrielle's reply. He smiled at the x's and o's his mate always added to the end of her messages. *The cell...of course.*

Eve's cell number. It was how they'd tracked her down in the first place. Through the chaos of Guerin's kidnapping, he'd almost forgotten about that small detail. But would she still have kept her phone? Could they be that lucky?

An hour later, Emily and Kenric emerged, the master's color looking better than earlier. A pang of hunger arrowed through Arran's midsection. He would have to take care of his own growing need for a meal before long.

"You've filled Emily in on our current situation?"

The couple shared a glance, and Kenric replied. "She knows everything."

"I was thinking," Arran began. "We still have Eve's last known cell number. What do you think of texting her and seeing if you could get her to talk to you? She could ignore your call or delete your voice mail, but maybe we'd get lucky and she'd read your message."

"Good point," Kenric said.

"Based on what had gone down inside her apartment before we arrived, she'd liked Guerin at one point. Maybe for his sake, she'd risk a meeting with us to save him."

"That's if she hasn't ditched the phone." Kenric retrieved his cell from the nearby table.

"It's worth a try at least," Emily chimed in. "I can't imag-ine what Guerin's going through, and I'm not even thinking worst-case scenario."

Kenric eased onto the edge of a sofa cushion, staring at the screen of his iPhone. "Now to find the perfect words so Eve won't ignore us…"

. . .

The sun had to be down by now based on the fact that some of the lethargy had left Guerin's body. But it didn't do a damn thing for the ache building in his joints and muscles from standing chained to a wall for more hours than he'd care to count. Nor did it help stabilize what little skin remained around his wrists where the silver continued to slowly fry his flesh. But hey, beggars couldn't be choosy, as they say. At least he felt more alert to enjoy it all.

"Well, well, well…" A female voice drifted across the room. A voice that had every hair on Guerin's body lifting. His stomach roiled, and an icy chill skated down his back. *Son of a bitch.*

And just when he was trying to see the bright side.

But if Daniela De Santis was involved, things couldn't be more dark. Desperation—powerlessness…hell, both threatened to choke him until he blew a lung. Dear God. There was no way in hell he could allow Eve anywhere near him. Not with Daniela wanting a piece of her.

Guerin straightened his spine and tamped down his emotions when it came to Eve. He dared not let Daniela see him flinch. If so, she would pounce on his weakness like a cat chasing a laser light beam. He narrowed his gaze in the direction of the sound although the spotlight continued to glare into his retinas, blinding him to anything beyond.

"I was highly annoyed to learn our minions had failed once again to bring me the hybrid. But imagine my surprise when Seth told me the name of our guest they'd returned with instead. Guerino Lombardi…"

The overhead lights switched on, stabbing their rays into the back of his eyeballs. Guerin blinked under the intensity, attempting to focus.

"It's been such a very, very long time." The spotlight's beam died, and the female stepped in front of Guerin.

"Not nearly long enough, Daniela. But I'm not surprised you're involved in something so vile."

"You sound bitter, pet." Daniela closed in and stroked the back of two fingers along Guerin's cheek. Reflex had him twisting his head away from her touch. She *tsk*ed. "And here I thought the years we'd shared had been so memorable."

"I can't deny that," Guerin scoffed. "More than two centuries and an ocean between us have yet to sufficiently incinerate you from my brain cells."

Daniela laughed, but quickly sobered as if she'd never heard the joke. "What a sweet thing to say." She smiled. "But you always were a sentimental male." Daniela reached over and plucked a long, smooth length of cane from a rack. "Remember this, pet?" She ran her fingertips over the surface.

"How could I forget?" Guerin said, pressing the back of his head against the stone behind him. "You introduced it to me many times across my back, my ass, and…other places."

A wicked grin curled her red lips. "Yes. I did." Daniela slid the end of the pole along the inside of his leg, dragging the tip higher over the thin cotton of his sweats.

"What do you want, Daniela?" Guerin gritted his teeth. For years, her attention had heated his blood. He'd lived to endure her games—to please her. Hell, he'd given up the sun for the opportunity to be with her forever. But now... Now, he could barely stomach her caress even through a six-inch piece of wood.

The tip of her cane nudged the length of his shaft, and her nostrils flared. "I can smell her on you." She lifted her chin and met his gaze. "Oh, how I remember the intensity of your tastes, pet. Was she able to get you off as easily as I could?"

"Despite how strongly you believe in your own inflated ego, you're not that unique, Daniela."

Her eyes flashed, but quickly cooled. "You're lucky I'm in such a good mood. I'm willing to overlook that remark and your past failures. Perhaps if you're nice, I might even give you another chance."

What?

"You're offering to forgive me?" The words barely exited his throat without the contents of his stomach.

"That's right." Daniela circled his groin with the cane. "Once we have the hybrid, you can come home again, pet." She looked up, her pupils devouring the white space of her eyes. "Everything could be as you remembered. You, me..." With her other hand, Daniela seized his nipple between her index finger and thumb and twisted. "All the games we played." Instead of turning him on, the zing went straight to his head, pissing him off. A surge of what he could only describe as satisfaction rolled through his core with his response. Whatever spell she'd cast over him years ago was broken.

"Too funny, Daniela. But I'm like the toy you buried in your bin and forgot. Now that someone else has played with it, you're getting all possessive and want it back." He cocked his head. "I don't need, or want, your forgiveness," he growled. "You can go to hell."

Her lip curled, exposing a twin set of fangs right before her palm connected with the side of his face with a hard *smack*. Stars whirled in front of his eyes, and it had nothing to do with his favorite spotlight. Well, Daniela certainly hadn't lost her touch. Guerin licked away the coppery taste of blood from the corner of his mouth and straightened.

"Feel better?" He lifted a brow.

"Not yet," she said, tossing him a sadistic curl of her lip. "But I'm about to." Daniela swung her arm back with the cane in her grip, then forward, aiming between his spread legs. The long tip struck his cock and balls with a hard *whack*.

Guerin's jewels made a leap for his gut, punching the air from his lungs. His knees threatened to cave. But secured to the cross, he had nowhere to go. Guerin clamped down on his eyelids and fists, calling for every ounce of what was left of his endurance.

Fuck. Me.

His day had just made a hard turn in the direction of *this is gonna suck.*

Chapter Seventeen

Twenty kilometers outside of Nuremberg, Eve paced the small confines of the cheap room she'd rented in the local *gasthaus*. If her indecision kept up much longer, she was going to have to pay the owners for new carpet. But damn, she was so confused.

Her head hurt from sifting through all the new versus old information. Who was right and who was wrong? Did her father hate her—want her dead as he had her mother? Or was her dream real, and he had had no clue about her existence?

Eve wasn't sure she'd ever forget the look in Kenric's eyes when she'd held him against the wall, her knife at his throat. He'd appeared stunned. Yet instead of lashing out in self-defense, he'd seemed fascinated with her presence, even though she'd threatened to kill him where he stood. Not what she'd expected from her first meeting with a father who was a master and leader of a group of warrior vampires.

And a male who her mother had sworn despised them both.

A fact Marguerite Devonshire had ingrained onto Eve's spirit since the day she'd been born.

The Enclave's master was either a damn good actor, or he'd been telling the truth.

"Why would you do that to me, Mother?" Had she been so selfish, wanting desperately to keep Eve all to herself, that she would convince her daughter that her father never wanted her? The idea made Eve sick.

God, she'd never been so conflicted and unsure of her judgment. A part of her insisted, *stick to what you know. It's kept you alive this long. Mother could not have been all bad or wrong.* But her other half wanted to run back to Nuremberg, take that leap of faith, and find the members of the Enclave. Yet would Guerin even want to see her face again after Seth's minions had drugged him and hauled him off? Her head knew Kenric and Arran had gone after Guerin, gotten him back. Yet her heart still ached from the memory of their attack.

Everything about her and Guerin had happened so fast.

They'd gone from zero to a hundred in a matter of days. But the connection she'd shared with Lombardi was something she'd never experienced—ever.

Then it had all gone to hell.

But that didn't mean it had hurt any less when it was over. Eve massaged her sternum and the dull ache that refused to let her go.

Stabbing pain radiated through Eve's abdomen and up her spine, bending her in half. "Damn!" She gasped. What was wrong with her? The intensity brought Eve to her knees, and she fell forward onto her palms. Inhaling through her nose, exhaling through her mouth, Eve tried to hang on and ride out the wave.

A lash of fire bloomed across her back. She cried out and collapsed onto the carpet. Then another wave of flames singed her spine. Eve blinked away the dark spots in her vision and groaned. It was as if she were being flogged with strips of burning leather.

Guerin.

"Oh, God. No... Guerin..." Eve rolled to her side and grasped for purchase along the bedrails. Her body trembled under the continued onslaught as she pushed herself up onto her knees. "No!" she cried out. "Damn you, Kenric! You were supposed to have gotten to him in time." She choked back the tears, rage at the Enclave's master's failure seething under her skin, but it was her own failure to save Guerin, when she'd had the chance, that consumed her.

Guerin and Eve were both vampires of more than two centuries. Powerful beings who'd shared blood equally over the last forty-eight hours. As a result, they'd formed a temporary link between their minds. Not only were they able to track each other, communicate telepathically over short distances, but they could sense any significant traumatic or emotional distress of the other as well. Having felt nothing through their link all this time, Eve had been lulled into a false sense of security. She *believed* Kenric and Arran had gotten to him in time.

Damn! She had to reinforce the walls around her mind. Had to be able to think. If she didn't, she would be worthless.

Eve fell over the side of the mattress and tumbled face-first onto the sheets. Searing pain clawed its way along her back like a rack of hot nails trying to peel her flesh open.

"Guerin!" Dear God, how could he bear it? This agony wasn't meant for sexual submission, a blend of pain and pleasure. This was a brutal attack meant to break him physically and mentally—if it didn't kill him first.

And it was all her fault.

Pull it together, Devonshire. Pull yourself together. He needs you.

Gripping the sides of her head with her palms, Eve closed her eyes.

Breathe. Breathe.

Her hands were the walls surrounding her brain. Picturing the physical barrier inside her head, Eve pushed past the attack on her nerve endings. Flesh became stone. Concrete blocks stacking one upon the other, growing thicker and thicker, formed an impenetrable barrier around her mind. *That's it.*

Slowly, she crawled her fingers away from her skull and twisted them in the sheets—waiting—testing the seal for leaks.

The assault had eased. The connection between her and Guerin had dimmed to a point where Eve could lift her head.

A ding sounded from the bedside table, drawing her attention. Someone had sent her a text. But who the hell had her number besides Ingrid from the club? Eve snatched the phone and stared at the display. Her pulse stuttered at the words.

Guerin's in trouble. You're our only hope if we're going to get him back. I know there's no reason why you'd ever want to help me. But can you do this for Guerin? He needs you. We need you, Eve. No trap.

Please... Kenric.

Oh, shit! Her mind whirled. Too many years of thinking of her father as the enemy had her leery as hell. But could she enter the heart of Seth's operation and rescue Guerin on her own? Probably not. It would be a suicide mission.

No one deserved to spend any amount of time inside Seth's colony as an unwelcome guest. She'd heard the stories of those who had never returned because of some perceived betrayal. Eve lived most of her days as a human, but it didn't mean she didn't lurk as a vampire on occasion, with her ear to ground. She had to, or end up in a master's torture chamber where Eve was sure they'd attempt to breed her... or dissect her if she failed to produce. Her ability to walk in daylight and the origins of her birth were too much of a temptation for those greedy for more power.

She studied the message once more. If she was true to herself, wasn't this the opportunity she'd secretly hoped for? One more chance to meet the Enclave's master on her own terms, not some sneak attack like their last encounter? This time, she would be better prepared. Guerin needed her, and Eve needed this — to find out once and for all what had happened between Kenric and Marguerite.

Eve tapped out a short reply:

Where do you want to meet?

And hit send.

Quick and simple.

One sentence.

Yet somehow she knew everyone's life, including hers, had just been changed.

. . .

Eve was very familiar with the hotel where Kenric and the other member of his team were staying. She'd driven past it many times. A six-story complex in the center of town. They were staying in suite 601. Yet she had no intention of using the door.

The view was spectacular from the roof. If one didn't mind the cold wind lifting your hair and crawling its icy fingers down your neck. Eve shivered and tugged the collar of her leather jacket higher.

Climbing up on the lip of the tower, she stared down at the row of balconies, their concrete slabs and metal railings jutting out from the white face of the building's exterior. She slid the toe of her boot over the edge, giving her stomach a hard flip. Her breath hitched. God, she didn't like high places even though she had the power to phase and never hit the ground. The human side of her spirit still rebelled at the whole idea of taking that first big step.

She could have phased up, but where was the excitement in that? Besides, she would have missed out on the view, and selecting the correct balcony was much easier starting from the top. Kenric's suite sat only one floor below.

Closing her eyes, Eve pictured the image of where she wanted to go and sent her body on the trip. Solid ground evaporated from beneath her feet, and she was flying. Except there were no wings. More like the dizzying rush of a roller-coaster ride minus the sights and the sounds. Bit by bit, she coalesced outside on the balcony and gazed through the window at the occupants inside. No one would spot her there unless she wanted them to. She'd made sure to keep her body in its ethereal form, a ghost-like mist giving her enough functions to covertly observe.

A couple was eating dinner—takeout, based on the boxes—in front of the TV. The female was blond, and the male...not the one she'd seen with Kenric from the other night. Too little hair and too much girth.

Wrong room.

Eve mentally directed her molecules over onto the next platform and rematerialized, yet maintained her translucent vapor form. The veil lifted on her vision and she found the patio door open to this room. Blocking the opening, a tall male with broad shoulders and dark hair, dressed in jeans, boots, and a leather jacket, stood with his back to the city.

"She should be here by now," the male stated to a beautiful redhead standing in front of him.

"We don't know how far away she was when she sent the message. But she did respond. What reason would she have to lie?"

Reflex had her hands clenched into fists for control. Kenric was discussing her.

"What reason did Marguerite have for any of her lies?"

Don't go there, Father. No matter what she'd done, Marguerite was still her mother.

"Still," he went on to say. "When I looked into Eve's eyes, I didn't see the same venom Marguerite possessed." He cupped the female's face. "Eve was furious with me, don't get me wrong. She was hurt. But deep down, I sensed more pain than evil."

"I'm glad to hear you say that. Because I have to admit the idea of putting Guerin's life in her hands, counting on her to come through and help us find him…it scares me. Half of her is you; it's the other strand of her DNA that worries me."

Eve slipped the knife from her boot, glided in behind her father, and solidified. Kenric was about four inches taller than her, but at six feet herself, putting the blade to his throat wasn't that hard.

The large male stiffened at the feel of the cold steel against his neck, and a gasp sounded from the woman.

"I'm my own person. How dare you judge me before you've even met me." Eve glared over the shoulder of her father at the female on the other side.

"Don't hurt him," Emily whispered. "Please."

"Not unless someone makes me. Now, get inside," Eve ordered. As a unit, they slowly stepped farther into the suite.

"Hey, have you two—" The tall blond she'd seen the other night marched in from an adjoining room and drew to a halt. "Shit!" His glare fixated on the knife at Kenric's throat. "You have heard from her."

"Leave her alone, Arran," Kenric instructed. "Again, this is between Eve and me." The other male nodded and flashed his palms as if in surrender.

"Kenric…," the female called out, her tone sounding desperate.

"She's my daughter, Emily, and she deserves to know the truth." His throat worked under the blade, the Adam's apple doing an up-and-down maneuver. "I have no idea what your mother told you about us, your conception. But the fact is that I've never heard about you until now, and I bet she told you a lot of lies."

Eve flinched, the serrated edge of the blade digging a millimeter deeper. She couldn't help it. Dammit. She felt like the ass end of a joke. Everyone else in on the plot and she was the last one to know.

"You have no idea how sorry I am that you've been hurt by her deceit," he said. "It kills me every day knowing because of me, so many of the people I cared about have been caught in Marguerite's cross fire."

This had to stop. He was talking about her mother as though she was a monster. Eve grabbed his shoulder and spun him around, putting them face-to-face. But she didn't lose the knife. Hell no. She kept it under his chin. "Don't act like you really knew my mother," she bit out. "You weren't around long enough to vilify her."

"No. You're right. I escaped as soon as I could. But I spent three years with her, unwillingly, before I got away."

"Escaped?" She shook her head. "What are you talking about*?" He had walked out on them. Kenric made it sound as if he'd been her mother's prisoner.*

"I want to show you something," Kenric said. "Trust takes time, and with Guerin's life on the line, time isn't something we have a lot of right now."

"What do you want me to see?"

"Kenric?" The redhead stepped closer. "What are you doing?"

Eve held up a hand, blocking her. "Stay right where you are."

"I'm fine," he said to the woman. Eve glanced up and Kenric added, "We're going to be okay."

"So what do you have in mind?"

"I can only think of one way to prove to you—show you who I am and the truth at the same time. I want you to look inside my memory."

Shit. Was he serious? A master vampire inviting another for a stroll inside his brain? That took guts. He would be completely vulnerable.

"Kenric!" This time it was the one called Arran. Her father looked up. "Are you sure about this, man?"

"Yeah. I am." He nodded and returned his attention to Eve. "She won't hurt me. If she'd wanted me dead, Eve would have tried a lot harder before now. Not that you would've won…" The corner of his mouth lifted with a hint of a smile.

Despite her best efforts, a part of Eve's heart warmed at the sight. She could see why her mother had been so enamored with the male.

"If I had known, Eve, I would have never stopped looking for you—no matter what the cost. I would have loved and cared for you, because you're my child despite who your mother was."

God, he came across so sincere. If he was playing her, Kenric St. James was a vile, manipulative bastard.

"Look inside my mind. I can feel how powerful you are, and I know you have the ability. There are no walls there." Kenric spread his arms wide in surrender.

The answers she'd been waiting for were right there within reach. So why was she hesitating? It felt as if she were back up on the rooftop and about to jump. But this time she didn't know if her powers would save her from crashing to earth.

"Do it, Eve," Kenric said, drawing her back in. "You deserve the truth, and the only way you'll ever believe or trust me is if you see for yourself there are no hidden memories of a daughter. No games here." His eyes welled with unshed tears. "No tricks."

"Okay," she said, the word barely audible. Eve fisted her free hand for courage. She couldn't wait, yet she wasn't ready. Didn't know if she'd ever be ready, but there was no turning back. "Look at me," she commanded, turning her vampire genes on full blast. Kenric zeroed in on her gaze. And exactly as he stated, his mind was wide open.

Eve dove in, peeling the layers back on his memories as if his gray matter were an onion. Kenric stumbled and cursed, but the other female in the room was at his side, placing an arm around his waist before he fell.

"Shit," he mumbled. "She's strong." Kenric chuckled.

How the hell he could even talk under the probe was impressive. "Stop running your mouth. You're not in charge right now."

"That's my girl," he whispered.

Her concentration slipped at his words, and she nearly lost her hold on his mind. "Quiet," she commanded, this time a little stronger. Flashes of faces she didn't recognize zoomed by. Echoes of conversations from long ago resounded inside her head. Then she heard the name—Marguerite. And she slowed.

The redhead was in the image. But she was tied down and Eve's mother loomed over her. Emily…the other woman was Emily, and she was his mate. A rush of emotion filled Eve's mind and heart, nearly staggering her. He loved this female.

Frame after frame she watched the interaction—no, battle—between him and his mother. Oh, my God, Marguerite was enraged. She wanted to kill them both.

As if the word had summoned the one image she had almost hoped she'd pass by, her mother's last moment. A sob she had no idea had been building burst from Eve's throat. Kenric had killed her. But then he'd turned from her body, scanning the room where she'd died, and the carnage was horrific. Eve's pulse hammered inside her ears. Had her mother been the cause of such destruction?

She had to go further back. See how it had all started. Why did her mother want to hurt her father in such a way? Back. Further back, she drove into his neurons, stripping away the years. Kenric's head flinched under the onslaught.

Annice. No! the haunting sound ricocheted in Eve's head followed by the image of a woman lying in a pool of crimson. His fiancée. Kenric's heart was breaking. *Marguerite.* She'd killed Annice, and Kenric wanted Marguerite dead.

Eve pushed harder. So much pain associated with her mother. But not once had she heard her own name mentioned. Nothing about a daughter? How could he not know?

"Stop…," Kenric whispered. "Enough."

"I'm not finished yet." A wall slammed into place, but as this point Eve was too far in for anything he erected to be effective. With a mental shove, she knocked it down. Kenric staggered, but Eve held on.

"Kenric! Say the word to make her stop, and I damn sure will," Arran growled from a few feet away.

Her father grabbed her arms. "Eve…," he rumbled. "Don't. Go. There," he forced out as if her invasion were constricting his throat.

Darkness. So cold. A cell. Kenric was in a cell. Chained. Her mother stood beside his supine form. *Oh, God.* This wasn't anything like the stories she'd been fed. *He was her prisoner.* None of what Marguerite had told her was true. *Lies!* Eve's stomach rebelled. Why had her mother done this to her father? Marguerite was forcing the blood from her wrist down his throat. He thrashed against her, and when he could get a breath, a litany of curses fell from his lips. Then the female vampire was above him, her long dark hair draped over her bare chest. She straddled his hips. Kenric arched his spine and cried out. *Oh God… No!* Marguerite was going to—

The force of the invisible blow knocked Eve backward, taking out a table lamp with her along the way. She slammed into the far wall with a *bang*, cracking her head against the wall. Any other woman would have been unconscious from the blow, but thanks to her hybrid nature, Eve shook it off. She straightened and massaged her skull.

Damn. How had her father managed to eject her from his mind? No other vampire she'd ever known would have been able to achieve such a feat. He was…impressive.

She glanced up at the powerful male who stood scrubbing a hand over his face. Kenric caught her gaze, his expression pained, weary. Impressive wasn't a sufficient enough word for what she'd witnessed and he'd survived. So many emotions tumbled around inside her. She felt as if she were on some crazy roulette wheel her mother had set in motion years ago with its white ball bouncing from slot to slot over words such as disgust, anger, hurt, and betrayal. But most of all…sorrow. Eve was so sorry for what her mother had done to Kenric.

"Are you hurt?" Kenric lowered his palm from his jaw as he approached.

Eve shook her head. "No. I'm all right." *Shit.* She felt like an ass after violating his memories, and here he was making sure she wasn't the one injured.

"I tried to get you to stop. I didn't want to do that, but it had to end."

"I know." She swallowed hard, doing her best to ignore the other heated stares in the room. "I'm sorry. I know I pushed too far." The lump in her throat wouldn't stay down, and her vision blurred. She blinked hard. *I can't cry in front of him. I wasn't the one tortured.*

"That was something I never intended for you to learn," he said inside her head. *"For anyone other than my mate to know ever happened. Especially not my daughter."*

"I'll never betray your confidence," Eve replied, the only way she could to her father. Her voice wasn't working, and thanks to the pathway he'd already opened, she was able to resurface on the perimeter and communicate. *"I promise."* She dropped her gaze to her boots. Too ashamed of her mother to look him in the eye.

"I only wanted you to see I wasn't lying about the extent of her malice. That your existence was kept from me. It should have never gone that far. Hurting you wasn't part of the plan."

She swung her head up. "Hurting me?" Eve shook her head, appalled. "How could you even want anything to do with me after what my mother did to you?" She looked to his mate. "And to you?"

Kenric reached out and with an index finger at her chin guided Eve's attention back to him. "Because a miracle has happened. Out of the darkness Marguerite created, a sliver of light has found me. And it's you."

He was killing her. A tear escaped and rolled down her cheek. Eve's heart was damn near splitting at the seams. She quickly wiped away the damp evidence from her face. This couldn't be real. But she didn't want to pinch herself and find out.

"You're a part of me, Eve." He brushed his fingers over her hair, so lightly she wouldn't have known if she hadn't witnessed the event. "I don't know how she did it, but how could I turn you away?"

"We've lost so many years…" Eve blinked and shook her head. "I don't know where we're supposed to go from here."

"Uhm…" Arran cleared his throat, drawing everyone's attention. "As much as I'm loving the fact that you two are having this family reunion…" Arran grimaced. "Can you figure out the rest after we find Guerin?"

"You're right," Kenric said. "Selfishly, I don't want to give up another second of my time with you, but we need to turn our focus to my second-in-command. He needs us."

Eve nodded. Even though she was nowhere near ready to change the subject either, Guerin was the priority right now. Besides, she had to put a stop to the Hallmark moment before she dissolved into a blubbering idiot and lost her entire kick-ass image. "Okay." She squared her shoulders. "What's your plan on how we're going to rain down some hell and yank Guerin out of this bastard's hold?"

Chapter Eighteen

Hell had a new zip code.

And if asked, your GPS would direct your ass to a dungeon in Bavaria.

Guerin could testify to the fact since he'd spent the last several hours sampling all it had to offer.

Dawn was coming. He could feel it in his bones, the prickle skating across his flesh.

"How was your visit with your sire?" Seth sauntered up, his gaze surveying Guerin from head to toe. "My, my." He clucked his tongue. "What did you say to the Mistress?" Seth chuckled. "I would have thought you, of all males, would remember her short temper."

"I'm so happy I amuse you." Guerin tugged on his wrists, straightening his spine despite the screaming of his muscles and the pull on the open wounds to his back and chest. He wasn't about to allow Seth to see him buckle.

"Oh, you do indeed." Seth smirked.

"I still can't imagine why you two haven't killed me already." Guerin shrugged. "It's been, what, at least two nights now, and I haven't seen Eve. Have you?" One pale brow lifted on Seth's brow. "She's not coming for me. I told you. She won't be. So why keep me around?"

Another laugh bubbled up from Seth's chest. "You're a terrible liar, Lombardi. You forget whom you're trying to scam." With a flick of his wrist, palm up, he continued. "We kill you. We destroy Eve's homing signal. The fact that you want to die tells me there is reason to think our little hybrid will show."

"What do you think you're going to gain even if she does show?" Guerin bit out, wrenching on his shackles.

The pale bloodsucker's eyes rolled back in his head. "You have no idea how long I've tracked her." Seth returned his gaze to Guerin. "Her talents mean power. And I plan to harvest every one of her secrets—including the mystery of her creation—or she will rue each day she hides them away."

"Eve will die first before she feeds your greed."

Seth grinned. "Fine. But I'll make more like her before she draws her last breath." He slid a palm over his crotch.

Rage surged like a fiery rod through his core. "You fucking bastard." Guerin's fangs burst from his gums.

"Not yet. But soon." He winked.

"I will kill you first," Guerin growled.

"Such arrogance for one chained against a wall with his flesh shredded." Seth whirled. "Eve has no idea how much she's going to bring to me and my colony," he added, strolling toward the stairs. "After my scientists take her apart, I'll find out how to replicate her tolerance to sunlight. I *will* walk in the morning sun again one day."

"Yes," Guerin growled. "You will. When I shove your disgusting flesh into its ray and watch you light up like foil in a microwave." Seth didn't acknowledge whether he'd heard Guerin or not. Guerin didn't really care. It was more of a vow to destroy the son of a bitch than anything else. A promise. Not a threat.

He had to make sure Eve had no intention of tracking him. Guerin had held off trying to contact her, because he didn't want to take the chance of drawing her here, alerting her to his presence and situation. But after the significant beating Daniela had given him earlier, Guerin was worried that if Eve hadn't known he was still a captive, she did now. They had shared blood more than once, plus something more, whether either of them was ready to acknowledge it or not.

He'd heard other vampires, including Kenric, talk about soul mates. He'd thought they were full of shit. After allowing one female inside his head and the disaster that had turned out to be, Guerin had doubted he'd ever find such a thing. But now... Perhaps Eve was his? All he knew for sure was the female had gotten under his skin and had left an imprint. One he couldn't seem to shake.

She'd made him feel. Made his heart beat again.

And he wasn't referring to an orgasm. Hell, he'd had plenty of those over the centuries—though the ones with Eve had been more than incredible—but the real kind of hammering pulse that drove hard through his veins, screaming that he was alive. Guerin never wanted it to stop. Eve was his addiction.

They'd spent only three nights together, but it had been enough to know he'd never be the same. She was different, and it wasn't just because of her DNA. And if dying meant Seth and Daniela wouldn't get their hands on her...then so be it. Kenric's daughter had to live.

"Eve," he called out to her inside his mind. *"I don't know if you can hear me. You may be far away by now. Shit. I hope you are."*

A few moments of silence passed, and he hoped like hell she was gone.

"Guerin! Oh, thank God you're alive!"

His heart skipped a beat at the sound of her voice inside his head, but at the same time, panic seized him. *"Yeah. I don't go down that easy."*

"Don't joke. I know you're in trouble, and it's my fault. But I'm going to make this right."

"I don't like the sound of that. And this is not your fault! Whatever you're planning, stop it."

"Too late, Lombardi."

"I only reached out to make sure you didn't do anything crazy like trying to track me. You can't take that kind of risk. I'm not worth it. I'm sure I don't have to explain what they'll do to you if they get their hands on you."

"Don't you dare say you're not worth it!" Even telepathically, Guerin could feel the anger in her voice. *"There's no way on this earth I'm going to let them torture you for another day."*

"You know...? You've felt it, haven't you?" The words were a whisper inside his head.

Silence.

He groaned. *"Shit! I'm so sorry that touched you. I tried like hell to keep it inside."* His chest ached, and not from his wounds. For her pain.

"*There's nothing you need to apologize for. My God, Seth can be brutal.*"

Seth... If only they were just dealing with Seth. "*That's what I'm trying to tell you, beautiful. Seth isn't the only one hunting you.*"

"*Who is it, Guerin? It's someone you know, isn't it? Because it felt personal.*"

Guerin closed his eyes. Damn, this female was perceptive. "*Daniela is here. She and Seth have partnered to hunt you down.*"

"*I'll kill her,*" she said, her growl resonating across his neurons. "*She'll wish she'd never been born when I'm finished with her carcass.*"

"*Oh, no, beautiful. That pleasure will be all mine. That's why you have to stay far away from me.*"

"*Don't worry about me. I won't be alone.*"

"*What do you mean? Who's with you?*" A streak of jealousy shot through his veins, shocking him with its intensity. Damn, he didn't like the idea of her around other males.

"*Kenric contacted me. They needed my help to find you, and I agreed.*"

"*You're with them? That's good. Don't get me wrong; I'm happy you've connected with your father, but dammit! They should have left you out of this.*"

"*They didn't have a choice. The Enclave's clueless to the power plays in this area and to Seth's long-running campaign to bring me in. It made sense that Kenric would reach out to me since they knew we'd fed from each other.*"

It did make sense. But he didn't like the idea of her coming anywhere near Seth and Daniela.

"*Don't come here, Eve. Please promise me you'll keep*

your distance."

"I can't make that promise, and you know it. This is too personal. They took you because of me, and I can't let that go."

"Eve…" Fuck. *"Dammit, Eve."*

"We're coming for your ass whether you like it or not. So don't you dare die on me, Lombardi. If you do, I'll be so pissed off."

How in the hell could she make him smile at a time like this, but damn if he didn't feel his mouth curling. *"And God help me, I don't want to piss off Eve Devonshire."*

"No. You don't."

. . .

Guerin had contacted her.

Eve's heart soared as she stared at the pinkening horizon off the suite's balcony.

She'd been too afraid to reach out for fear of what state she'd find him in. And a part of her didn't want to know if he would hate her for abandoning him. She wouldn't have blamed him if he did. But it sounded as if that wasn't the case, and it was too good to be true. Guerin had said he wasn't worth the risk. He had it all wrong.

After Kenric shared his memories, he and Eve had come to an understanding. But there weren't enough hours of darkness left for them to make a run on Keller's estate. For the remainder of the night, she, Kenric, Emily, and Arran had discussed Seth, the reason behind Guerin's kidnapping, and their plan for getting him back. Eve was sure she could track Guerin from his blood. But she'd never been inside the walls of Seth's home, so she wasn't much help regarding what to expect once they were there.

They would stand a better chance if they hit the place during the morning or late afternoon. Then they would have only the colony's human minions to battle. Eve could handle it during those hours. But that wasn't a possibility for the rest of the team. Kenric being the eldest would be able to tolerate a small amount of early-morning sunlight. Yet after a short period of time even he would begin to sizzle.

So they'd settled on sundown tonight to load up, survey the property for any weakness, and hit them hard and fast. With the power of a master vampire, Eve's additional talents, Arran's strength and fighting skill, and Emily's ability to tap into her mate's arsenal—they had a chance.

Odds were, Kenric was still awake. Eve had to let him know Guerin had contacted her, and he was still alive. She stepped back inside and slid the glass door shut with a click. Her father and his mate's room in the sprawling suite was off to the left of the living space. Eve made a beeline for their door but before she could knock, hushed voices brought her to a halt.

"There's no way I'm letting you go with us tonight." Kenric's voice.

"Letting me…? Since when has that ever worked with me?"

"You can't expect me to put you in that kind of danger. You're my mate!"

"Funny you should remember that now and not when you learned about Eve," Emily snapped in return. Their voices were low, but the hurt and angry tones carried, despite that fact.

"You know why I couldn't tell you. We've been through this."

"I know," she said. "But it's all fresh to me, and I'm still working through it. How is it even possible this happened?"

Eve clutched her neck. The raw pain in Emily's voice threatened to steal her ability to breathe.

"That's how I felt when Arran told me," Kenric said. "I had to work through it. See for myself if she was even real before I brought her into your world. Damn," he groaned. "I didn't know how I was supposed to tell the woman who was the other half of my soul that I'd given a child to the sadistic female who'd raped me and attempted to kill her." A heavy sigh sounded from the other side of the wood. "Based on everything I've learned over the centuries, we'll never know the joy of our own little one. And ultimately, because of Marguerite, you'll never feel a life growing in your womb. Yet my seed somehow placed one in hers. I don't even know how it happened. How was I supposed to ask you to accept it?"

Kenric's words drove into her gut like a fist. Eve staggered away from the door. Holding an arm to her abdomen, she rushed toward the patio door. She needed to feel the breeze on her face. Clear her head. She slid back the metal and glass along its track and raced for the railing.

With her fist white-knuckling the metal, Eve released the flood of tears she'd been fighting. No matter how eloquent and compassionate his words had been to Eve earlier, it was clear, her presence cut him to the quick. She was a painful reminder of the past to them both and of what they could never have. Just as Eve had suspected.

Eve didn't "fit" anywhere. She didn't quite belong in the human world, nor was she well suited for the vampire realm. And she certainly wasn't what Kenric and Emily needed glaring across from them at the dinner table. Then there was Guerin… A dull pain prodded her breastbone, and she closed her eyes. Wasn't it exactly the same for him? God, she was making herself sick wallowing in her pity party. She wasn't about to stand there and feel sorry for herself. That wasn't her MO. Dammit. She was stronger than that. And after what her father and Emily had suffered at the hands of her mother, didn't they deserve a better future?

Turning, Eve stared at the empty living room, the sun's rays splicing around her head and bouncing off the glass. Her next step was obvious. She had to be the one to stop the cycle of abuse.

It was the right thing to do.

Eve straightened, wiped her cheeks, and sniffed. As usual, tears never helped. They only clogged her nose.

Chapter Nineteen

Crash!

Bang! The sound of something hard slamming onto the floorboards above Guerin's head jarred him from his unconscious state.

"What the hell?" Guerin turned his gaze to the stairwell across the room. At least after his last round with Daniela, they'd left the spotlight turned off, and he could see who came and went. Another loud *crack* echoed inside the dungeon followed by what had to be shattering glass.

The Enclave.

Kenric, Arran, and Eve had finally found him.

A loud clatter echoed from the top of the stairs, then the heavy thud of boots pounded off the wooden treads. At the bottom, Seth turned the corner along with three others trailing behind him.

"Look who decided to pay us a visit, Guerin." Seth stepped aside, revealing Eve's bruised body held by two of his vampire minions. *Oh, fuck!* Guerin jerked and pushed himself a little taller. *Where was the rest of the Enclave?*

Eve's gaze fell on Guerin, and her eyes widened. *Yeah.* Based on the lingering ache in his body, and since he'd lost the feeling beyond his wrists, he couldn't be a pretty picture. Hunger gnawed at the lining of his gut and his veins burned. His body was unable to heal at its normal pace due to the lack of blood.

"You have me," Eve spat. "Now let him go!"

"My, aren't you the bossy one," Seth replied.

"We had a deal." She swung her head in Seth's direction, dark strands of her hair clinging to her cheeks. "I surrender, and you release him."

"Eve! What are you doing?" *Hell no!* This couldn't be happening. What was left of his adrenaline reserves coursed through his veins, making his head pound and the room sway.

"That's true," Seth replied. "I did agree to your deal."

"But I didn't," Daniela's voice filled the room.

Eve stiffened, and even though Guerin was still a few feet away, he hadn't missed the flash of fire inside her irises.

Daniela glided from the foot of the staircase and over to the minions holding Eve. "You made quite an entrance, hybrid." She palmed the back of Eve's head. "I imagine Seth is going to want a little payback for the loss of a few of his treasures."

"Whatever." Eve tossed her hair over her shoulder. "As long as he keeps his end of the bargain and lets Guerino walk out of here."

"But my dear…" Daniela circled them, stopping in front of Eve. "We finally have a party. Why would I want to let him go when the fun has just begun?"

"No!" Eve cried and yanked against her captor's hold.

Oh, shit! What was she thinking, coming here on her own? Guerin watched as Eve closed her eyes and a vibration rippled through the air. A blur of color flashed across the open space and the cool steel of a blade was at his neck.

"You stop whatever it is you're up to this second, Eve, or I swear your lover will be minus his head." Daniela pressed the serrated edge into his flesh. The stinging nick followed by the warm trickle onto his chest meant she drew blood for effect.

And it worked.

Eve's eyelids popped open, and the trail of fire across his skin ceased.

"That's better," Daniela crooned. She lowered the dagger and returned to Seth and the others. Guerin tightened his fist. Being chained for Daniela's and Seth's entertainment was one form of hell, but having to stand there while the bastards fucked with Eve was beyond fire and brimstones. Guerin would rip his wrists free from his arms if they hurt her.

"I don't think we've been formally introduced," Daniela said, closing in on Eve. "I'm Daniela De Santis, but I have a feeling you may have heard of me already." She glanced over her shoulder at Guerin. "Guerin and I go way back. I'm sure he told you I was his sire, yes?"

"Something like that," Eve muttered.

"I thought he might have." Daniela pivoted, her stiletto heels clicking off the concrete floor. She'd dressed in her best Dominatrix attire, including black leather pants and a red corset that barely contained her breasts. Her blond curls were pulled back, and they hung down her back almost to her rear. So very different from her look more than two centuries ago. But a lot had changed since then, and not just in her choice of clothing.

"You see," Daniela went on to say, "while Guerin has been our guest, he's done his best to try to convince us that you two were nothing more than a fuck."

"Why would you think otherwise?" Eve shrugged. "I ask for his release because there's no reason for him to hang around. He serves no purpose."

"I see," Daniela said and nodded. "But I'm not done with him yet." She whirled around and called out for additional forces. Two more males hustled down the steps, both looking as if they'd recently taken a few blows to the face. Guerin had to suppress his grin at what had to be Eve's handiwork.

"What are you planning to do with him?" Eve tugged on the beefy hold of Seth's minions.

"Why do you care, dear?" Daniela turned her attention to the new arrivals, then pointed at Guerin. "Put him in the cage."

Dammit! He couldn't allow them to lock him up behind silver bars. He didn't give a shit about the ramifications to his body, but if he attempted to escape he would come apart in pieces. He would never be able to save Eve.

Daniela knew this.

Out of the corner of his eye, Guerin caught sight of a minion ripping away the dark material covering the tall rectangle of bars. With gloved hands, the male wheeled it closer.

"Daniela," Guerin hissed.

The blond female swung her gaze to his.

"Don't do this. Whatever you're planning...don't go there." He would destroy her if she hurt Eve. Before he took his last breath, he would make her pay.

Two of the vampires unhooked Guerin from the wall, leaving the shackles in place around his wrists and ankles. Gravity forced his arms to his sides despite his joints rebelling. The change in position lit up his nerve endings. His muscles cramped, bowing his back. Guerin gritted his teeth as the males dragged him forward. Which is exactly what they had to do—drag him. Because no matter what he told his legs, his knees refused to keep him upright.

They tossed him on the paneled floor of the containment box and sealed the door. The cage was narrow, tall enough for him stand, but not wide enough to stretch his arms out to full length. As a result, the combined effect of the metal hit him like a Mack truck on a downhill slope, sucking away what was left of his energy reserves. His flesh sizzled as if the bastards had dumped him on top of a mound of fire ants. Guerin closed his eyes and sucked in a deep breath. He had to take his mind to a happy place. *Focus.*

Think.

He couldn't lose it now. Somehow he had to get them both out of this.

"Place her on the table," Daniela commanded. "Cover her with the mesh."

No, no, no!

"Eve!" he called out.

"Worry about yourself, Lombardi," Eve snapped. Daniela chuckled. He watched as they positioned Eve on her back, her upper body facing Guerin, and draped the silver netting over her midsection and upper legs. Eve had somehow blocked their connection in an attempt to save him from experiencing her misery, but the look on her face spoke of agony. Yet she didn't make a sound. Daniela might as well have reached inside and clawed his heart from his chest. Because he wouldn't have known the difference based on what was happening behind his breastbone.

Daniela hovered over Eve's form. "You be a good girl now," Daniela said. "Whether or not Guerin's head remains on his shoulders is up to you."

She struck.

And the blow resonated through Guerin as if Daniela had targeted him instead of Eve.

Eve arched and her mouth fell open in a silent cry as Daniela sank her fangs into her neck.

"Let her go!" Guerin forced himself to his feet and slammed into the bars, his flesh searing under the contact with the toxic metal. "Damn you, Daniela!" he cried out, his voice hoarse. "Eve! Fuck!" He rammed into the door once more with his shoulder, jarring the hinges, but the lock didn't budge. "Daniela, don't do this! I swear I'm going to rip you apart with my bare hands."

Laughter rolled from Seth, who stood watching from his spot in the dungeon, making sure he had a good spot to observe Guerin's reaction to Daniela's attack.

His former Mistress reared back, blood forming a macabre trail down her chin. She turned toward her partner in crime and Seth sped to her side. Guerin fought back the taste of his bile as Keller attentively cleaned the other female with his tongue.

"Fucking delicious," Seth groaned, and Daniela sealed her lips over the other male's for a brief kiss. "Thank you, Mistress," he said breathlessly.

• • •

Eve watched as the vampires standing over her savored the taste of her essence. In the distance, Guerin snarled, the sound ricocheting off the stone walls of the dungeon. He was enraged, and had thrown himself repeatedly into the silver bars. Each time, he tore another piece of her heart away.

This was not how she'd planned for this to go down. Guerin was supposed to be gone. Giving herself over to Seth was supposed to save him, Kenric, Arran, and Emily from any further harm.

"I thought you'd enjoy a taste," Daniela crooned at Seth. "What an exotic flavor." She licked her lips.

"You win," Eve declared, snagging Daniela's attention. The elder female's brows lifted. "You succeeded in getting under Guerin's skin again. So let him go now. You've got me. I'm not going anywhere. Why do you still need him?"

"Yes, I do have you."

"Stop it, Eve!" Guerin yelled out. "Don't bargain for me with your life. I'm not going anywhere without you, so give it up."

Frustration boiled in Eve's gut, a nauseating mixture of pain, hurt, and bitter defeat. And it was nasty as hell.

Daniela's laughter rang out. "You two crack me up, acting as if you have a choice. I'll keep Guerin around as long as it pleases me."

Shit. She was one sadistic bitch.

"But perhaps you and I could come to some sort of deal?" Daniela sashayed over to the dungeon's wall of toys and plucked down what looked like a heavy-duty cattle prod.

Eve closed her eyes and tightened her fists. Damn, she'd never been a fan of electro-stim. She'd seen one in action at the Rose's Thorn, and based on the shrill scream that had come off the sub, the device hurt like a mother.

"What did you have in mind?" Eve forced the words out from the constriction in her throat.

"You answer a few questions." She shrugged. "That's all. And if your answers please me, I don't use this." She waved her weapon over Eve's face and pressed the button. Blue lightning bolts buzzed between the prongs. Eve could have sworn hairs on top of her head lifted from just the proximity of the damn thing. "In the end, if you tell me everything I want to know, we can discuss Guerin's future."

"What kind of questions?" As if Eve didn't already know.

"I want to know how your mother managed to conceive."

Bingo. Of course that's what Daniela wanted. It's what they all wanted. That and the secrets locked away inside her genetic code that gave her tolerance to UV. "Do you really think my mother told—"

Eve never saw it coming. White lights danced in front of her eyes, and the world went mute. Every muscle in her body contracted under the electrical overload to the point Eve thought her spine would crack. It went on forever, yet it was over in seconds.

On a long wheeze, Eve filled her starved lungs and the volume inside the room clicked on.

"Stop this shit, Daniela!" Guerin's voice. His cage rattled, like a wild beast taunted to the point of blind fury. Oh God, Guerin was going to destroy himself if she didn't get them out of this. "You want to hurt someone? Hurt me." Guerin slapped his bare chest, the veins in his forearm distended. He paced in a tight circle, the fluorescent lights bouncing off the fluid-filled blisters littering his shoulders and back. "Come on, Daniela!" He faced forward. "You know you love to make me scream," he roared, his voice rusty. Then in a move that shattered Eve's heart, he dropped to his knees and bowed his head. "Please…Mistress," he chewed out. "Hurt. Me." His sides sawed in and out.

"Guerin," Eve cried out. *Oh, God.* A sob burst free. "I'm okay." She gasped. "Don't…" This was her fault. Dear God, why did Guerin have to be in the middle of this? He shouldn't have to pay for her problems—for her existence.

Daniela's eyes lit with renewed fire. Eve swore the female had nearly orgasmed at the sight of Guerin's submissive form. "Now, isn't he incredible?" Daniela sauntered over to the cage. "It's not every day a female Dominant finds such a gorgeous prime alpha specimen with a taste for sexual submission. Am I correct, Eve?"

Eve swallowed the curse she'd been about to spew. She wasn't about to give the bitch more ammunition to hurt Guerin. What was she going to do? If it were just her life at stake, there weren't enough cattle prods in hell to make her give Daniela one blip of information about her conception. Eve would rather die first.

But Guerin didn't deserve this. Yes, he'd lied to her about his motives for seeking her out. But he was loyal to his friend and the Enclave. Guerin's reason behind his search was to protect Kenric. That was evident. At his core, Lombardi was a decent man. More than likely why she'd been so drawn to him in the first place.

"So I take it you're asking for my forgiveness, pet?"

"Yes, Mistress," he whispered. "Forgive me and return your attention only to me."

Helpless under the silver mesh, Eve watched as a grin spread across Daniela's face. Right before she jabbed the end of the cattle prod between the bars and into Guerin's flank. He bowed under the assault with a strangled yelp.

"I can keep this up all night, Eve. Though I'm not sure how long Guerino can."

Guerin swayed on his knees. "Hurt me more, Mistress," he begged, the words slurred.

Eve's mind spiraled, going under, drowning beneath a dark wave of impossible choices.

"Tell me everything about how Marguerite did this!"

"Eve. Don't give away that you can hear me."

Oh shit! It was Kenric.

"We're here," her father said. *"We can discuss why you bailed on us later. Right now, I need to know what's going on in there."*

She wanted to shout for joy, but Eve bit her tongue instead. They had hope. *Guerin* had hope.

"I don't know what you think I would know," Eve said, directed toward Daniela.

A loud grunt burst from Guerin's lungs under the prod's volts, and he tumbled onto his side, falling against the silver bars. The smell of singed flesh scented the air, but Guerin didn't move. *Oh God, he'd passed out.* "Help him up!" Eve cried. "Please."

Daniela *tsk*ed, then waved to one of the gloved minions to push Guerin over.

"I don't understand how you found me. It's not like we've ever shared blood."

"That's just it. In a way, we have. About three hundred years ago."

"What?"

"After our encounter last night and your trip through my mind, you must have triggered something inside me—a recognition of sorts of your mental fingerprint. When we discovered you'd left without us, I tried reaching out for you to see if I could sense you. And I could feel you. Locating my daughter was like finding a piece of myself. I followed your trail here."

"I'm glad you did…because I made a terrible mistake," Eve whispered inside her head. *"And Guerin is paying for it. You have to get him out of here."*

"Are you saying that if I were to ram this down his throat," Daniela cried out, fisting her cattle prod like a branding iron at Guerin, "it wouldn't jar your memories about your talks with mommy dearest?"

"I don't know anything!" Eve screamed. "She never told me how she did it."

"Open this thing up," Daniela commanded one of her minions and banged the rod in her hand onto the bars. The vampire male pulled the key from around his neck and shoved it in the lock. "Put the collar on him, then drag him out of there and onto his knees in front of me."

"Daniela, wait!" Eve cried out again. "I swear. There's nothing I can tell you." Sweat beaded across her body and ran cool trails down the sides of her face. Yet inside, she was on fire from the metal covering her torso, and she couldn't do a damn thing about her situation or Guerin's. She was as trapped under the cloth as Guerin was inside his cage.

A grunt registered from Guerin's throat as two minions

hauled him from behind the bars, secured a wide silver collar around his neck, and deposited him at Daniela's feet.

"Eve? What's going on? Don't go silent on me."

"Open his mouth," Daniela barked at the two minions still at Guerin's side. Eve's gut twisted. Was Daniela really going to do this?

"Kenric! Focus on my location and get ready. I think Daniela is going to kill Guerin."

"Daniela? Guerin's sire is here? Fucking hell!"

One male grabbed Guerin's head, holding it steady as the other gripped his jaw and began prying it open. Guerin squirmed under the attempt but he appeared drained, too weak from blood loss and his prolonged exposure to silver to fight them off.

"If you're useless to me alive…" Daniela waved the wand in her hand, as if it were magic, in Eve's general direction. "I guess I'll just kill you, too, and we'll decipher what we can from your remains."

"You're not going to kill her!" Seth cried out from behind Daniela and lunged with a knife for her throat. "I'm not done with her!"

It happened so fast, Eve never saw Seth move into position. In fact, she'd forgotten about him. Apparently, so had Daniela. Seth swung his arm around the female's head, his blade glinting under the fluorescents. Daniela screeched as the edge buried in her flesh. She went for her attacker's wrist with both hands, and spun out of his hold, blood spraying.

"Now!" Eve cried out inside her head. *"Kenric, now!"*

Before Eve was finished with her last thought, Kenric's form coalesced a couple of feet from her side. Their gazes locked, and he charged for her.

"Eve," he blurted out. Then Emily was behind him, followed immediately by Arran.

"Don't worry about me." Eve shook her head. "Take care of Guerin."

"I'll take care of her." Emily rushed forward and brushed past Kenric. "Go!" she ordered him. Emily yanked her jacket from her shoulders and tossed it over the silver. Carefully, she pulled the mesh free from Eve's body and tossed it to the floor.

And it was as if the air itself were cool water drenching her overheated flesh.

"Are you able to move?" Emily brushed the hair back from Eve's eyes. "You're sure?"

Eve pushed up onto her elbows, and the compassion in the other female's gaze knocked her off balance.

"Yeah." Eve nodded and continued until she was upright. "Let's kick some ass."

Emily grinned. "No doubt you're related to my mate."

Chapter Twenty

Guerin had to be hallucinating.

Daniela shrieked and clutched her throat as blood sprayed from between her fingers. *Seth had attacked her? What the hell?* She whirled, and like a towering midsummer storm, Daniela descended on her former submissive comrade.

Movement in his peripheral vision caught Guerin's attention. His vision was blurry, but he could have sworn Kenric had appeared near Eve. His pulse surged, breaking through the cobwebs in his mind. He shook his head and blinked.

Holy shit! The cavalry had arrived.

Kenric pounced on one of the vampires at Guerin's side. *Yes!* With a one-two blow to the male's face and midsection, the Enclave's master toppled the lesser vampire to the floor. Guerin lunged from his knees and dove for the male's throat. He needed to get into the action, and that meant he must restore his resources. The male only had a half second to flinch before Guerin sank his fangs into the minion's artery. Guerin pulled hard, drinking in his prey's life essence and soaking up the vampire's strength.

More. He gulped. Christ, he was starved.

Injury upon injury combined with the toxic metal had dwindled Guerin's power down to fumes. The only thing that had kept him going for the last several hours was the need to save Eve. And he hadn't given a fuck what that had required.

A hard slap to his back halted Guerin's feeding.

"Hey, slow down, man," Kenric said. "There's more where that came from."

He was right. Eve needed him, and there was some serious payback at hand. Guerin pushed away from the listless male and onto his feet.

The stairwell echoed with the loud pounding of feet. Reinforcements were on the way. A fierce growl erupted from the other side of the room, and Guerin turned in time to witness Daniela shoving Seth away. The flow from her neck wound appeared to have slowed to a trickle. Seth's wound hadn't severed an artery. *Good.* Because the bitch was Guerin's to destroy.

Scarlet drops clung to the end of the blonde's tresses and blended with her corset. Seth's white shirt looked as though he'd been caught in the center of a bloody war. Her wound hadn't been enough to put her out of commission, but Daniela had lost a significant volume of blood.

"Look what you've done, you fool!" Daniela screamed at Seth, her fingers raking through her hair. "You've ruined everything."

The clash of metal against metal rang out behind Guerin. He glanced over his shoulder and found Arran surrounded by four vampires. "I've got Daniela," Guerin rumbled, with a nod to Kenric, indicating the other male was free to jump in and help Arran.

Guerin returned his attention to his sire. She stilled, but her head cranked toward Guerin. Their gazes locked, and her eyelids narrowed over enlarged pupils. Daniela blurred, but Guerin intercepted, blocking her exit. Her chest heaved, cresting the top of the crimson leather cinched around her torso.

"You wouldn't dare touch your sire," she growled, fangs glinting from beneath her upper lip. "Kneel." Daniela lifted her chin, giving him her best arrogant glare.

Perfect opening.

Guerin seized her neck and tightened his fist. Her eyes bulged. "You said it best, Daniela. Outside my Mistress's bedroom, I'm an alpha male." Curling his lip, he added, "And I'm done kneeling for you." With preternatural speed, Guerin crossed the dungeon floor, his sire in tow. He came to a stop in front of the table where she'd been torturing Eve and thrust the female onto the stainless steel top. Daniela gasped under the impact. With his bare hands, Guerin nabbed the silver mesh near his feet and slung it over the vampiress. She cried out under its paralyzing and sizzling effect.

"Guerin!" It was Eve.

He spun and Eve darted toward him. But before Guerin could act, Seth stepped in behind her, lashed out with expert precision, and coiled a silver-laced whip around her throat. Eve stumbled back, clawing at the noose.

Hissing out a curse, Guerin lunged for the duo.

"Stop right there!" Seth yanked hard, wrenching Eve's head. "Or I swear I'll snap her neck." Seth edged back, dragging Eve with him. Frantically, the male's gaze darted back and forth between Guerin and the rest of the Enclave.

"Wrong move," Kenric said, spinning a dagger in his gloved palm. Seth and Daniela's former minions lay dead, their carcasses scattered at the Enclave's feet. "You leave with my daughter, and I will hunt you down like the filthy dog you are. And when I find you, I swear I'll bring the wrath of hell down on your head, until you die screaming for mercy." Kenric inched forward. "You think you know pain—understand what it can do to a male's mind?" The cruel edge to the curve of Kenric's lips would've had a smart man shaking in his boots. But it didn't look as if Seth's IQ was going to measure up.

"Shut up!" the blond vampire barked.

"No," Kenric stated and shook his head. "I don't think we've been properly introduced."

"I would listen to him, Keller," Guerin joined in and moved closer. "He's a mean motherfucker you don't want to mess with."

"Get back. Both of you!" Seth spat, heading toward the stairs. "I don't give a shit! She's mine! You have no idea how long I've waited—plotted for this night." He huffed. "No one is going to take her from me."

"I'm not going anywhere with you," Eve gritted out between her teeth. Arran circled in behind Seth while Emily, Kenric, and Guerin approached from the paranoid vamp's front.

"Oh yes, you are," Seth demanded. "There's no way in

hell I'm allowing you to slip through my fingers." Seth jerked her against his chest, placing his lips at her ear. "You're my ticket to once again feeling the sun on my skin, dear."

"You want to see the sun?" Eve's brows lifted.

Shit. What did Eve have in mind?

She lowered her hands from the noose and with superhuman speed, reached up and grabbed Seth's head. "I'll show you the sun," Eve growled.

Seth screamed, the agonized sound bouncing off the walls. He scrabbled at Eve's fingers, his eyes wide, unseeing. "Stop!" he bellowed. "Get her off me!"

Eve spun, never letting go of his skull, taking the male down to his knees. "You wanted the sun?" She rolled back her upper lips, exposing her fangs. "How does it feel rising inside your brain?"

Damn. Eve was absolutely amazing—more powerful than Guerin had imagined.

"Please," he begged. "Too much! I can't see. You're blinding me." He sobbed. "It burns."

"Then allow me to give you a taste of the mercy you would have never granted me." Eve nodded to Guerin, and he stepped forward, pulling a sword from the wall in the process. She released the cowering male as Guerin moved into position. With a *swoosh*, Guerin swung high, his pulse thundering inside his ears, and in one swift downward motion, removed Seth's head from his shoulders.

As one, they lifted their gazes, her blue eyes holding Guerin's—and time slowed to half-speed. Eve's long midnight hair clung to her face and cascaded around her like a dark cloak. Blood splattered her cheeks and beads of sweat glistened on her lashes. Yet he'd never seen anything more beautiful in his life. How had he lived on the earth this long without her?

"What about Daniela?" she asked, breaking the spell.

Guerin released his grip on the hilt of the sword, letting it fall to the dungeon's floor with a loud *clatter*. "She's mine."

He pivoted, faced Kenric, and held out his palm. "May I?"

Kenric nodded. He placed the pearl handle of his silver-plated dagger into Guerin's waiting hand.

Slow and steady, Guerin made his way across the smooth concrete toward the female he once would have died for. Daniela glared at him from across the room, the black filling the whites of her eyes. "What do you think you're about to do, Guerino?"

He fisted the pearl handle, the surface cool and the weight perfectly balanced in his palm. Eve followed on his heels, but the sound of her footsteps faded before he reached Daniela's side, putting distance between them. She knew he needed to handle this alone.

"You're not a murderer, pet. Don't you remember? You couldn't even kill the girl on my dungeon floor, and I'd given her to you as a present." Daniela swallowed and licked her lips, her neck oozing from her encounter with Seth's blade, the blood pooling beneath her head. "So what do you think you're going to do with that?" Her gaze flicked to his hand where he held the dagger, then back to his face. "Come on, pet. Release me and all is forgiven." She made a weak attempt at a smile. Guerin didn't fight back his chuckle of laughter. His gut churned at her words—*forgiven*.

"You're right about one thing, Daniela." He lifted Kenric's weapon, the blade vertical and pointing south. "I'm not

a murderer." Guerin shook his head. "I don't kill the innocent. But that's something you lost touch with a long, long
time ago." He sank the dagger into her heart until only the
hilt remained visible, and twisted. Like a balloon rupturing,
air burst from between her lips. Daniela blinked, the expression on her face puzzled as if she couldn't wrap her mind
around what he'd done. Then with a crackle, her flesh bubbled. Bloated. Smoked and imploded.

Daniela was gone.

Guerin waited for the dark thrill of triumph, the feral
glow of satisfaction that should've welled inside him like a
bubbling, overflowing fountain. Instead…nothing. He was
empty. Numb. And really…really tired. He swiped a hand
over his face and the warmth of Eve's touch moved up his
spine.

"You gave her a much better death than she deserved,"
Eve said. "Most would have wanted her to suffer—taste the
pain she inflicted on others."

"A part of me wanted her to pay long and hard," Guerin
said, his voice raw, scratchy. "I contemplated how I should
drag out her last moments in the most agonizing way imag-
inable. But then I realized, wouldn't that make me the vampire she'd tried to create all along?" He turned to Eve. "She
would have won."

Arran came into view behind Eve. "We're going to get
this mess cleaned up, and then get the hell out of here."

"That sounds like the best idea I've heard in days."
Guerin sighed.

Less than an hour later, they'd cleaned up the evidence
of the bodies and burned what was left of the bloodstained
clothing. Together the five of them stepped into the night air.

"Before you make some excuse about where you need to go," Kenric began and moved to block Eve's path, "I want you to come back to South Carolina with us."

Every muscle tensed in Guerin's body waiting for her response. The thought of boarding the plane and leaving her behind… Yeah, he couldn't go there. Yet the emotions Eve had unearthed inside him…the lengths he'd go to protect her. The intensity of his reaction inside that dungeon had shaken him to the core. Eve turned him inside out.

She glanced to Guerin, then Kenric and Emily. "That's not going to happen." Eve crossed her arms beneath her breasts.

Guerin's heart stuttered. What was she thinking? His body vibrated with the urge to shake her. How was he supposed to protect her across the Atlantic? But at the same time, how in the hell could he live with her under the same roof and not be in her bed, not belong to her body and soul? He would go mad.

Chapter Twenty-One

Kenric had to be out of his mind.

After what he'd just gone through with his team—his mate—he wanted her to return to the United States with him? He must have taken a blow to the head when she wasn't looking.

In a move identical to hers, Kenric crossed his arms. "Then at least come back to the suite with us so we can talk?"

"There's nothing to talk about." Eve moved her palms to her hips.

"Where do you plan on going tonight—tomorrow?"

"I'll be fine," she ground out. *Enough already. I'm fine*

"Okaaay," he said. "Then try this one on for size. We just saved your ass. Guerin almost lost his life because of your impulsive move. You owe me an explanation about why you bailed on us, and I'm not standing around outside this hellhole holding a family conversation. You're coming back with us for the next few hours, and I'm not asking."

Who the hell—? How dare he? She couldn't even find the words. Frustration rolled through her on a tsunami level, but she stopped short of stomping her foot like a little girl throwing a temper tantrum. Eve was three hundred years old, and her father had just ordered her home like a naughty teenager caught sneaking out at night.

"Fine," she huffed. "What's next? You plan on taking the keys to the car or grounding me?" She shot him her best scowl.

"Don't tempt me," he growled. Emily joined him at his side and wrapped an arm around his waist. "Meet us at our hotel room." His eyes narrowed on her. "Don't make me come looking for you again."

"Fine. I'll be there," she grumbled.

"Since you two have lost a lot of blood," Arran said, with a nod to Eve and Guerin, "I'll phase Guerin back to the suite. That way he doesn't have the stress of trying to track your essence, since he's never been to our hotel." He turned to Guerin. "Okay with you, man?"

"It's cool." Guerin met her gaze as Arran swung an arm over his shoulder. Creases she'd never noticed before were etched around the outside of his eyes. She couldn't help but wonder if she was responsible for putting them there.

"Hang on," Arran said to Guerin. "And I know it's hard, but *try* not to cuddle. You're really not my type."

"Kiss my ass."

Eve watched as the quad shimmered, then dispersed into their molecular state, and began their trip back to their temporary residence. It would be so easy to just fade away in the opposite direction. She didn't want to follow and listen to all the explanations regarding why she should return to the States with them. Eve had already overheard the truth and the regret, and she wasn't about to be the cause of any more.

But Kenric would only hunt her down again. She could already tell from the glare he'd leveled on her earlier that he wasn't the kind of male to leave things alone.

Closing her eyes, Eve pictured the patio outside the Enclave's suite and allowed her body to melt away. Moments later, she opened her eyes as the concrete solidified under her feet.

On the other side of the glass, the rest of the group were together, cleaning up and talking about the recent battle. Kenric sat in the chair facing the door, Emily on the arm. Arran was across from the pair, his blade out in front while he wiped down its length. Guerin stood between them, his mouth in a thin line, grim, but surrounded—supported—by his fellow Enclave members. The whole scene exemplified how she felt. Her father and his team inside, her on the outside. A part of him, but not quite fitting into his world.

Eve turned away on her heels, intending to grab on to the rail, but her head kept spinning. She missed and stumbled, knocking one of the low tables on the patio onto its side. Damn, Daniela must have taken more from her than Eve had realized, and her adrenaline levels were taking a nosedive.

The sliding door opened with a *swoosh*. "Whoa!" Guerin slid an arm around her, steadying her.

"I'm fine," she blurted out and batted away the hand cradling her hip.

"No. You're not."

She tugged on her leather vest and tossed her hair back over her shoulder. "I just lost my footing. That's all."

"I was there. Remember? You lost a lot of blood."

"Everything okay out here?" Kenric's dark, leather-clad form filled the doorway.

"I'm fine."

"No. She isn't. Eve needs to feed."

"I'll handle it later," she said, not bothering to hide the annoyance in her tone.

"I can— " Guerin began, but a strange expression flashed across his face, and his words halted.

"What? Were you about to offer to feed me?" She scoffed. "You're not much better off than I am." Eve brushed past him and Kenric stepped aside, letting her into the suite.

"I can help," Emily stood from one of the leather chairs. The statement brought Eve to an abrupt halt along with the next beat of her heart. *No way.* How could Emily offer such a thing when Eve knew the other female had to resent her very presence? "There's no need for you to go out and hunt tonight after what you've been through. Let me feed you." Emily began rolling up her sleeves.

"No…" Eve backed up and bumped into Kenric's chest. This was the worst idea she'd ever heard. *Oh, my God.* What was Emily thinking, offering to feed the spawn of the woman who'd tried to kill her? Eve couldn't imagine anything more awkward and uncomfortable for both of them. Why would Emily want to put herself through it? "Please. You don't have to do that. It's not your place." She shook her head, the cold fingers of panic sinking into her chest. If there was ever a reason to flee a scene—this was it. And Eve was about two seconds from flipping the kill switch on this whole little get-together.

The other two males joined them in the room, their gazes swinging back and forth between the two females.

"I'm the logical choice, Eve. Arran is mated, and I'm sure if there were any other way, Elle would prefer he not feed another female. And for reasons we don't need to get into right now, Kenric isn't available to donate to anyone. Guerin, as you've stated, isn't in any condition to lose any more blood. He needs time to heal." Emily closed in on her. "Eve," she said, her voice softening. "If you will allow it, I would be happy to care for Kenric's child."

"Are you for real?" Eve cocked her head, then glanced up at the female's mate—her father. Kenric smiled down at Eve.

"One of the many reasons I love her." His gaze moved to Emily. "She's smart and has the biggest heart of anyone I've ever known."

"Why don't the three of us step into the other room?" Emily motioned for her and Kenric to follow.

As if her legs had grown a mind of their own, Eve shuffled forward. Kenric trailed into the couple's bedroom behind Eve, and Emily closed the door.

"Now that it's just us, do you think you can tell me why the thought of feeding from me bothers you so much?" Emily brushed past Eve and sat on the edge of the bed. She patted the spot beside her. "Please, sit with me."

Kenric sauntered over near the windows, pretending to look outside. She lowered onto the mattress as requested.

"I don't need a connection to your mind to see I've upset you. It's all over your face."

"It's not that I'm upset or angry," Eve said, then sighed.

She might as well go ahead and tell them, get everything out on the table. "After what I heard you two discussing, I don't know how you can stomach the thought of being near me — much less allowing me to drink from you."

"When did you hear us talking? Before you left?"

She nodded. "I came to your door at sundown to tell Kenric I'd heard from Guerin." Kenric pivoted and faced them. "He'd contacted me telepathically to try to keep me away. I wanted to let you both know he was alive." Eve studied her hands, finding it hard to keep her gaze trained on the couple. "That's when I heard you both discussing what my existence meant to your relationship." She swallowed back the lump doing its best to choke her. "I'm the product of a horrible crime I'm sure Kenric would much rather stay buried and not have walking around in front of his face." Eve sprang from the bed and turned away. Whoever said the confrontations you dreaded were supposed to end up easier than one imagined was a liar. "Guerin was tortured at the hands of Seth and Daniela because of me, and I'm a constant reminder of what you'll never have." Eve stared at the broad brushstrokes of color in the abstract painting on the wall. Blues, reds, yellows in giant swirls forming a tighter and tighter ring. Sort of like the band constricting her heart. "I needed to face Seth—alone. Turn myself over to him so you, Kenric, and Guerin could find peace."

Kenric's broad hands circled her upper arms. She'd never heard him move. Gently, he turned her to face him. "If you left feeling so hurt, you obviously didn't stick around to hear the rest."

Eve glanced up, her gaze falling into familiar azure eyes, but this time, his shimmered with tears.

"Because if you had stayed..." Emily moved in beside Kenric, reached over, and brushed her palm over Eve's forearm. "You would have heard me tell Kenric that his joy is my joy. You're a part of him. And from what I've seen...the best part." Emily smiled. "I won't lie and say it doesn't sadden me that we'll never have our own child. But how can I resent you? My God. You were willing to give your life to save ours. That shows character and strength."

"Thank you," Eve whispered, a strange wave of warmth washing over her bones. *Acceptance...? Was this what it felt like?*

"Now please. Let me help you." Emily's palm slid down and into Eve's. "I'll be fine until we get home tomorrow night."

Home.

"And by 'we' I mean you, as well," Emily added.

"Leaving you here, after only just discovering you, would kill me," Kenric said. "We haven't had any time to get to know each other. You could always return here, if you're not happy. But we really don't have a choice. We have to go home as soon as possible." Kenric checked the clock on the bedside table. "Actually, I should call the pilots and see if they have time to file a flight plan tonight." He pulled out his cell. "Please tell me you'll come with us. Give us a chance?"

Emily took her seat on the bed and held out her wrist. Eve lowered onto her knees in front of the other female and looked up, taking her hand in hers.

"Are you sure?" She couldn't help but ask one more time, the question twofold.

"Absolutely." Emily nodded.

Eve glanced over at Kenric, and she had to smile at the

anticipation simmering in his expression. "Okay. I'll go with you. But I can't promise I'll stay."

"Fair enough." He punched a number in his phone, and Eve returned to Emily.

"Thank you," Eve whispered.

"You're welcome." Emily smiled. "Now feed."

Hunger cramped her stomach at the reminder, and her fangs slid into place. Eve lifted Emily's wrist to her lips. A sweet floral scent wafted into her nostrils—wildflowers. *A perfect fragrance for the female. It reminded her of the warmth of sunshine.* As quickly as possible to minimize the pain, Eve sank her fangs into Emily's vein. The heady essence of her blood flooded Eve's mouth, making her head swim. Emily must feed mostly from her mate, based on the potency of the crimson fluid. Eve's veins hummed under the influence of the cocktail. It didn't take but a few pulls on Emily's wrist before Eve's strength returned. She sealed the puncture with her tongue and lifted her head.

Her skin tingled and her heart raced. "Wow." Eve blinked. "You have quite a kick there."

Emily laughed. "You're feeling better?"

"Much." Eve stood, her head no longer spinning.

"Good," she said and nodded in the direction of the door. "I think someone in the other room will be interested in learning about your decision to return with us."

Eve's gut tightened. Yeah. She didn't know whether to be excited or anxious about the idea of moving to the States with Guerin. Would he be happy to spend more time with her, or resent the fact that he'd have to deal with her presence? He certainly had enough to come to terms with without a daily reminder of the shit he'd been forced to confront to save her. Eve's anger reheated, remembering how Guerin had swallowed his pride and submitted to Daniela—to save her. Her fist coiled at the thought. The female hadn't deserved the years of trust and devotion she'd had bestowed on her from a male like Guerin. Daniela had been given a treasure like none other, and she'd crushed it under her heel.

"Yeah, well, we'll see." Eve gave Emily a tight smile. "He endured a lot because of me. I'm not sure how he's going to feel about me tagging along."

"I think you might be surprised."

"All right, ladies," Kenric interjected. "Pilot said we're cleared to leave at six a.m. So that gives us about four hours to get ready."

Stepping into the living space, Eve scanned the room and found Arran watching TV, and Guerin in the bar area with a bottle of water in his hand. He froze mid-swig, then slowly lowered his arm as she approached.

"How did it go in there?"

"It went well," she said. Guerin had cleaned up since she'd left him. He'd changed into a pair of ripped jeans and a black *Hysteria* concert T-shirt. "Def Leppard?" Guerin followed her gaze to the graphic. "For some reason," she added, "I just can't picture you rocking to an eighties big-hair band." He glanced up and she grinned.

"It's Arran's," he added with an eye roll. "He lent me some clothes since my stuff is still at the *gasthaus* room I rented before I went looking for you—hopefully."

"Ah. I see. You'll probably need to head over there in a few minutes and collect it since we're leaving for the States at dawn."

He stilled, as if his brain were mulling over what she'd

said. Guerin took another swallow. "We? Does that mean Kenric convinced you to come back with us?"

"Would it bother you if he did?"

"No." He plopped the bottle on the granite. "Of course not. I was actually surprised that you hesitated."

"I've survived on my own for many, many years." Eve crossed her arms. "Moving back with the Enclave—my father—isn't something I ever expected to happen. I needed to clear the air first."

"You two were able to do that in there?"

"Yeah. We got some things out in the open."

He clutched the half-empty bottle and rocked the contents, his gaze following the waves. "So your reluctance to move back was based on your relationship with your father?"

"Most of it." Her pulse spiked at her next thought. "Maybe you and I should talk? A lot of things went down in that dungeon…"

"No." He swung his head back up. "God, no. I'm fine. You really should do this—come back with us." He nodded, his smile tight. "It'll be a great new beginning for you after all…this shit with Keller and company. Plus you'll have the Enclave always at your back—added protection going forward."

"Sooo, you and I, we're good?" Eve added a smile. "I haven't had a chance to thank—"

"We're fine." His smile broadened, but a shadow lurked behind his eyes, dampening the full effect. "Nothing for you to thank me for, or for us to talk about. I'm glad you'll be coming. I'll rest easier knowing you're on our side of the Atlantic." He brushed past and headed over to Arran.

Well, that couldn't have been more clear. He wasn't anywhere near ready to discuss what had happened between them in Seth's dungeon.

"Eve said we're leaving in a couple of hours," Guerin said to Arran. "I'm going to pop back over to the *gasthaus* where I rented a room and get my things. I'll be back in a few."

"Okay, man." Arran dropped his boots from where he'd propped them on the coffee table.

Without another word or a glance back, Guerin phased from the suite. A twinge of hurt nudged her breastbone at the barricade Guerin had slammed into place between them. But there was a part of her that wasn't surprised, and she'd halfway expected it. He'd opened up a very old, festered wound in the past twenty-four hours, and no doubt, he was reeling from the anguish.

Eve knew he cared about her. She'd witnessed firsthand the hell he'd allowed himself to endure to try to protect her. And after what they'd experienced, Guerin had to know how much she cared about him. She just hoped the sacrifice Guerin made, submitting to Daniela once more—for her—hadn't erected a defensive wall so thick Eve would never be able to penetrate.

Chapter Twenty-Two

Their plane touched down during the late-morning hours on the East Coast of the US and taxied into a hangar. Luckily for Eve, their flight over the Atlantic had launched at sunrise, and the passengers, including Guerin, had slept for the duration. Eve had barely closed her eyes and was anxious to escape the close quarters of the tin box. Kenric and Guerin, being the senior vampires of their posse, were now up, but groggy.

After their pilot had confirmed that the area was secure and their ride had arrived, Kenric carried Emily's sleeping form to the darkened limo. Guerin managed to awaken Arran long enough for him to lumber toward their ride. Eve climbed inside the stretch vehicle and found a spot between the two warriors while Kenric held Emily in his arms. Kenric tossed a blanket over his mate for added security and warmth. Eve squirmed inside over the display of affection and deflected her gaze, but she wasn't sure where to look.

The windows in front of her were dark. To her left, Arran was a nice-looking man, but it was totally inappropriate to sit there and stare at the mated male. To her right…Guerin. Eve swallowed, her throat suddenly as dry and dusty as the bottom of her boots. She glanced at the strong vampire beside her with his dark Mediterranean good looks, and her stomach did that girly crush flip-flop thing. *Good Lord.*

She was *not* a teenager.

But watching him sleep during the flight had given her way too many hours to reminisce about the good times they'd shared. And her libido had kicked into full alert. As if Guerin sensed her perusal, he cocked his head from where he studied his fingers, his forearms resting on his legs. Their gazes connected, and Eve could have sworn someone had cranked the limo's heat to high. His nostrils flared. Eve crossed her legs and cleared her throat.

"How far of a drive is it to your home?" Eve looked over at Kenric and rubbed her thighs with her damp palms.

"About an hour," Guerin responded before Kenric had the chance, dragging her attention back to the male.

"That long, huh?"

"Afraid so," he said and lifted a brow. "Restless?" He leaned against the seat's backrest and propped a boot over his knee.

"Yeah. A little," she said.

Guerin's expression darkened as he surveyed her from beneath eyelashes the color of coal. The corner of his mouth curled, and the tip of a fang emerged from under his lip. *Okay. Nope. That did not help.* Why did she have a feeling the one-hour drive to the Enclave estate was going to feel a hell of lot longer than the flight across the Atlantic?

Sixty minutes later, and not a moment too soon, the limo came to a complete stop and the engine went silent. Thank God. She needed some air.

The door to the passenger compartment opened. "Everything's secure, sir," the human male she'd heard Kenric call Michael stated. Her father stepped from the vehicle with Emily in his arms, his movements fluid, as if Emily's added weight were an extra jacket, not an adult female.

Eve grabbed her small bag from where their driver had placed it beside the vehicle and followed Kenric from the multi-vehicle garage into the house. They marched through a dimly lit corridor until it opened to a chef's kitchen. A large island with an inlaid stovetop and seating for six dominated the center of the room; white cabinets contrasted the black granite countertops and dark stained wood floors. Stainless steel appliances topped off the overall design. *Nice.*

Vampires didn't require human food to survive, but some still enjoyed the act of eating. And apparently this group did. Thank goodness, because she needed both to remain at her best.

"Eve," Kenric said, slowed to a stop, and pivoted. "I'm heading upstairs to put Emily to bed, but Michael will show you to your room and help you find anything else you require. Later, after sundown, I'll give you a tour of the place."

"That's fine. I look forward to it."

He smiled, his eyes soft and warm, and proceeded into the house.

"I can show you to your room now if you're ready," Michael said, coming up beside her.

"No," Guerin interjected. "I'll show her."

"Uh, how about I show myself? You can just point me in

the right direction, Michael. I'm sure I can find my way." She did not need Mr. Tall, Dark, and Testosterone-Filled taking her to her bedroom.

"Did you give her the vacant room next to Alexandria's?" Guerin proceeded on, completely ignoring her protest. Michael nodded.

"Guerin." She propped her hands on her hips. "I don't need a tour guide. It's a house, not the Louvre."

Guerin scrubbed a palm over his face, his beard sounding bristly on his flesh, and exhaled. "Follow me." He took her bag from her hand and headed off in the direction Kenric had gone with Emily. Eve grumbled, but relented and fell into step behind him. He hadn't left her much choice.

"You look like you should be finding your own room," she mumbled. Guerin drew to a halt at the foot of the stairs and looked over his shoulder.

"Are you saying I look bad?" He crossed his arms.

Doing her best to keep the grin off her face, Eve gave him her best innocent expression. "I didn't say that, exactly. We've all been through a lot these last few days. You're tired, Lombardi. Sheesh... Vain much?" Eve brushed past him and began climbing the stairs.

"I am *not* vain," he huffed behind her.

She chuckled under her breath and stopped at the top to wait for him to catch up.

"This way," he said and smirked before heading right. "Your room is at the end, facing the side of the house. But you should also get a nice glimpse of the front and back."

Eve couldn't pull her gaze from the way the dark jeans hugged the rear of the male in front of her. The denim perfectly encased the tight muscles and then molded itself down his thighs. Eve had to bite her lip to keep from groaning. Yes. She did have a nice view of the back.

Guerin opened the door and stood aside, allowing her enough space to pass through. Eve surveyed the floor plan and furnishings. Rich dark woods, mahogany or cherry, filled the room. A comforter designed with a cream, chocolate, and blue geometric pattern covered the bed. White wooden shutters sealed the windows, but she surmised the house must use some kind of exterior or tinted covering for the glass itself because no UV light filtered between the slats.

"You have your own bathroom in here," Guerin said and sauntered over to a darkened doorway and clicked on a light inside. Eve joined him and peeked inside.

"Great." The bath came with a separate soaker tub and freestanding blue-and-white-tiled shower. Kenric and Emily certainly had good taste and obviously took care of the members of the Enclave. Eve moved to the other side of the room and found the double doors to the closet. She pulled them wide and surveyed the deep space. Damn, she could actually sleep inside there.

"You like?" Guerin was behind her. His presence—warmth—sent a shiver up her spine. He was so close, she could swear his breath tickled her nape. Yet he hadn't touched her.

"Yeah," she whispered. "What's not to like?"

"Good." He hadn't moved. Eve tightened her grip on the door handles.

"Where's your room?" *Damn.* Why had she blurted that out loud?

"I sleep downstairs in the basement." Eve could hear the smile in his voice. He was loving that she'd asked.

"Oh. There's a basement?"

"It's where the Enclave handles its business, plus there are a couple of bedrooms. Since I'm not mated, I prefer to allow the others to have the suites up here. They're a little larger."

"How considerate of you." Electricity virtually hummed inside her head. It was as if the space between them had become a Tesla coil, and the current zinged between her nipples and her core.

And then he touched her—not her shoulder, or her back. A gentle brush of his fingers in her hair, moving the strands aside and exposing her neck. "I do try," he breathed on her flesh. His lips feathered along the curve up toward her ear, and the effect had her tugging hard on the closet doors. The hinges groaned in complaint.

Eve released her grip and spun, and his mouth found hers. She wanted to shout at the exquisite bliss. She opened and Guerin dived inside. God, Eve loved the taste of him— sweet and spicy. Her heart raced as he pulled her against his chest, her nipples hard, aching, demanding more of the contact. He rocked into her, pressing the hard length of his shaft into her abdomen. She moaned, but not from the desire alone.

This was too easy.

And what they had was anything but easy. Their history or baggage couldn't be swept away with a roll between the sheets. Sure his body wanted her, but what about his head, his heart? She'd been the reason he'd traveled back down a very ugly dark road. How could he be ready to be with her— completely—after he'd been forced to relive a nightmare of Daniela's creation?

And if she were honest, the thought of him calling the bitch "Mistress" chapped Eve's ass. She knew why he'd done it, but the green monster inside didn't care. God, she didn't want to be the reason he ever hurt again. But dammit, Eve didn't want him if she got half his trust and only a small piece of his heart.

Giving in now to satiate their lust meant neither would be truly happy, nor in the end, receive what they needed from each other.

She couldn't do this.

Eve bit down hard on Guerin's lower lip, and the spicy flavor of his blood shot over her tongue. He grunted and jerked back on a hiss.

"I never gave you permission to kiss me," she stated.

Guerin stilled, and fire flashed, then swirled around his pupils. With the back of his hand, he wiped away the scarlet stain from his mouth and reversed his step until there was room to breathe between them. "No, you didn't," he snarled. "And I didn't ask."

"You want to pick a fight now, vampire?" She raised an eyebrow. "A second ago, I got the impression you wanted to fuck. Or maybe you were just begging me to punish you?"

Any evidence of the flames in his gaze was vanquished with her words. His eyes went coal black, the pupil swallowing up the white. He growled. "That's the last damn thing I need." The tips of his fangs glinted beneath his upper lip.

"Good. Because you're not getting either from me." Eve moved around him, her knees more wobbly than she'd like to admit. At the door to her room she stopped and grasped the edge of the door, her back to Guerin. She couldn't look at him. Her will wasn't strong enough. "So why don't you and I keep our distance until you figure out exactly what it is you do need." Her words were fierce, even though in her heart, the venom behind them wasn't nearly as potent.

"You know…," Guerin stated from behind her, his voice gravelly and deep, his proximity so close, the heat from his body warmed her backside. "I think you've verbalized exactly what has needed to be said for a long time."

Mentally, Eve flinched. She couldn't help it. She was pissed, and she'd pushed, but this wasn't really what she'd wanted.

"You and I both know this, you and me, isn't going to work," he went on to say. "What we had was good—hot as hell. While it lasted. I know what I need, beautiful, and un-less what you've got in mind is killing bad guys, anything more than that isn't it."

He brushed past her through the bedroom door. Eve closed her eyes and tightened her grip on the wood to keep from crumbling. The heavy thump of his boots faded as Guerin made his way down the hall. *Maybe he was right.* That was what she was going to have to keep telling herself when she crawled into bed without him each day.

A couple of hours after sundown and a restless day of tossing and turning later, Eve sat at the bar in the kitchen. Michael had made a wonderful chicken salad, and Eve was attempting to make a good show of enjoying it. She didn't need the entire Enclave to know her heart was breaking.

"There you are." Kenric stepped into the kitchen, wear-ing dark slacks and a navy turtleneck, his gaze going straight to Eve, then swinging to the other male in the room. "Good evening, Michael. How are you doing?"

"Good. Thanks." Michael smiled. Eve guessed the other

guy was probably in his midthirties. He was a good-looking male with a head full of wavy sandy-brown hair. Perhaps a little too tall and thin for her personal taste, but he was friendly and pleasant to be around. It was refreshing to see a human who worked for a vampire of his own free will, and judging by the lack of marks on his neck, one who wasn't being used as a calyx. "Nice to have someone in the house who enjoys my cooking." He chuckled.

"Well that is truly a rare find, indeed."

"Bite me," Michael snapped, but it appeared all bluff.

"Another time. Already eaten."

Michael flicked Kenric his middle finger, but Kenric laughed and circled the bar toward Eve. "I promised you a tour," her father said. "Is this a good time?"

"Of course." Eve slid from the chair. "The sandwich was delicious, Michael. Thank you."

"You're welcome. Anytime." He gave Eve a nod.

Kenric guided Eve through what seemed like every inch of the house. He mentioned the house was their second. They'd moved a little over a year ago because someone on the inside had betrayed their whereabouts, and their headquarters had come under attack by a group of DEADs.

"Did my mother have anything to do with that?" Eve had a feeling she already knew that answer.

"She did." He nodded. "But this location is secure," Kenric went on to say. "We have the latest in electronic surveillance available, and the warriors in the Enclave are as loyal as they come." He placed a hand on her shoulder. "One of the reasons I wanted you with me—to make sure you're safe and protected. Seth and Daniela are dead, but we can't be sure of who else out there knows about you. I'm so pleased you agreed to come to the States with us."

"Me too," she whispered, and a part of her really did mean it. This was an opportunity to get to know her father firsthand. She just wished... Wished for a life with another Enclave male that wasn't meant to be.

He finished off the tour of the library with a stroll outside and to the pool. Eve rubbed her bare arms under the chilly night air.

"South Carolina summers are hot," he said. "So even during the night, the water and breezes are warm, and you can enjoy a swim."

"That will be nice." Eve stared out over the still blue waters of the large rectangular pool, the underwater lighting serene and inviting. The grounds were lined with large evergreens, giving a swimmer the feeling of complete privacy for a midnight dip.

"Lastly, I'd like to take you down to the basement and show you where we meet each evening."

The basement...where Guerin sleeps.

With a palm to her back, Kenric led her back inside, past the kitchen, and down a corridor that dead-ended at an interior door. "When most of us aren't trekking to Europe"—he chuckled and opened the door—"we rotate shifts to monitor the streets of Elizabeth Bay and the surrounding area for DEAD activity. My team feels strongly about protecting the human population from vampires who can't control their urge to kill and end up addicted to Death Euphoria." He started down a set of wooden treads and Eve followed.

"My mother mentioned you and the Enclave before she left."

"She did?" At the foot of the stairwell, he glanced back

over his shoulder.

Eve nodded. "She just neglected to inform me of a lot of other important details."

Kenric grunted in acknowledgement, then placed his hand over a flat surface. A beam of light flashed on and proceeded to scan the surface of his palm. A lock clicked and Kenric pulled the door handle.

Inside, Eve would have sworn she'd stepped into an enormous bachelor pad complete with a flat-screen TV, video games, an air hockey table, and a pool table. Yet at the far end, the elaborate computer and security monitor setup said the place held a higher purpose. Sitting at the helm of the controls was a beautiful young woman with long dark-brown hair.

"Eve, this is Elle, Arran's mate," Kenric said. Elle looked up and gave her a warm smile.

"It's wonderful to meet you." She stuck out her hand and Eve slid her palm inside for a shake.

"Likewise," Eve said. "I've met Arran. He's a fierce warrior. Loyal."

"Yes, he is." the woman nodded, her eyes bright. No one would have had to tell Eve the woman was in love. One mention of Arran's name, and she practically radiated. How nice it must feel to have the feeling reciprocated. Something Eve wasn't sure she'd ever know. "I'll have to introduce you to my sister, Alex," Elle added. "She's not home right now. Maybe we can get together later? I'm sure she'll love having another female in the house."

"Sure," Eve said. "I look forward to meeting her."

Eve turned to head out with Kenric when a door opened a few feet away and Guerin appeared. Wearing a pair of black leather pants, boots, and a white T-shirt, along with his dark hair and eyes the male was a lethal combination—to her sex drive.

"Hey, Guerin," Kenric said and headed over to him. "I'm glad you're here." Eve joined her father at his side. "I'm overdue to take care of Markus. It's been way too long. Would you mind keeping Eve company? This shouldn't take long." Kenric slapped him on the shoulder and marched off, not waiting for a reply. Guerin swung his gaze in her direction, and from the look on his face, Eve guessed he'd prefer a roll in fire ants.

"*You* do *not* have to babysit me," Eve chewed out and started toward the exit. "I can find my way around and am certainly capable of entertaining myself."

"Wait," he called out. Eve slowed and came to a stop, but she didn't turn around. God, why had she agreed to this tour? She'd rather be upstairs alone in her room than spend time with a male who couldn't make up his mind what he wanted. Because after a while, the forced togetherness would only end up making each other miserable.

The fresh scent of sandalwood and leather drifted into her nostrils. Guerin stood behind her. Her pulse leaped. Eve curled her fingers into a tight fist under the response. "After earlier this morning...I wasn't sure how you'd feel about his request."

She pivoted and faced him. "How do you feel about it?"

"We're going to be living under the same roof, so I think we'd better get used to spending time in the same room."

He had a point. It was a big house. But not so big they wouldn't run into each other on occasion. She sighed. "I'll try if you will." Eve scanned his attire once more, noting the sheath strapped to his thigh. "You're going out tonight?"

"Yeah. I've been gone a while, so it's way past my turn on rotation."

Eve nodded. "I see." She didn't know why she'd assumed Guerin's returning home would put him in less danger. He was a member of the Enclave. Putting their lives at risk was what they did, yet the idea of him being out there didn't sit well with her at all. A part of Eve wanted to cry out "mine" and keep him all to herself. But since when had he become *hers* to worry about? He'd made it perfectly clear that what they'd shared was in the past.

"Kenric said he needed to take care of Markus," she said, needing a different subject to direct her focus. "Who is he?"

A look she could only call rage flashed across Guerin's face right before it morphed into disgust.

"Wow," Eve stated. "Maybe I don't want to know. Or maybe I do, because based on that look on your face, he's someone whose ass I need to kick."

Guerin chuckled, and the sound warmed her heart. "And you would be right." But the smile that had ridden along with his laughter quickly died before he glanced down at her and proceeded to tell her about Markus, the male's abduction, and subsequent alliance with her mother. Guerin revealed to her that Markus was the one who had confirmed her existence and had put them in contact with Ana, whom Guerin had met on his arrival in Nuremberg.

"I remember Ana from when I was young."

"She was the one who sent me to the Rose's Thorn."

"I still can't believe my mother told Markus about me." Eve's chest tightened. "She must have truly thought she had him completely ensnared." She whirled around. "I have to see him." Eve made for the door. He was the last person to spend time with the Marguerite she never knew, and Eve had to know what secrets this male kept.

"I don't know about this." Guerin put his palm to the wood, halting her exit. "Kenric asked me to keep you here."

"No, he didn't." She glared up at Guerin. "He asked you to keep me company. So you can do that from anywhere, even in the other room with Kenric and Markus." Eve yanked on the door, and Guerin reluctantly lowered his arm.

"You're determined to give me an aneurysm, aren't you?"

They exited the Enclave's common area and Guerin accessed the door that led into another wing of the basement. The lock secured behind them. Ahead, a light shone through the bars of a silver holding cage. Eve craned her neck, peering inside before stepping in full view of the occupant. Guerin stood behind her, within reach, but allowing her to take the lead. Unlike the cells she'd seen in the past, this one was much larger. Bars enclosed its front side, but the other three sections of the square were contained behind the whitewashed wall The silver would keep a vampire from escaping, but the room was large enough so the prisoner wouldn't be tortured with an overdose of the toxic metal.

A humane approach.

Kenric stood over a thin male who sat on the edge of a cot, his broad palm holding the back of the seated male's head to his wrist. Markus's long pitch-black strands covered the side of his face, but she could tell he was feeding from Kenric's vein. This had to be what Emily had referred to back in Germany when she said Kenric wasn't an option for blood. Sweat glistened on Kenric's forehead as if nourishing the male took great effort.

Several long minutes later, Markus reared back, gasping, crimson streaks dripping from his chin.

"Dammit, Markus!" Kenric raised his arm and sealed the punctures to his flesh. "I'm doing everything in my power to give you another chance. But you fight me even to take my vein."

Slowly, Markus cranked his head in her direction. His nostrils flared, and then a smile she could only define as sinister curled his lips. "She's here, isn't she?"

"Who?" Kenric growled.

"Marguerite's daughter." The thin male rose, staggered, but kept coming toward the bars. "I smell you, Eve. Your scent is similar to your mother's. I'd know you anywhere."

From behind him, Kenric wrapped his hand around Markus's throat. "Leave her alone, or I swear I'll end your pitiful life right now where you stand." Markus didn't flinch.

"It's okay," Eve said and moved closer to the front of the cage. Markus's eyes widened, yet no light reflected back. Her gaze captured his, and she grabbed the bars for added security as if the dark void staring back at her could somehow suck her in if she didn't hold on tight. Markus followed where her hands had gone and smiled. He hadn't missed the fact that she'd touched the silver without retreating. It burned, but thanks to her hybrid nature, there wasn't enough of an overall concentration to blister or to have her writhing in agony. Not like the dose she'd received under the silver mesh that had had her nerve endings on fire. The contact with the metal was uncomfortable, but it was nothing compared to the disturbing vibe radiating off the male on the other side.

"Fascinating," he said, then lifted his head. "You look exactly like your picture, Eve."

"What picture?" She'd never known her mother to have a photo of her. Marguerite had always said it was too dangerous to have her image documented.

"She kept one locked away," he said. "Marguerite showed it to me one night as proof she truly had a child with Kenric. She'd been in an especially melancholy mood, and after some encouragement, she finally told me why — that particular day was her daughter's birthday." His gaze roamed from toe to head. "Damn. Except for the eyes, you look so much like her." Markus seized the bars, hissing as his flesh sizzled, and thrust his hips at the cage. Guerin circled her waist with his arm, pulling her against his chest. Kenric roared, yanked Markus away, and tossed him onto the floor.

"That's my daughter," he growled. "Show some damn restraint."

Markus laughed. "You had better keep an eye on her, Master. But I don't think it's me you have to worry about. I'm just having a little fun." Markus's gaze shifted to the man behind Eve, and a corner of his mouth curled into a sneer. "Oh, I'm thinking you're too late, though, Dad. I suspect your best friend's already had her."

A deep growl rolled off Kenric as he spun away. He exited the cell, slamming the door with an ear-ringing clatter. Markus rolled to his feet, his attention never wavering from Guerin. "Does she have her mother's taste for domination?"

"Shut the fuck up," Guerin snarled.

"I'm taking that as a yes." Markus winked and turned to Eve. "Unlike myself, I don't think your daddy enjoyed your mother's flair for the darker side when it came to sex." His gaze raked her once more. "I wonder how the copy compares to the original."

"That's enough!" Kenric barked.

Rage vibrated off the male behind Eve. "Let's get the hell out of here," Guerin said, and he grabbed her shoulder. But Eve didn't budge. She wasn't finished yet.

"My, you are a *bad* one," she said, her tone mocking, and placed her hands on her hips. "But I'm afraid that's a question, Markus, you'll be left to ponder for the rest of your miserable days," she said, the tips of her fangs nipping her lip. "Because *you'll* never know for sure." Eve spun and headed for the exit.

"Ouch. Touché, little beauty." Markus's laughter echoed off the walls.

Chapter Twenty-Three

"Hurt me, Mistress," Guerin begged, his voice ragged. His heart galloped inside his chest, each beat a thunderous clap inside his head. How the hell the muscle hadn't ruptured by now, he'd never know. He'd rather walk into the sun than grovel for Daniela. But he had no choice. He couldn't allow Eve to suffer. It was worth swallowing his pride and shattering his vow.

The lash cracked, then licked his spine with its fiery tongue from where he kneeled on the floor. He writhed under the bite, and his head lolled between his shoulder blades. The click of her heels resounded off the wood as she neared. Guerin opened his eyes, and the image of the female he'd expected to find morphed. Daniela's blond waves darkened, and her brown eyes shifted to blue.

Eve. *What the hell?*

They were no longer in Seth's dungeon, but had somehow leaped into Eve's basement.

His cock pulsed—thickened until it was rock-hard. "Fuuucckk." The word ripped from his throat on a groan. How could it be? But damn if he cared. "Again!" he cried out. "Don't stop until there's nothing left."

She spun and resumed her position. Guerin bowed his head and curled his fingers. The tip of the whip snapped in the air, then struck.

"Yes!" This was what he needed. Needed her to eradicate every memory, every nerve ending that had ever responded to the other female. "More," he growled. "Rip me apart!" He tore at what was left of his shirt, the popping of the seams competing with the crackle of the whip. Christ, he was so dirty.

Contaminated.

How could Eve ever stand to touch him, to love him, after where he'd been, the things he'd done with Daniela? His very tongue was tainted from the word "Mistress" he'd uttered for her. The whip crashed over his shoulder, and a strangled cry burst from his lungs.

A loud clatter filled his ears, and Guerin lurched forward, his eyelids popping open. He scanned the darkness of the bedroom. His bedside lamp lay busted on the floor. *Shit.* He was dreaming. Again.

Guerin swung his legs over the side of the bed. Beads of sweat covered his body, and he shook from the chill of the air flowing over his naked flesh. Yet the AC had done little to bring down his raging hard-on.

For the last two weeks, he'd requested every shift Kenric would give him to avoid time alone with Eve. Removing a couple of DEADs from the planet had felt damn good, but it hadn't taken care of the problem he was dodging inside the walls of the Enclave. It was still there every time he stepped across the threshold and his gaze fell on Eve. Whether or not he was ready or willing to verbalize his issues, the fact was, he had way too much crap going on inside his head that needed to be fixed before he was ready or worthy for a female, especially one as amazing as Eve.

Padding across the carpet, he made his way to the shower. What he needed was a cold one, but he was already freezing. He pulled open the stall's glass door, twisted the faucet, and stepped inside.

He plucked the bottle of shower gel from the caddy and lathered up, doing his best to wash away the memories of his dream. With a slick palm he gripped his shaft and swallowed a moan under the warm, slippery feel. He gave his length a few hard tugs with his fist. A quick and easy release. That's all he wanted. Nothing too complicated. He leaned back against the cool tile, working his cock—praying for the familiar tingle at the base of his spine to hurry and appear, the signal his orgasm was imminent. Damn, who was he kidding? It wasn't enough, and he knew it. He gave up on his jerk-off session and moved under the spray to rinse.

Would he ever rid himself of Daniela? How many centuries would he have to endure before her taint wore off? Before Eve could ever love him?

The words his mind had conjured during his dream came flooding back to the surface. *Love...* He bit back a laugh. He was three hundred years old, and the ridiculous fantasy was for those much younger and far less impure.

Yet an ache pulsed and radiated behind his breastbone at the concept of Eve's love. He rubbed a palm over his chest. Yeah, maybe he liked the idea more than he wanted to admit.

When Eve had pushed him away from her bed the day of their return, she'd known better than him that what they needed couldn't be found in a hot and fast fuck. They'd shared something in Germany, but when she'd pressed for more, Guerin could only go so far, could only let her in so deep.

Perhaps his dream was trying to tell him something his conscious mind hadn't been ready to accept. The only way he was ever going to mend his soul was to open up and allow Eve inside to heal the wounds.

The thought scared the hell out of him.

Yet the idea of waking every day to Eve upstairs and him in the basement was driving him mad. The last hour was proof.

Guerin turned the shower off and stepped out onto the bath mat. Beads of water sluiced down his torso as he stared at his cloudy image in the fogged mirror. He pulled a towel from the stack on the shelf, draped it around his hips, and sidled up to the sink. With his palms, he worked a lazy circle over the glass, revealing a clearer view of his face.

"You know what needs to be done, Lombardi," he whispered at his reflection. "Admit it to yourself." Eve belonged to him. She was his soul mate. There was no getting around that fact. Every cell in his body desired her. Hell. Guerin needed Eve on a level he never knew existed.

He craved her touch.

Her taste.

And he wanted nothing less than for her to possess him—body and soul.

Now he just had to prove it.

After midnight, Guerin lit the wick to the final solid

white cylinder candle on his dresser. The flame danced to life and joined the twenty others in the room, giving his room a magical glow. He tossed the lighter onto the wood beside the wax with a *clunk* and pivoted to survey his work. The tray on the stand in the corner where he'd suspended a large ring from the ceiling contained a nice assortment of tools and toys for Eve. Everything she might want should be there.

Guerin crossed the room, reached in the top drawer of his desk, and pulled out a pad and pen. He straddled a chair, put ink to paper, and reached for the words he'd practiced inside his head all night. His chest tightened, his heart heavy like a rock. *Christ.* He hoped this worked.

Looks like we've come full circle. Except this time, it's me sending you the note. But one thing remains the same—I'm still looking for you, Eve. I've been searching for you my whole life. I just didn't know until now. Meet me in my room in ten if you want to be found.

He signed it with a single G, folded the paper, and slipped it inside an envelope. On the outside, he wrote "Eve," then sealed the flap. Guerin palmed the house phone and rang Michael, asking him to stop by; he needed a favor. The guy was at his door a couple of minutes later. He answered, making sure the younger male couldn't get a full view of his room.

"Thanks for getting down here so fast," Guerin said.

"No problem." Michael shrugged. "You never call for anything, so I figured it must be important."

Guerin passed the other man the envelope. "Would you give this to Eve for me?"

Michael took the note and slipped it into his back pocket. "Consider it done." He nodded and turned to leave.

"One more thing," Guerin said and Michael looked back. "Discretion is appreciated. Keep this between us."

"I got your back." Michael grinned.

"Yeah. Right." Guerin coughed. "I'm going to owe you big-time for this, aren't I?"

"So big," Michael mouthed the words, and spread his hands wide.

"That's what I thought." Guerin shook his head and laughed.

Back inside, Guerin quickly washed once more and brushed his teeth. Then with nothing else to do, he stripped down to his boxer briefs, folded his clothes and set them neatly on a chair. Standing in the center of his room, he clutched his wrists behind his back—and waited.

Time yawned and Guerin thought he would crack before a knock finally sounded at his door.

"Enter," he called out, not worrying if it were someone else. The vibration in his soul said it was her.

"Guerin?" she called out. Staring at his feet, he listened for the sound of her footsteps. "What's going on?" Eve's voice was barely above a whisper, then her movements stopped a couple of feet away, and he could swear Eve had ceased to breathe.

Dampness pooled inside his clenched fists as he lifted his gaze to hers. Her midnight locks fell down her back and over her shoulder in a raven waterfall. So different from Daniela in more ways than her appearance alone. Eve wore a white blouse with a few of the buttons left open at the top, a black leather skirt that stopped a few inches above her knees. Below, she'd finished the outfit with a pair of sexy black ankle boots. His shaft pulsed at the mere sight of her.

"I can't do this any longer," he said, the words tumbling from his lips. "I lied. What I need is you."

Her mouth parted, but no sound escaped.

Guerin lowered one knee to the carpet, his quads trembling. "I want you," he added. His heart clogged the back of his throat. Then his other knee fell beside the first. Guerin swallowed hard, clearing his vocal cords, and he bowed his head. "Tear down my walls until there's nothing left but you inside my head. I want only you there." He gasped. "Please… Mistress," he uttered, his voice ragged.

Her breath hitched, then silence.

Damn.

What the hell was she thinking?

He listened as Eve began to move about the room, imagining her taking in all his preparations, but Guerin kept his gaze lowered.

"I approve of the items you've chosen," she finally uttered in her best Dominatrix voice. His pulse raced under her praise. "Now on your feet."

Guerin did as he was told—stood, and released his grip on his wrists.

"Clasp your hands in front." Eve closed the distance between them, and with metal cuffs she'd retrieved from his stash, secured his arms together. "Come with me." She directed him to the area beneath the suspended metal ring. Earlier, he'd mounted a tire swivel to the ceiling. The ball joint inside allowed him to rotate on the attached ring but kept him from moving no more than a step in either direction. "Arms up," Eve commanded. Guerin lifted them over his head, and Eve hooked the links between the shackles to the device. His pulse kicked into a higher gear. But he could do this. Guerin scanned the profile of the female who heated his blood—this was Eve.

She returned to the collection he'd gathered on the stand, selected a black silk scarf, and turned toward Guerin. Sweat popped on his forehead. *Shit.* It wasn't as if he'd never been in the dark before. Yet for some reason, he didn't like the idea of losing sight of his beautiful Domme.

"Let's take your senses higher," she said and placed the cloth over his eyes, then wrapped it around his head. Her vanilla and cinnamon scent invaded his nostrils—his mind—taking him to rock-hard. Eve's fingertips teased his shoulders, then brushed over his nipples. He sucked in a harsh breath. Lower still, she trailed over the ridges of his abdomen and down to the waistband of his briefs where she slipped under the material. Slowly, she explored his flesh there, teasing the end of his rod with her nails, sending darts of electricity down the shaft. "What's your safe word?"

Safe word? He wanted to laugh, never having been asked for such a thing in the past. Guerin scrambled for something common enough he wouldn't have any trouble recalling it if he were under duress.

"Black," he said.

"Black, it is." Then with a *snap*, Eve released the elastic. Guerin jerked, and her footsteps moved away.

"Where are you going?"

"I haven't given you permission to speak freely," she stated, her voice firm. Guerin sealed his lips, reaching mentally for his patience.

The strike across his chest took him by surprise, and Guerin reared back on his restraint. Instinct drove his fingernails into his palms in anticipation of the next blow from what had to be a riding crop. Again the leather seared his other pec and nipple, locking his molars together. Over and over she struck the muscles of his chest, then the tops of his thighs. His neurons fired, sparking memories to life with every blow.

Daniela's dungeon.

The sting of her whip, her blond tresses clinging to her face from her exertion.

No, no, no!

He swerved and pivoted, doing his best to divert the next unseen blow.

"You're running, Lombardi," Eve said. She grabbed him by the band of his boxer briefs and held him in place. The sound of cotton popping filled his ears, and his rigid cock sprang free. Cool air washed over his heated flesh. "Spread your legs." Guerin did as he was told, and Eve yanked his briefs from his hips.

The bite of the crop returned, and Guerin spun. Eve didn't let up. She showered his back, his buttocks, his hamstrings with the tool.

Pain spiked, crested.

With only the images from his past inside his head along for the ride. His stomach churned. This wasn't what he wanted. The bitter taste of anger surged from his gut.

"Turn around," she commanded. Sweat ran down the sides of his face, and air sawed from his lungs. *Dammit.* Why had she taken his sight? He could hold on, give her what she wanted if he had her to focus on.

"Take off the blindfold," he bit out.

"No." Another strike seared across his ass. "Turn around."

Rage festered. "Fuck you," he spat.

"Not till I damn well say so," she retorted.

Multiple blows of leather rained down on Guerin's back, and he swiveled hard sideways. *Son of a bitch.* Eve had switched to a flogger. Again. And again. She covered his shoulders with solid whacks and then lower across his cheeks. His pulse roared inside his head, his nervous system responding to the assault like a thunderhead, rising, swelling under the influx until he was about to blow. Yet not for *her.* Not like this. His mind in the past—his body in the present.

"Stop!" Guerin cried out, swinging away from the incoming strikes.

"You're still running, Lombardi."

He spun, facing his Domme, and the tips of the flogger skated across his erection. His balls drew tight. "Shit! Take this thing off me or stop," he growled.

"Why?" She struck again, wringing a hiss from between his teeth. "If you really want me to stop, you know what you need to do—say the word."

His molars squeaked under the pressure. He didn't want it to end. Not really. Guerin loved mixing pain with pleasure, being taken into subspace where his will wasn't his own. But with Daniela, taking him there had become a weapon of manipulation.

So he'd run.

Run from his memories and his desires for fear of ever opening up again, letting his defenses fall. Because if he did, he'd lose himself.

But he wanted this with Eve, right? Being kept behind the damn blindfold had his mind frazzled.

"So do you want me to stop?" Eve danced the flogger once more off his dick. The shock wave launched up his shaft, arching his spine. *Yes…! No!* Blood leaked onto his tongue from where his fangs had pierced holes in his lip.

"Just take the blindfold off," he rasped, and shook his head.

"But I want your senses on high. I like it."

"I don't," he barked. Panic seeped under his skin, a parasite seeking to dig its mandible in and snap his control. Eve crashed into him again with the flogger, and the leather seared his chest. Guerin's head reeled.

"This isn't about what you want."

The image of Daniela's laughing face loomed in front of his mind's eye. "I can't do this," he stated, panting.

"Why?"

"Get this off me!"

"Why?" Another whack to his groin.

"Because I can't let go," he cried out. "Not like this. She's inside my head—in the dark. Daniela's there. I need to see you," he whispered. "Let me see you."

Eve tugged on the knot behind his head and tore the blindfold away. Guerin gasped. He blinked, clearing his vision and absorbing the one in front of him—Eve. The room spun, but somehow Eve bound him to earth.

She reached up, detached him from the loop, and pulled Guerin into her. He stared down, lost in the liquid pools of blue that were her irises.

"I want you…," he growled. "I want you to crawl inside me until I don't remember anything that came before where you and I began."

"Shh." Eve placed a finger to his lips. "I've got you." She hooked a finger on a bit gag from his assortment and brought it forward. "Open wide," she said. A groan left his throat but Guerin obeyed. Eve stuffed the narrow bit into his mouth, making sure it fit around his fangs. The thick rubber padding was soft, allowing him to dig the sharp points in if needed. "After having seen the kind of endurance you possess, and the fact that you're the most stubborn male I know, this is probably a waste of time. But this needs to be said. With the gag in place, you won't be able to speak, so if you need me to, shake your head a few times, and I'll stop."

He nodded, and she removed the shackles from his wrists, then ordered him on the bed, face up.

Guerin climbed onto the mattress and centered himself. His cock jutted up toward his abdomen, veins distended. Wrapping his fingers around the shaft, he stroked the sensitive flesh. He couldn't resist. The damn thing ached. A moan erupted from his throat, sounding choked behind the bit.

"Hands off," she demanded. "That's mine."

His arms slammed onto the mattress at his side, held in place by Eve's mind. *Damn.* He loved it when she did that. His heart pounded like a heavy bass drum, each beat a pulsing reminder of the need inside his cock.

Guerin watched as she went for another object from the table. She held up her new find for his inspection, stroking the long cylinder of a blue silicone vibrator. With a smile, she brought the toy up to her mouth and slipped it between her lips. *Damn.* Guerin couldn't drag his gaze away if he'd tried. His cock flexed as she worked the toy in and out like a delicious dessert. The end shone in the candlelight as she aimed it toward his groin.

"I remember during our last time together you touched yourself here." She placed the tip to the backside of his shaft, clicked the on button, and the device came alive with a rapid buzz. The vibration went straight to his balls, boiling the cum inside. Guerin's hips left the mattress on a grunt, needing more. Eve traveled his length to the root. With her other hand, she lifted his balls. "And you wanted me here," she added, and tucked the item against his ring. His breath hitched, and reflex tightened the pathway. Chills raced over his flesh in anticipation. "I'm going to fuck you with this, love," Eve said and tossed him a seductive grin. Guerin's eyelids shuttered at the thought. *Shit.* He could come from the visual image alone. But damn if he would allow his release before Eve got inside and gave him permission.

Pressure ramped below, and he bit down on the rubber inside his mouth. Air surged in and out of his nostrils. His pulse thumped in his temples.

"Let me in," Eve crooned.

Focusing on the invasion knocking on his back door, Guerin closed his eyes, relaxed, and Eve slipped inside. *Oh God.*

Burned.

So damn good. He moaned.

"Look at me," she called out. Guerin lifted his lids. Eve released her hold on the toy, clutched the hem of her shirt, and pulled it over her head. Her breasts filled the cups of her white bra to near overflowing. He licked the roof of his mouth, remembering the sweet taste of her nipples. Shit, he wanted to see them again. Suck on the hard tips. His cock jerked, and his bottom clenched on the hard length of the probe. The vibrations bounced off a sensitive spot inside, and Guerin's back arched. He cried out. Too much. He couldn't come yet.

Eve latched onto the base of his shaft and clamped down. Guerin slammed the back of his head into the pillow. *Breathe…* He sucked in a cleansing breath through his nostrils. *Breathe.*

"That's it," Eve crooned. "Relax for me."

Guerin blinked, his heart rate gearing down a notch.

"Okay?"

He nodded.

"Good," Eve said, then uncurled her fingers and went for the zipper at her hipbone. Slowly, she peeled the black leather away, a seductress tightening her noose around his heart with every move. Did she even realize the power she wielded over his soul?

Toeing off her boots, Eve shimmied her skirt down her legs. She tossed it onto the floor, leaving her lower half bare. His palms itched to touch, to smooth his hands over her curves—stroke the petal-soft folds between her legs. His mouth watered at the thought of burying his face there. *Damn*, nothing compared to the nectar of her arousal.

Suddenly, the vibrator surged forward, and her fingers latched onto his dick once more.

"Do you want to come?" Eve pumped his cock with one hand, matching the pace of the vibrator sliding in and out of his rear. His head roared, and Guerin drove his fangs into the rubber of his bit. All he could do was nod. "But you're not going to come yet, are you?"

Guerin couldn't form the words around his gag. He groaned and shook his head.

The plunging sensation in his ass ceased, but the vibrator remained on. Eve uncurled her fingers from his erection and slinked over his torso until her legs were on either side of his hips. She seized his cock once more and positioned the head at her entrance. *Oh fuck.* The walls around his mind trembled, fractured. The tip penetrated her wet, hot core, and a brick toppled, leaving him dazed. He moaned. With every inch she sank over his shaft, another one fell.

"This is mine, Lombardi," she stated, her voice low, husky. Eve's head lolled, and her channel devoured his length until she sat balls-deep. Guerin cried out around the restriction in his mouth. She reached behind and twisted the rod inside him. "All of you. Mine. Do you hear me?"

His head buzzed. White spots danced in front of his eyes. *Son of a bitch.* He had to come. Hard pants burst from his lungs.

With a click, Eve released her bra. The material fell away, and her breasts swayed free. Dark, rosy nipples stood erect at the tips. Dear God, she was glorious. An angel of darkness and light, and the only one strong enough to delve into the black abyss of his mind.

Up and down, she rode his shaft, milking him. Taking him to the edge and back again. "Are you ready to come?"

God, yes!

Leaning forward, she worked at the buckle to his gag. Within seconds, Eve tore it away. His fangs ached. He wanted her.

Her blood.

Her body.

Her every pleasure to be his own.

"Are you ready?" she repeated, looming over him, his

cock hard, throbbing inside her heat. Eve's pupils swirled with fire, and the tips of her fangs glinted beneath her upper lip. Sexy as hell.

"Yes," he growled.

"Yes, what?"

"Yes, Mistress," he whispered. "Let me come." Eve's hips stilled, and Guerin stifled a groan. "Please, Mistress." Her inner muscles squeezed the length of his shaft, and it was as if she'd backwashed his pulse into his skull. His head pounded. Guerin clamped his eyes shut under the pressure.

"Who does this serve?" She clenched the walls of her core again for emphasis.

"My Mistress," he bit the words out.

"And who is your Mistress?"

Guerin opened his eyes, his gaze locking with hers. "You."

"No one else?"

"Only you," he rasped. "Oh, fuck." He groaned. "I only see you, Mistress."

Eve surged up onto her knees, then drove down onto his rod. "Come for me," she shouted. "Now!" She rocked up and down on his cock.

And Guerin erupted.

"Eve!" he cried out, and suddenly his arms were free. He clasped on to her, needing something to hold on to as his orgasm filled his Mistress. Colors exploded in front of his retinas. Then Eve was beneath him, and he pistoned into her core, giving her everything.

"Take from me," she ordered and turned her head, exposing the smooth column of her throat. *Holy hell.* Eve didn't take his trust and twist it to her will; she held it in the palm of her hand.

Stroked it.

Strengthened it.

His pulse stuttered with the realization. Getting lost inside her was the first time Guerin had found himself. Became more than he was when he was alone.

He teased the rapid beat of her carotid with his tongue, and gooseflesh popped along her flesh.

"Do it," she whispered.

Guerin struck, driving his fangs into her artery. Eve shuddered, the walls of her sex in spasm along his shaft, and his name ricocheted off the walls. The sweet and salty essence of her life flooded his mouth, his throat, veins, swelling his heart. How had he ever existed before her?

No. Guerin was dead wrong.

He'd never lived before Eve.

Chapter Twenty-Four

Eve pulled the silver Mercedes coupe into the garage and killed the engine. "That was a great idea," she said and turned to Alex, who had invited her out for some girl time. "I can't remember the last time I went shopping with a girlfriend."

"No problem. A woman can never have enough clothes or shoes." Alex laughed and popped open the passenger door. Eve grabbed their bags from the backseat. "It was nice to spend some time away from the house with someone other than my sister. After what happened last year, she doesn't like letting me out of her sight." Alex met her at the front of the vehicle, tucking a few strands of her long blue-black hair behind her ear. "I'm sure Guerin has filled you in on how I came to live with the Enclave." She retrieved her two bags from Eve.

"Yeah." Eve gave her a gentle smile. "He told me a little

about everyone who lives here. Anytime you want to get some fresh air, come look for me. The house is big, but I imagine it can get claustrophobic in there, especially with who's locked away in the basement."

Alex nodded. "If it weren't for Elle…" She sighed. "I'm not sure what I would have done. I kind of have a love/hate relationship with this place."

"I can understand." Eve opened the door to the main house, allowed Alex to pass, then followed her inside.

"Anyway. Jeez. Enough depressing conversation." Alex glanced over her shoulder and hit the light switch with her free hand. "It's time to party."

"Party?"

"Surprise!" Voices filled the room, coming from every angle around the kitchen. Eve froze, trying to take everything in. Balloons covered the ceiling with blue, red, and yellow streamers crisscrossing among them. What the hell? Guerin maneuvered around Alex and palmed Eve's upper arms, drawing her attention.

"Happy birthday, beautiful." He cupped her chin, then dipped his head, covering her mouth with his for a gentle kiss. But it was enough to have her pulse racing.

"What have you done?" She grinned. "How did you—?"

"I hate to give the bastard any credit, but Markus was the one who mentioned learning about you on your birthday. So Kenric and I pried the date out of him." A sly grin formed on his face. One that said they hadn't minded a great deal having to get the info out of the male. "Did we get it right?"

"Yes." She placed her palms over his chest, wishing for a moment that they were alone so his shirt wouldn't be between them. "You did."

"Happy birthday, Eve," Alex said, and Guerin moved aside to allow the other female in for a quick a hug.

"Did you know about this?" Eve chuckled as she pulled away.

"Guilty." Alex chewed her lower lip. "But I did have a good time doing it." She snickered. "We must go shopping again soon."

"Happy birthday!" Elle called out and maneuvered her way in, elbowing her sister over for an embrace.

"Thank you," Eve said, finding it difficult to get the words around the lump in her throat.

The gang ushered her farther inside and around the table for a boisterous, although slightly off-key, round of "Happy Birthday." Eve cringed, but at the same time was bursting with joy. Who could have imagined how much her life would change in a few months?

The overhead lights dimmed, and Kenric appeared at her side. Her father beamed, carrying a three-tier cake draped in chocolate icing and ablaze with candles. He placed it on the table in front of her and straightened.

"Happy birthday, my daughter. May we have many more to share." He tugged Eve in by her shoulders and placed a kiss to each of her cheeks.

A knot of emotion swelled in the back of her throat. *Oh my God. I will not cry!*

"Now make a wish and blow out these candles before we start a fire."

She burst into laughter, then swiped away a tear.

"Hope you like chocolate cake?" Emily asked from the other end of the table.

"Hey, what girl doesn't love chocolate? Perfect!"

"That's what I was hoping." Emily chuckled. "I told you she'd like it," she said, grinning in Elle's direction.

A firm hand rested on Eve's lower back, then Guerin's warmth surrounded her. "Make your wish, beautiful," he whispered at her ear.

Eve closed her eyes, and the room quieted. It took only a moment to conjure up the perfect request, because there was only one thing she wanted. *Please never let this end, or if I'm dreaming, don't ever let me wake up. I love them...I love* him, *with every piece of my heart.* She lifted her eyelids, inhaled, then leaned in and blew at the twinkling flames. The candlelight died, and a thunderous roar of applause filled her ears. She looked up from under her lashes at the smiling faces around the table. They didn't care whether she was human, vampire, or both. *How novel.* Eve just...belonged. Such an incredible feeling she could hardly contain or describe.

This was home.

This was her family. And she'd die before anyone or anything dared to touch either.

A perfect hour later, Eve sat her second empty plate in the sink. The cake had been delicious, although she was pretty sure only the females in the room had partaken of the dessert. Even though they had met only a few weeks ago, she couldn't believe how thoughtful everyone had been with their gifts for her birthday. Kenric had purchased her a gorgeous dagger with a pearl handle, matching his own. He was sentimental, and she loved that about him.

Emily had found a fierce pair of black leather boots with buckles adorning the entire length of her calves. The woman had taste.

"Are you ready for my gift?" From behind, Guerin

snaked his arms around her. She smiled to herself. Eve had wondered why nothing had appeared from Guerin.

"If *you're* ready," she stated.

"It's upstairs in your room." He nipped the shell of her ear, shooting chills over her flesh.

"Oh, really?" Eve bit her lower lip. "It's something you don't want to show the others?"

"Hmm… No. It's the kind of a present meant for a private audience."

"Wow. Sounds intriguing." She turned inside his hold.

"Come with me and let me show you." A corner of his mouth curled. Guerin found her hand and laced their fingers.

"I will. But can you give me a minute first? There's something I really need to handle that can't wait any longer."

"Sure." Confusion drew Guerin's brows together, but he released her.

Eve sauntered back to the group and over to where Kenric stood by the gift table with an arm around his mate. "Hey there," Eve said to her father. "Do you have a minute?" The couple turned her way. "I won't take too much of your time, but I would like to talk to you in private."

"Sure." He looked to Emily, and she nodded. "Let's go into the other room." He moved away, and Eve followed. Inside the study, Kenric headed to a couple of leather chairs near the fireplace. A low flame smoldered in the logs behind the wrought iron screen. "Do you want to have a seat?"

Eve perched on the arm, too anxious to sit still. "I'll get right to the point," she began, staring at her hands, the words spilling out. "I've never told anyone—ever—the few details my mother shared with me about my conception." She glanced up. Kenric stood motionless, his expression stoic.

"And it surprises me you've never asked."

"I have no doubt you've been hunted most of your adult life for that information." He swiped a wide palm over his mouth and chin, inhaling. "I hoped in time, when you were ready, you would come to me. I didn't want to pressure you. You've lived through enough of that."

"Of all the people on this planet, you alone have the right to know what happened. How *I* happened."

As if someone had released the air from his limbs, Kenric sank in the chair across from Eve. "I'm listening."

"Honestly, I don't know everything, of course. Only what my mother revealed over the years—piece by piece. Marguerite mentioned taking high doses of a plant or herb called chasteberry for several months. After she experienced the resurgence of her monthly cycle, she turned you. It was during the process of your change, she told me, when I was conceived."

"I see...," he said. "So it was the residual part of my humanity—my fertility—that made her pregnancy possible."

"That is how it seemed. And of course, you know my mother was an unusually powerful female. I don't know of any other vampire, even with the assistance of the herb, who would have been able to rebirth her ovaries. But no one ever accused Marguerite Devonshire of being weak when it came to her will."

"That's an understatement."

"I wish what information I have would have been better news for you and your mate," Eve said, her heart heavy.

"It's okay." He shook his head. "The life I lead is dangerous enough for my mate. Bringing a child into this dark world probably wouldn't be my smartest move," he stated.

"Present company excluded."

She released a short laugh. "No insult taken." Eve stood, releasing a sigh. "I should probably get back to Guerin."

Kenric stood, then pulled her in, placing a kiss to her forehead. "Thank you for trusting me enough to tell me." A wave of relief bloomed in her chest alongside an overwhelming sense of what she could only term as rightness.

Eve cupped his face to see his blue eyes shimmering in the firelight. "You deserved to know." She turned and walked away. This was how it should be. Kenric had been the central focus of her mother's obsession—her madness. And she was so grateful no one had ever learned their secret before her father had the chance to know what had been done. Over the last several weeks, he'd stated many times he was happy she'd chosen to stay, be a part of his life and the Enclave. Eve only hoped Kenric would never regret his decision to invite her to live among them, and that her presence wouldn't someday thicken and deepen the scars from his past. She would make sure that never happened.

A few minutes later, Guerin hustled her upstairs. Outside her door, he stood, knob in hand, grinning, waiting for her to join him inside. She couldn't begin to imagine what he had planned. Eve entered, and her eyes widened. Apparently, while she'd been shopping, Guerin had filled every corner of her bedroom with roses. Red, white, yellow, pink... the view and the smell were stunning.

She spun, facing him. "I can't believe you did all this for me." Eve blinked back another flood of tears. "My party... then this." She shook her head.

"Roses remind me of you, and the first time we met." He stroked her cheek with his thumb. "Even when I didn't know it was you at the Rose's Thorn, there was still this underlying connection I'd never felt before."

"I know," she whispered. "When I saw you crossing the dance floor"—she swallowed—"you took my breath away."

Guerin kicked the door shut behind him. Eve's heart slammed against her sternum, not from fear, but excitement—anticipation. A rumble vibrated off the male. "I'm dying to kiss you."

"Do it," she snapped, breathless. Then his mouth was on hers—hard, claiming. Their teeth clicked right before his tongue drove inside. God, she could devour him. Eve would never get enough of the way he felt, smelled. Like sandalwood and hot nights. She wanted to climb inside his arms, demand he fill her, drive into her core until her throat was raw from crying out his name.

Something crashed to the floor, maybe one of the vases, and her back was against the wall. Eve wrapped her arms around his neck, her legs around his hips. Guerin thrust into her, the hard ridge of his erection nudging the vee between her thighs. *Yes!*

"Too many clothes," she stated and pushed at his shoulders. Eve had to get her jeans off. "I want you naked."

"Wait," he said, and slowly lowered Eve until her feet touched the floor.

"Wait?" She lifted a brow.

"I haven't had a chance to give you your birthday present yet."

"But I thought…?" She pointed to the flowers and then swung her index finger between the two of them.

"Well, that's part of it." Guerin stepped away, smiling, and grabbed the remote to the stereo system. A click sounded, and a guitar began to softly play. Christina Perri's "Arms" filled the room.

"You keep surprising me, Lombardi. Such a kick-ass alpha warrior, but deep down, you're a romantic." Eve grinned. "I would have never guessed."

Guerin shrugged. "Only for you," he whispered. He reached over and retrieved a pouch she'd never seen before from the surface of her dresser. "You bring out the best in me. Parts I never knew existed. You make me want to fly, beautiful. And then you make me want to crawl for you," he said. With one hand, Guerin tore his shirt over his head and dropped it to the carpet. He lowered to his knees at her feet and lifted the velvet bundle in offering. "Blend with me, Eve."

She couldn't breathe.

Hell, she didn't even know if her heart still beat.

On automatic, Eve accepted the pouch, tugged the strings, and glimpsed its interior. Silver bindings lay coiled inside. He was serious.

Oh my God.

This male wanted to bond with her. Connect them on a level where they would never be parted. Forever.

Her hands trembled at the monumental impact of what he asked. "Guerin," she said, after finding her voice. "This is something you should really think about."

"It's all I've thought about since you returned with us. I would have never believed it possible for someone like me to receive such a treasure. Yet here you are. And you're my soul mate, beautiful. Everything inside me screams it with shrill intensity any time you're near—you're mine."

Her vision clouded. "This is almost too much." She

swallowed, wetting her throat. "When I'm with you... My heart fills. My veins warm. You give me a sense of belonging. Something I never allowed myself to dream about. And it's not only because I'm living in the same house as my father. Which in itself is still hard to believe and amazing." Shaking her head, she closed her eyes. "But it's because this is where you are." She reached down, opened her eyes, and threaded her fingers into his hair. "You're right. The only thing missing is having a piece of your soul where it should be." Eve placed her free hand over her chest. "In here." She pulled her arm away. "Please...stand." Without hesitation, Guerin rose. "Yes." Eve nodded. "I would be honored to blend with you, my fierce warrior."

Guerin seized her mouth, stealing her breath for a moment, then retreated. "I can't wait another second to be inside you, in every sense of the word." He ripped at his fly, and the buttons popped, scattering across the carpet as he made his way over to the mattress. Guerin shoved his jeans down, plopped onto the edge of the bed, and yanked his boots off. "Are you familiar with the ritual?"

She nodded. "I've heard about it." Eve closed the distance between her and her intended mate. "I bind you with the straps and drain you while you submit to me during sex, correct?"

"That's right," he said, and moved into position on top of the comforter, facing the ceiling. His shaft at full salute.

"No second thoughts?" She couldn't help but ask. The ritual required her to drink from him until his heart stopped. Not a final fate for a vampire, like a silver blade to the heart or decapitation, but he would be completely at her mercy if she didn't bring him back.

Guerin turned his head, his gaze drawn to hers. "I trust you," he said. Three simple words, but after everything he'd been through—what *they'd* been through—it was a powerful statement she didn't take lightly. Her gut clenched.

"I trust you as well." She moved to the head of the bed, an aura of absolute peace settling in her soul. This was what—who—she'd been waiting for her entire life. He was the yin to her yang. The key perfectly carved to open her heart, and it was his to possess. "Hand me your arm, please." Guerin complied, and Eve secured his wrist to the bedpost with the binding—silver side down next to his flesh. A small hitch in his breathing told her the metal was doing its job. She went to work on the other side, making sure to move at a fast pace. Guerin had spent enough hours sizzling beneath the toxic metal. Eve cinched the last knot in place, wringing a grunt from her lover's throat.

"And for more than any other reason, Eve Devonshire," he added, his voice strained, "I do this because I love you." That stopped Eve in her tracks. She closed her eyes, steadying herself.

"Say it again," she stated.

"I love you, Eve Devonshire." The deep rumble of his voice caressed her spine, and her heart pounded. *He loves me.* Her nipples tingled, growing taut, and her sex ached. "Eve?" Without a word, Eve shed her clothes. She couldn't speak. Too much emotion had paralyzed her vocal cords.

Eve climbed onto the mattress beside him. With her index finger, she traced the outline of the Enclave symbol over his right pec, then moved to the dark cluster of fine hairs down the center of his chest. *Damn.* He was sexy. Every muscle perfectly defined and not an ounce of fat anywhere.

She traveled over the ripples of his abdomen, her fingertips riding the waves. His cock met her near his navel, fully erect, a drop of precum beaded inside the slit. The shaft twitched as if beckoning her for a caress. Her core clamped down, needy. Too empty.

She couldn't hold back any longer.

In one fluid motion, Eve swung her legs over Guerin's waist and impaled herself on his shaft. Air punched from her lungs under the sheer ecstasy of the intrusion. Her lover cried out and thrust upward, meeting her downward stroke. His thick shaft stretched her, igniting every nerve ending inside her channel. Her bottom tapped his thighs as the length of his rod bumped her cervix. Eve had never been more perfectly filled—in every way.

Tossing his head back and exposing his throat, Guerin hissed. "Yes!"

Eve fell forward, her palms catching her weight near his shoulders. Her fangs erupted and her mouth watered. The sound of her pulse was a melodic beat of desire, need, and hunger in her ears. But most of all…

"I love you, too," she breathed and scored the flesh above his artery with the sharp points of her fangs. "I love you more than I ever believed possible."

"Oh, fuck, beautiful." He sighed. "Take me."

And she did. His blood filled her mouth, hot and spicy, and Eve gulped it down. God, he was delicious. With every pull, Guerin rocked into her depths—faster and faster, massaging the bundle of nerves at the apex of her sex. His essence electrified her veins. His cock took her higher and higher.

"Don't stop," Guerin cried out and jerked beneath her.

Heat flooded her channel with his orgasm, sending Eve over the edge along with him. Pleasure spiked where they were joined, and a hard quake rocked her body. She gasped, the intensity taking her sight, leaving her with nothing but swirls of black spots before her eyes. *So damn good.* "Keep going…" It was Guerin, but the sound of his voice was so far away. She had to come back to earth. He needed her.

Drink. She had to drink. Eve worked her throat, pulling the last few mouthfuls she could manage from her mate. That's when she noticed…Guerin wasn't moving any longer. She licked the wound, sealing her holes with her tongue.

"Okay, Lombardi," she whispered. "It's your turn." She closed her eyes, waiting. "Come on, you stubborn warrior. Let me feel you." Then as if a ray of sun, too hot, too bright, warmed her spine, she felt him. She arched into the prickling sensation, welcoming it. The heat grew in concentration, penetrating her.

"Guerin," she called out inside her mind. As if the room were suddenly alive with static electricity, every hair on her body lifted. Hard pants escaped her throat.

"I'm here," Guerin's voice whispered inside her head.

It was all she could do not to jump from the bed from the thrill of it all. His spirit was inside her. Hundreds of tingling sensations roamed her insides, filling every centimeter of her body, leaving nothing untouched. Christ, they were truly becoming one. Guerin was blending with her soul.

"Wake me before I can't come back," he said, shaking Eve from her dreamlike state. *"Too damn beautiful, inside and out. You make it hard to leave."*

Shit. She had to feed him. *Now.* Eve brought her wrist to her mouth and sank in her fangs. Crimson fluid erupted from her artery, and she leaned over, placing the wound to his mouth. The scarlet liquid coated his lips. Eve tugged on his lower jaw, creating a small opening for her blood to enter.

"Come on, Guerin," she demanded. "Swallow."

Eve cupped his nape, tilting his head back up slightly so he wouldn't choke. "Feed!" A steady stream of her essence trickled down his chin and pooled on the sheets below. "Your Mistress commands you to feed!" she shouted. Suddenly Guerin coughed, then gulped. Eve gasped. Shit, how long had it been since she'd last taken a breath?

The razor-sharp tips of his fangs stabbed into her wrist. Eve gritted her teeth under the impact. Guerin clamped down hard, drinking in greedy swallows. Her womb tightened, shooting an erotic wave of desire into her clitoris. A tremble rolled over her.

"I love you. More than you can ever imagine," Guerin whispered, but the words were a caress inside her mind.

"I love you too." Eve ran her fingers through the dark waves of his hair. His tongue brushed over the punctures to her wrist, and he looked up.

"I'm so glad I found you," he said.

"Me too," she whispered.

"I hope this birthday was all you dreamed, beautiful." Guerin smiled.

"More than you know." She lifted his chin with her finger for a kiss. "Because my birthday wish was you."

Acknowledgements

To Naima, the best critique partner and friend a girl could ask for: I'm eternally grateful for your incredible support and fabulous talent. I don't know what I'd do without you.

About the Author

Almost every author's bio states they've been writing since they learned how to read. It's what they've always wanted to do. Well, my journey wasn't so straight and narrow. I was a nurse for more than twenty years and hold a bachelor's degree in science with a major in biology. So as you can see, my career path had originally gone in the opposite direction. I didn't discover my passion for the craft until after I'd had my son and decided to work part-time. I've always loved to read but had never read a paranormal romance. Then one night at work on break, I began reading Karen Marie Moning's Spell of the Highlander. I couldn't believe what I'd been missing, and I immediately fell in love with the genre. I wanted to write like that. I wanted to create worlds where others could fi nd the same escape and fascination I did when I read my first sensual paranormal romance. And I hope that's what I've accomplished in my work. Please dive in, hold on tight, and enjoy the adventure. Just be careful in the dark—you might find more than you expected waiting for you there.

Jessica Lee lives in the southeastern United States with her husband and son. She loves writing and can't wait for that quiet time each day when her son is in school, and she can get lost in another place and world with the fantastical, sexy creatures in her head.

She's a member of Romance Writers of America, FF&P, and Carolina Romance Writers.

Also by Jessica Lee

UNDYING EMBRACE

Arran MacLain is a vampire on a suicide mission, driven to kill his former partner who betrayed him and the Enclave they served. But two things stand in his way: Gabrielle Stevens, the human female who holds his heart, and the past that won't let him go. When Gabrielle's hunt for her missing sister brings her face to face with Arran, their missions combine and thrust them into the heart of evil. Will their passion be enough to overcome the pain from their past, or will their dark desires destroy them both?

UNDYING DESTINY

Emily Ross just wanted a fresh start. She's a survivor, coming off the tail end of an abusive relationship, and craves time alone to learn who she is and to save the home that holds her heart. The last thing she needs is a controlling, alpha male calling all the shots. Meeting Kenric might just change her mind, though. He is wrong for her in all the right ways. But in order to keep her heart from breaking, he has to keep the hordes of evil vamps from stealing her very breath.